10/2015

LI W9-CNE-313

print

RANDOM HOUSE LARGE PRINT

Undercover

DANIELLE STEEL

Undercover

A Novel

RANDOM HOUSE
LARGE PRINT

· All rights reserved.
Published in the United States of America by Random House Large Print in association with Delacorte Press, an imprint of Random House, a division of Random House LLC, a Penguin Random House Company, New York.

Cover design by Lynn Andreozzi
Cover images: © Roy Bishop/Arcangel (Paris), © Tom Hallman (man)
Cover illustration colorization by Tom Hallman

ISBN: 978-1-62953-575-3

Printed in the United States of America

This Large Print Edition published in accord with the standards of the N.A.V.H.

To my wonderful children,
Beatie, Trevor, Todd, Nick, Sam,
Victoria, Vanessa, Maxx, and Zara,

You are my greatest blessings,
and I love you more than words can ever say.
May your challenges be small ones,
and your blessings and victories huge.

I love you so much,
Mommy/d.s.

The ideal person is not the one
with whom one can be happy,
but the one without whom one
can't be happy.

—Anonymous

Undercover

Marshall

Chapter 1

The birds calling to each other in the early morning just after the dawn heralded another perfect day in the lush jungle south of Bogotá. Pablo Echeverría, his skin a deep tan, his eyes the darkest brown, his hair almost to his shoulders, pushed back behind his ears, and his beard slightly overgrown, walked out of the hut where he and Paloma lived. She was expecting their first child, and the date was coming near. Paloma was as fair and light-skinned as he was dark, and her name suited her. In Spanish Paloma meant "Dove." She was a bird of peace in the jungle where they lived and Pablo worked. He was her brother's right-hand man. Raul Vásquez López was one of the most powerful men in Colombia, despite the simple way they lived. Pablo had been with him for three years, working his way up through the ranks since he had come from Ecuador, and gaining Raul's trust. They called

Raul "El Lobo," the Wolf. He was cunning, daring, and quick, like a wolf.

Pablo was the son of an Ecuadorian general who had been killed in a military coup, assassinated by rebels. Pablo had turned to the drug trade, and after three years of working on a smaller scale in Ecuador, he had found his way to Raul. And the three years he had spent working for him since had been a satisfying and productive alliance.

Pablo and Paloma weren't married, and no one cared, he was planning to marry her soon, after the baby was born. For now, he and Raul had other things on their minds. Raul liked the idea of Pablo being with his younger sister. Pablo was not only smart, capable, and trustworthy, he was a good man. Paloma had had no medical care through the eight months of the pregnancy, but at nineteen she was fine. And she was planning to give birth at the camp. Pablo had been reading books about how to help her, and if things started to go wrong, he could drive her the two hours to Bogotá. Her brother was twenty years older than she was, and Pablo was twenty-eight, young to have risen so high in Raul's operation, but Raul knew pure talent when he saw it, and his inquiries about Pablo in Ecuador had proved him right. He prided himself on his infallible judgment about his men, and Pablo had never let him down. He executed Raul's orders flawlessly, and handled their purchasing and transport operations brilliantly. There had been no problems, and no slips in the three years he'd been there.

Their simple life at the camp suited him. Pablo went to both Bogotá and Cartagena for Raul regularly, but he was always happy to get back, meet with Raul, who was like a brother to him now, live with the other men, and come home to Paloma, waiting for him in their hut. He had built it for them himself. In his first year at the camp, he had lived in a military surplus tent with the other men, but once he was with Paloma, they wanted privacy and a space for themselves. She had grown up in Raul's camps, after their parents died. Her three other brothers worked for Raul as well. And Pablo had rapidly caught her eye, as she had inevitably caught his. Raul had defended her virtue fiercely until then. It was a sign of his deep respect for Pablo that he had entrusted her to him, and given him his consent. To Pablo, she was the ultimate prize. He loved the sweet scent of her skin as he nestled with her at night, her gentleness in all things, and her full belly now, heavy with their child. Raul wanted it to be a boy. Pablo didn't say it, but he didn't care. He just wanted it to go easily for her, and the baby to be healthy when it was born. She was a brave girl, used to the primitive conditions in which they lived, and said she wasn't afraid. Pablo could feel the baby kick him, when she slept behind him with an arm gently cast over him, in the cool night air of the jungle.

Pablo was wearing his old military jacket from Ecuador, with an undershirt, fatigue pants, and his old army boots, as he lit his first cigarette of the day, and took a long drag. He had slipped out, as he always did, without waking Paloma, and had his first cup of coffee with Raul every morning, while they discussed the missions of the day, and the state of their activities in process. They had dealings in Panama, Ecuador, Aruba, Venezuela, Bolivia, and Mexico, and exported literally tons of cocaine to Mexico, Canada, Africa, Europe, and the United States. Raul ran the largest and most successful drug operation in South America. They exported it by land, air, and sea via ships and speedboats out of Cartagena. Pablo was in charge of coordinating their transport operation at the highest level. While Raul ran everything from their camp, Pablo slipped quietly into the two cities, checked on operations, conveyed Raul's orders, and then came back to the camp to report to El Lobo, who ran his vast empire with military precision. Raul was a man worthy of respect and admiration, for the sheer efficiency with which he ran his business. And he had built it all himself, adding one piece of the giant operation to the next, until his arms encompassed much of South America. Pablo was his most trusted legman, but they all knew that Raul was the heart and soul and brains of their business, and ran it all on a grand scale.

Pablo finished the last of his cigarette as he walked

into the clearing where Raul made camp. His tent was military and heavily camouflaged, but no one was ever sure where he slept at night. The location was always kept secret even from Pablo, although they met at his tent in the morning to discuss work. But the joke in the camp was that El Lobo slept with the other wolves. The women he slept with were temporary and of no consequence to him, he considered them more of a liability than an asset, and he teased Pablo that he didn't have his romantic ideas. But it was a weakness he tolerated in him, since it benefited his sister, and Pablo treated her well. Raul was all about business, nothing else mattered to him, except the loyalty of his men. He considered their total dedication to him a sacred trust. And those who failed him in some way rapidly disappeared. Their families, attachments to women, and personal lives were of no interest to him.

He was smoking a Romeo y Julieta limited edition Havana cigar, as he did every morning, when Pablo arrived. He offered one to Pablo from the box on his desk every day, and Pablo always declined. He smoked a cigar with Raul sometimes before he went home at night, but didn't have the stomach for it first thing in the morning. But he liked the familiar, pungent smell when he walked into the tent, and often brought the cigars for Raul from Bogotá. They were common here, for men like Raul. Despite the way he lived in order to run his business, he was a man of distinguished tastes. He had been educated in Europe, and had gone to Oxford for two years. It made for interesting conversations with Pablo, when they shared a brandy and a cigar late at night. Pablo had been well educated too, from a respectable family. It gave them something more in common than the business interests they shared.

The moment Raul saw Pablo, there was a brotherly light in his eyes. He clapped him on the shoulder, and they embraced. The two men even looked somewhat alike, although Pablo was younger and taller and in flawless shape. Their coloring was similar, as was their military style.

"How is my fat sister?" Raul said, teasing him, as Pablo helped himself to the strong dark brew of coffee that Raul made himself, and drank gallons of, every day. His coffee cup was never empty.

"Getting bigger," Pablo said proudly. "I think it will be soon." He was mildly worried about it, but knew better than to say it to Raul, who called him an old woman when he did. Raul knew that Pablo's soft spot was Paloma, which he always considered a dangerous thing. It was why he never allied himself with any woman, he just used them. He thought women were too risky for that reason, and easily became an Achilles' heel, but it was a flaw he forgave Pablo, only because Paloma was his sister.

Raul had been sitting, looking at a table full of maps and a list of transport ships, when Pablo walked in. He pushed the list toward Pablo as soon as he sat down, pointing the cigar in the direction of the maps.

"So what do you think? We ship to North Africa tomorrow? And Europe at the end of the week?" He liked to keep things moving and not let the shipments sit for too long after they came in. They had gotten a huge shipment in Cartagena from their supplier the day before, and he wanted to get it out quickly. Despite what they paid in bribes to government officials at all levels, El Lobo knew better than to let the goods sit in warehouses longer than they had to.

"That sounds right," Pablo said, studying the maps. "I don't see why we can't ship to Europe tomorrow too. Why wait till the end of the week?" He pointed to the name of a ship that was smaller than the others but had served them well before. "And Miami, when the next shipment comes in." Raul nodded. Pablo always planned ahead and was as careful as Raul was himself about moving and storing the goods. They wanted to ship it out as fast as they could on ships they knew were safe.

As they discussed the details and mechanics of it, four other men walked in. Two were in camouflage, the other two in garb similar to what Raul and Pablo wore. They were the silent army of the dark side. And a few minutes later, six more men arrived in the tent, awaiting instructions. Pablo dispatched five of the ten to Bogotá for operations there, and he was planning to take two of the men to Cartagena with him. He didn't need more. He was an expert marksman, and he preferred traveling in smaller groups. Raul listened while Pablo gave the men instructions, nodded, and silently approved as he relit his cigar. He didn't offer his cigars to the others, only to Pablo when they were alone, as a mark of the brotherhood they shared.

Half an hour later, five of the men were gone. Three were staying at the camp, with another dozen peppered through the jungle, part of the protection of the camp. Pablo and El Lobo exchanged a few last words then, and Raul nodded as Pablo left with the two men he wanted with him.

"See you tonight," Pablo said over his shoulder. Pablo always reported in when he got back, to let Raul know how things had gone. They had a vast communication network that functioned efficiently, but Raul and Pablo communicated by phone and e-mail as little as possible, and both preferred it that way. They met in person before and after Pablo's missions.

Pablo trudged silently through the fierce brush of the jungle for half an hour, until they reached a heavily concealed Jeep. Pablo got behind the wheel, as the two men took away its protective covering, and then they both got in. They drove along a barely serviceable dirt track for a while, and eventually joined a battered narrow road, and stayed on it for half an hour, until they reached a clearing with a narrow airstrip that was barely more than a dirt track but was just long enough for the small plane that landed ten minutes later. Pablo had radioed for it before he left the camp, and it would make it possible for them to cover the thousand miles to Cartagena and return by that night. None of the three men spoke on the flight, and Pablo didn't say a word to them until they reached the landing strip they used regularly on the outskirts of Cartagena. Pablo was a man of few words.

He was thinking about their various operations being carried out that day, shipments coming in to several cities, others waiting to be moved. They picked up a car at the airstrip that was parked for them there, and drove to a warehouse just outside the city, and from there to a small battered building, which housed their office. It looked completely innocuous, and no one would have suspected the millions of dollars of business being conducted there. Pablo parked the car behind a neighboring house, with chickens wandering through the yard, and walked into the first building through a back door. One of Pablo's men stayed at the back door, the other moved to the front door. All three of them were armed. And Pablo walked up the creaking stairs to meet three men waiting for him there. He met with them for just under an hour, delivered all of Raul's instructions, and ascertained that the plan was clear and that they were ready to carry it out. The cocaine was being shipped, concealed in farm equipment, to North Africa, which worked well for them. And the shipment to Europe was being sent with textiles going into Marseilles. It had all been successfully done before without a problem.

Less than an hour later, Pablo was back on the road, to the airstrip, and in the air minutes after they arrived. The mission had gone well. When they reached the camp that night, they carefully concealed the Jeep where it had been before. Raul was waiting for him. Pablo assured him that all had gone according to plan. They handled all their shipping through Cartagena. Raul told him he needed him to go to Bogotá the next day, which was standard procedure for Pablo. He went to one of the cities where they did business almost every day.

"Did you eat?" El Lobo asked him with concern. One of the men had bought sandwiches on the way to the airstrip outside Cartagena. They had other things to occupy them than to worry about meals.

"We ate." Pablo smiled at him, touched by the fraternal gesture. When they were alone, Raul treated him like a younger brother. And with that, he poured a glass of brandy, pushed it toward him, and offered him a cigar, which this time Pablo accepted. Raul was pleased with how things had gone. He knew he could always count on Pablo to execute his orders to perfection. He had earned the brandy and cigar and El Lobo's praise.

"My sister can wait," El Lobo said, as the leader of their operation, and Pablo smiled. Whenever

Pablo came back to the hut, Paloma was happy to see him, asked no questions, and never complained. Her life with Pablo had been a little piece of heaven for the past two years, in the rigors of their world. It was a hardcore man's world with no room in it for women's needs and demands, which she knew well.

The two men enjoyed the brandy and cigars, in a civilized moment at the end of their day. The business Raul ran was a high-stress operation where millions of dollars were involved on a daily basis, and there was no margin for mistakes. There had been none so far, which had won Pablo El Lobo's trust.

It was nearly midnight when Pablo went back to his hut, and found Paloma half asleep in their bed, which was a thin mattress on the floor. She smiled sleepily in the moonlight as she felt Pablo slip into bed beside her, naked. He pulled aside the covers to look at the velvet of her body, and her belly seemed to get bigger by the hour as their child grew inside her. She put her arms around his neck, and he kissed her and held her as she slipped back to sleep again with a soft purring noise, and he lay admiring her until he fell asleep himself.

The next day, after meeting with Raul in the early morning, as always, Pablo drove the Jeep to Bogotá, and this time he went alone. He met a man at a house in the Macarena district, who handed him a battered suitcase full of money, the fruits of their work a few days before. Pablo often brought large amounts of cash to Raul. He asked no questions about where it went or how it was handled, although he had heard long ago that Raul had personal accounts in Switzerland and in other countries in the Caribbean. But if so, Raul had never shared that information with him. There were some things El Lobo kept to himself, no matter how much he trusted him. Pablo knew where some of the operation's accounts were kept, but he knew better than to ask any details. When Pablo returned to camp that night, Raul told him that he needed him to return to Bogotá, for a smaller operation than the one he had carried out that day. There would be no money pickup this time, but only some directions that needed to be verbally given, and Raul said it wouldn't take him long. He wanted no record of the transaction, and they were laying the groundwork for the transfer to Miami, which usually went smoothly, with operatives they had dealt with for a long time.

The two men chatted for a few minutes, but Pablo was eager to see Paloma, who he knew had dinner waiting for him, since he had told her that he was only going to Bogotá. She was smiling and held her arms out to him in a simple white cotton dress she had made herself, and she was wearing gold sandals he had brought her from the city. He loved bringing her small gifts whenever he could. Raul always warned him about spoiling her, and told him he would regret it one day. Women were like that, according to El Lobo, who had never trusted a woman in his life.

They sat down to dinner to the familiar sounds of the jungle, and Pablo could hear a small plane droning overhead. He knew that there were several men coming in that night from Ecuador. They were part of Raul's empire, and Pablo knew he would be meeting with them and Raul the next day when he got back from his mission in the city.

Paloma didn't ask him what he'd done that day. She never did. Her brother had trained her well. They had other things to talk about, and for now, all she could think about was the baby. She hardly ate that night, she was too big. And after dinner, they lay down on the bed, listening to the noises around them, and were comfortable lying side by side. He rubbed her back, and she fell asleep, after she tossed the white cotton dress onto the floor beside the bed. Her body was so spectacularly beautiful, even now with the enormous bump that made him smile each time he saw it, and her breasts were large and full, bigger than they'd been before, and she had long graceful legs, which hadn't changed. In another world, she would have been considered a remarkably beautiful girl, but here she lived concealed and isolated in her brother's jungle camp, in a place that paid no attention to her, except as an occasional object of envy or admiration. As Raul's sister, she was unattainable, except to Pablo. And only he really appreciated how beautiful she was, and what a kind, gentle girl. Here, no one cared.

She was still asleep when he left the camp early the next morning, when he went back to Bogotá, to carry out the mission he'd been assigned. It was a brief meeting with a man he knew well and had met with many times before. They agreed to the amount of cocaine to be transferred to Miami, and how much it would cost. The funds would change hands later on.

After the meeting, Pablo walked for a little while, and stopped at a café. He ordered a cup of strong black coffee, which the waiter served him, as he sat on the terrace in the sun. When he finished it, he ordered a second cup, although the brew was strong, and the waiter spilled it accidentally, as he was about to set the cup down. The hot coffee spread across the table but missed Pablo. The server apologetically mopped it up, with an embarrassed look. Pablo didn't look like the sort of man one would want to annoy. There was a tension about him that was reminiscent of a lion ready to strike.

And as the waiter wiped up the last of the coffee, he whispered almost inaudibly, "Now." Pablo's eyes grew steely the moment he said it, and he glanced back at the waiter with a murderous look, then looked away. Pablo stood up and threw a few coins on the table, as the waiter watched him mournfully, and just as inaudibly, Pablo said, "No," strode away from the table, and walked to the Jeep. He was back on the road a few minutes later, and his eyes were cold and hard as he drove.

Chapter 2

Pablo met with Raul and the men from Ecuador late that night. They were making plans for the transfer of goods from Ecuador to Panama, but there was nothing remarkable about the meeting. And at the end of it, Raul offered him a cigar, which Pablo took. As he lit it, he saw Raul watching him, as he always did. One always had the feeling with him that he could look into your thoughts.

"So what do you think?" Raul was asking about the meeting.

"It sounds all right to me." It wasn't one of their bigger deals, and seemed like business as usual. They talked about the upcoming shipment to Miami then, which was far more complex, and more interesting, for a much larger amount. Raul told him then that he had to go back to Bogotá again the next day. Sometimes Pablo didn't go for a week or two, and at other times, when they were moving several shipments, he had to go to the city every day. He didn't mind.

It was nearly two in the morning when Pablo finally left the tent, and Raul disappeared into the shrubbery to dissolve into wherever in the jungle he would spend the night. The two men had embraced as they parted, as they always did. And when Pablo went back to the hut, Paloma was sound asleep. She was sleeping more now, he had noticed, as her time came close, and something told him it would only be a few days. He lay quietly next to her and fell asleep, and was up and dressed before first light.

He didn't stop to see Raul as he left, as he had to be in Bogotá early that day. But he was hoping to be back late that afternoon. The only thing that bothered him about going to the city now was not being there for Paloma if labor started. There was no one else to help her—she was the only woman in the camp.

He was thinking about her on the way to his meeting, when a man jostled him hard on the sidewalk. He apologized in Spanish, and locked his eyes into Pablo's. Pablo recognized him immediately and didn't want to be late.

"Not now," he said under his breath, and the man responded just as quietly, seeming not to even speak to him.

"Now."

No expression crossed Pablo's face, as he headed down a narrow street, turned a corner, walked be-

hind a small dilapidated building, and took a key
from under a plant. With startling speed, he had
turned the key in the lock, entered the house, and
closed the door behind him. He ran up a flight of
stairs, threw open a door, and glared at three men
in jeans and ordinary street garb, who were waiting
for him.

"What the fuck is this about?" he shouted at them.
"I told you yesterday, not now. I have a meeting in
five minutes about the shipment to Miami. Why
don't you guys back off?" He sounded angry and
looked tense, and he was speaking to them in English, not Spanish. The collective look they aimed
at him was like a wall. There was no give in it, and
no emotion. This was pure business, of a different
kind.

"You're out, Everett. You're done. There's a leak
somewhere in the chain. It's going to get to Raul
any second. Maybe it already has by now." Pablo
thought of the men who had flown in from Ecuador, and wondered if one of them had said something to Raul. There had been no sign of it the
night before. But El Lobo was cagey that way, and
he would have wanted to check it out. Maybe that
was why he had sent him to Bogotá for the third
time in a week. But Pablo wasn't ready to quit. He
was too close in, knew too much, and with Paloma
ready to give birth, he wasn't going anywhere.

"The hell I am!" he shouted at the men again.
There wasn't even the slightest shift in their eyes.

"For chrissake, I've been here for three years. My woman's about to have a baby any minute." He was shaking with rage and emotion and looked like he was about to cry.

"You're risking everyone in the operation if you try to stay. You're a marked man, Everett. We're talking about hours before Raul knows it, if he hasn't already heard. You're out. There's a plane waiting for us now. You may not even make it that far, if El Lobo is on to you. You've got five minutes. You know what you have to do." Pablo hesitated for an endless beat and glared at the man in charge. His name was Bill Carter, and he was a senior special agent of the DEA. He had flown down from Washington to get him. They knew he was hotheaded, and they didn't want any mistakes.

"And if I quit and walk out of here and go back?"

"You'll be dead by tonight, and so will the girl. The only thing that might save her is your getting the hell out now. Does she know?" Pablo shook his head miserably. "You know the deal. You can't destroy everything you've built by going back now." Pablo knew that too. Other operatives like him were planted throughout Raul's operation. If he was marked now, he was liable to blow their cover too. He had to get out. But it nearly killed him to leave Paloma, with their baby days from being born. He would never see the baby now, and possibly not Paloma ever again. He had known that all along, that inevitably this day would come. He just thought he would have more time with them, and that maybe he could get her to safety one day. It had been a futile dream. He knew that now.

"I have a life here," he said sadly.

Bill Carter spoke with compassion. "We all did when we were undercover. I was in for seven years. That's a long time. You've got to get ready." He handed him a small kit.

Pablo hesitated for an instant before taking it from him and heading to the bathroom. He thought about climbing out the window and going back, but he knew how many men would be killed if he did, and his getting killed himself wouldn't help Paloma either. He had no choice, he knew, as he took out the razor, and shaved his beard and his head. He put some dark makeup under his eyes, which aged him instantly. There was theatrical makeup, which allowed him to create a long ugly scar down one cheek, and contact lenses, which changed the color of his eyes. They had left clothes for him in the bedroom, similar to theirs, with a baseball cap, and as Pablo dressed, all he could think of was Paloma at the camp. It was inconceivable to him that he would never see her again, and he was determined to return. He would find her wherever she was, and do whatever it took to bring her home with him. But for now, he knew there was no way out. He had to leave.

As he emerged from the bedroom of the small apartment, looking like a different person, one of the men handed him his passport with his real name, Marshall Everett, and the badge he hadn't carried for three years, as a special agent of the DEA. The Drug Enforcement Administration had placed him in Colombia three years earlier, and for three years in Ecuador before that, to set up his identity for El Lobo's operation. The three men were standing, each carrying a shoulder bag, and they were ready to leave. They wanted him in the air and out of the country within the hour, before all hell broke loose and Raul sent his men after Pablo.

The man who had been Pablo Echeverría for six years of diligent undercover work said not a word as he followed them down the stairs to the car parked discreetly outside. He got into the backseat, and looked out the window in agony as Bogotá slid by. All he had to do was make a run for it, get to the Jeep, and drive back to camp, but he knew that if he did, the whole undercover operation would come down around their ears and other men would die.

They drove swiftly toward the airport, showed their badges to security, and boarded a small military plane that was waiting for them.

Security didn't look closely at any of them, and moments later they were in the air on the plane heading to Washington. There was a terrible unreality to it, as Pablo, now Marshall Everett again, watched the countryside shrink below them, knowing that the woman he loved was still there and he had just abandoned her. The only thing that re-assured him was that she was Raul's sister, which at least would provide some protection to her. She had never had the remotest suspicion that he was an undercover agent for the DEA. And Marshall knew better than anyone that there was nothing he could do for her now. Later, if he was lucky, he hoped he could find a way to return, without endangering her, which would be a delicate mission at best.

Bill Carter looked at his watch half an hour after takeoff and informed Marshall that they were raiding the camp within the hour. They had had close calls with Raul before, and this time they didn't want El Lobo to get away. It was why they had wanted to move so quickly. Everett had already stalled them for a day. He should have gone straight to their meeting point the day before, when the waiter spilled the coffee, and instead he had ignored them. That came as no surprise to Bill. Marshall was known to be stubborn and independent. He was a brilliant operative, willing to take unlimited risks, but he had defied his superiors a few times over the years, which was why Carter had come himself. He was taking no chances. They wanted Marshall out, before he was killed, once they knew about the leak.

"Tell them I have a woman there, and she's almost nine months pregnant, and to watch out for her when they take the camp," Marshall said tersely, then turned away and closed his eyes. None of the three men accompanying him attempted to speak to him for the rest of the trip.

An hour after Marshall's flight left Bogotá, Raul was warned by informants in the city that American DEA agents were about to raid the camp. He had just been told about Pablo, and after gathering up his papers and giving instructions to his men, he hurried to the hut where Paloma was taking a nap. He grabbed her arm roughly and dragged her off the bed.

"You knew about him, didn't you?" he accused her, his face inches from hers.

"Knew what?" She looked suddenly terrified. She knew how dangerous her brother was in a rage.

"He's an undercover agent . . . the sonofabitch . . . I trusted him like a brother. . . . He's a lying bastard, and he doesn't give a damn about you. You and that baby were just part of his cover, to fool us. What did he tell you?"

"Nothing . . ." She looked horrified. "That's not true . . . he can't be."

"It's true. He's gone. He left the car in the city and disappeared."

"He'll come back. I know he will," she said in a choked voice.

"He's smarter than that. You were just part of his game. And now what are you going to do with that?" He pointed at her belly in disgust, as her hands instantly went around it to protect it.

"He'll be back for me. I know he will." Raul believed that too. Pablo may have been a fraud, but he knew the kind of man he was, the kind of soft-hearted guy who would risk his own life for the woman he loved. And all Raul wanted now was vengeance for the lies Pablo had made him believe and for making a fool out of him. Without hesitating for a second, Raul pulled his gun out of the holster he wore, aimed it at his sister, and shot her in the head. Paloma fell to the ground. He wanted Pablo's men to find her and tell him what he'd done. The woman he loved and the child he wanted so badly were dead. And with that, Raul turned on his heel and left.

Marshall had been asleep for several hours when Bill Carter was called to the cockpit, an hour before they landed in Washington.

The message relayed to Bill in code was that the camp had been raided. Marshall's woman was dead, shot through the head, and El Lobo had escaped before they got there, yet again. He had vanished into thin air, and their suspicion was that he had flown to either Venezuela or Ecuador to take refuge until things cooled down. Without commenting, Bill went back to his seat and told no one what he'd heard. It was too soon to tell Marshall about the woman. He had three weeks of debriefing ahead of him, and they would tell him at the right time. It had been three years that he was with Raul in Colombia, and he had only returned to the States for two weeks to be reassigned after his successful mission in Ecuador, which laid the groundwork that allowed him to enlist in Raul's operation. He had essentially been undercover for six years. He had fully lived the life of Pablo Echeverría, and Bill knew it would take time now for him to get over the shock of being removed so quickly. And they wanted his full cooperation for the debriefing, to tell them everything he knew and had done for Raul. He had sent back regular coded messages to make them aware of shipments, locations, quantities, money laundering, and the people they did business with. But now they wanted the rest of the details.

Bill knew how hard reentry would be for Marshall after being undercover for so long. He had been through it himself. For a moment, they'd been afraid that he would refuse to come out at all. But he was responsible about his work, although Bill sensed it was a close call this time. The threat of costing lives other than his own had been the deciding factor, as Bill knew it would be. Marshall would never endanger another agent, no matter how willing he was to risk himself.

Marshall woke up as the plane touched down at

Andrews Air Force Base in Maryland, just outside Washington, D.C., and he looked exhausted and pale under his tan. He had removed the scar, the colored contacts, the makeup, and the baseball cap. But as he looked in the mirror in the bathroom of the plane, he no longer recognized himself. His head was shaved, his beard was gone, his eyes looked dead, and his heart had turned to stone. Pablo Echeverría had vanished into thin air, and what was left of Special DEA Agent Marshall Everett had come home. It was the last place he wanted to be. He felt like a robot instead of a man. A part of him had just died.

When they disembarked from the plane, Marshall knew he would be taken to the Drug Enforcement Task Force Center, where the OCDETF, Office of Crime Drug Enforcement Task Forces, was located, to check in. And a helicopter was already waiting to take him to Quantico, the facility the DEA shared with the FBI. He would be there for three weeks of debriefing, and reentry readjustment, including heavy psychological testing, to determine his state of mind. He had been debriefed for two weeks after Ecuador, but this was different. He hadn't been as deep into operations in Ecuador as he was in Colombia. And when he left Ecuador, he was twenty-five years old, and he had moved on to his assignment in Colombia very quickly. Now he was three years older, had infiltrated deeper into Raul's organization, and had left behind a universe and a life that he cared about deeply, a woman he loved, and a baby about to be born.

He was thinking about Paloma, wondering about the baby, when he was driven to the center on the base and was shown into an office, where a task force officer evaluated him briefly, handed him his papers, and released him to leave for Quantico. He arrived there half an hour later and was taken to his room. It was a small cubicle, with a bed, a chest, a chair, a desk, and a small refrigerator. It had a military feel to it. And he knew that other undercover agents would be at the DEA facility too, some of them in seclusion, which was all he wanted now. He wanted to be left alone with all his private thoughts, rather than being poked and prodded and having his mind emptied into a computer, the information to be stored at the DEA and the OCDETF fusion center, to be analyzed in depth by highly skilled agents.

He stood at the window of his room finally, and felt like he was in prison. He was far away from everything familiar to him. In a matter of hours, he had become Marshall Everett again, a man he no longer knew and didn't want to be. He ached to be in a hut in a jungle camp south of Bogotá with the woman he loved. And as he thought of her, and who he had to become again, he wished he were dead. There was nothing he wanted here. He felt like a stranger in his own country. Even speaking and hearing English seemed foreign to him. He had been thinking in Spanish for years. And as he closed his eyes that night and lay on his bed, he dreamed of the familiar jungle sounds and the velvet of Paloma's skin.

Chapter 3

The vigorous debriefing Marshall under-
went at the DEA facility in Quantico was harder
than he had expected or remembered from the last
time, after Ecuador. Or maybe it was just more difficult for him this time. He resented all their questions and everything he had to tell them, but as
he had been taught to do, he emptied his mind
and told them what he knew. He had gathered an
incredible amount of information about Raul's
operation, far more than his superiors had hoped.
He had a meticulous memory for every detail, and
knew more about Raul's operation than anyone had
been able to discover before. He knew by then that
the camp had been raided, and that El Lobo had
escaped. Marshall wasn't surprised. Raul had been
prepared at all times for such an event. He would
have trekked through the jungle, hidden for as long
as he had to, and managed to survive. Marshall was

sure that he had escaped by speedboat on the river, or even flown out from a hidden airstrip somewhere in the jungle. A man like El Lobo couldn't be contained, or stopped. But Marshall had given them enough information to hamper his operation severely and slow him down for a while.

His superiors left to the psychologist the unpleasant task of telling him what had happened to Paloma. They waited until two weeks after he'd arrived. Marshall had been talking about Paloma and the baby for the past two weeks. It was all he could think of, particularly knowing that the baby must have been born by then. He hoped Paloma was all right. The psychologist told him that she had been killed before the raid, and her brother had shot her himself. When Marshall heard what had happened, he was shocked.

"He did it to hurt me," Marshall said in a cold voice, shaking with rage.

"No," the psychologist said gently, making note of Marshall's appearance. His eyes were blazing, but he looked controlled. "I'm sure he did it to punish his sister." He hadn't expected that, or that Raul could be cold enough to kill his own sister, heavy with child. It told Marshall who he really was. He had known Raul was capable of coldhearted cruelty, but not to this extent. "I don't think he did it to punish you," the psychologist reassured him, touched by the look of devastation on Marshall's face and, worse, in his eyes.

"You don't know how these people think," Marshall said coldly. "He wanted to destroy what I love most, to punish me." It seemed a little extreme, and slightly paranoid to the psychologist, but anything was possible. The psychologist assigned to him was bilingual, and they had conducted many of their sessions in Spanish, as Marshall often seemed more comfortable in Spanish now. He had lived his role for a long time, and it only confirmed to her that it had been time to bring him home. Everyone agreed. The psychologist was well aware that it would take years for him to recover from the loss of Paloma and their baby. And there was no one to comfort him—he had lost his parents years before in a car accident when he was in college. And his days of undercover work in the countries where Raul operated were over.

Her final recommendation was to keep him in the States at a desk job for a year. He needed time to calm down and heal, especially now, after Paloma's death. All he talked about was how much he wanted to return to undercover work in South America again, for revenge, anywhere they were willing to send him. He wasn't ready for his days of working undercover to end. Even if it meant working on lesser operations in Mexico, where Raul had less control. He didn't say it to the psychologist, but he wanted to find a way back to Colombia, locate Raul, and kill him, for what he had done to Paloma and their unborn child.

The psychologist had confirmed that the baby had not survived its mother's death. Only sophisticated methods in a hospital setting would have saved the baby after its mother was shot. That had been Raul's whole purpose, to kill them both, taking away everything Pablo loved. And now Marshall knew that Pablo Echeverría was as dead as Paloma and their child. He had been destroyed. All that was left was the shell of the man he was now: Special Agent Marshall Everett of the DEA.

After he heard the shattering news about Paloma, he spent another week in Quantico being debriefed, but he had already told them everything he knew. He felt empty and hollowed out, and after a night of sobbing over Paloma, he had not cried again and felt nothing. He was released at the end of the third week. He was given the keys to a furnished apartment in Georgetown, in a building reserved for returning undercover agents, and was assigned to a job at the South American desk at the Pentagon. It felt like a death sentence to him, and he could barely make himself go to work on the first day.

It was snowing, on a bitter cold day the last week in February, and his new office was as barren as his life. He had grown up in Seattle, but after his parents' death while he was in college, he had left and never returned. He had entered DEA training as the youngest member of his class, and had gone into undercover work, shortly after he graduated. Now after six years of it, he had no close friends,

no family, no hometown or base, no one he wanted
to resume contact with, nothing to do when he
left work, and nothing to say when he was there.
He analyzed the reports that were given to him,
and handed in meticulous in-depth memos that
showed how well he knew his subject, the area, the
people involved, and their activities. He knew everything about the drug trade in Colombia and the
countries he had dealt with for Raul. He inquired
occasionally, but there had been no word of Raul,
since he escaped while they raided the camp. And
by the spring, Marshall felt as though he had been
at his desk at the Pentagon for a hundred years. He
turned twenty-nine and didn't care. He spent his
birthday alone in front of the TV, as he did every
night.

There was a Colombian restaurant he went to occasionally to eat the familiar food, and after banter-
ing with the waiters in Spanish, when they asked
him where he was from, he would say Bogotá. It
was easier than explaining why he spoke Spanish
the way he did. Anyone would have taken him for
a native, which was how he felt. He had more in
common with Latin Americans than with North
Americans now.

Bill Carter checked on him from time to time,
and knew he was doing extraordinary work, but
talking to Marshall always unnerved him. There
was something dead about him, as though his soul
were gone. A part of him had died with Paloma, as

Marshall knew only too well. The only thing Marshall wanted to know was when he could return to some kind of undercover work, anywhere in South America where he would not be remembered or associated with Raul. And Bill had the uncomfortable feeling that he wanted to go back for revenge. Marshall couldn't imagine spending the rest of his life at a desk. Undercover work was in his blood— he couldn't seem to get back to real life, whatever that was for an undercover agent who was expected to take on all the traits and habits and customs of a country and become a native in every way, then, when ordered to do so, forget all of it and come home again and turn into someone he could barely even remember. "Real life" was so much less interesting than the dangerous and exciting life he had led undercover.

The DEA was determined to keep him home for a year and reevaluate his situation then. They had no idea what to do with him after that, although Marshall had requested Mexico several times and insisted no one would recognize him there. But the psychologist had suggested that he needed an extended time in the States to reacclimate, and for a smooth reentry. Marshall felt as though he were living somebody else's life. He missed his missions for Raul, their morning meetings, their nightly brandies, and a last cigar while they recapped the day. Although he knew what he had been doing there and why, they had become friends. However much he hated Raul now for what he'd done to Paloma and their baby, Marshall missed their camaraderie, and the intelligent conversations and decisions shared, just as he ached for the exquisite beauty of Paloma, and everything he had known with her. It was a lost world for him, with nothing to replace it in the States. He felt like he had been sucked into a vacuum and was hanging in space between two worlds.

By May, it was hard for Marshall to believe he had only been back for three months. It felt like three years, and he couldn't imagine another nine months with a desk job at the DEA, let alone a lifetime of it, if they never sent him back to the field. By June, he was putting serious pressure on them to reassign him anywhere in the Spanish-speaking world, where the drug activities would put his experience to use and challenge him again. What he wanted more than anything was to work undercover and get out of the Pentagon.

By September, after a long, hot, dreary summer in Washington, he had spent every weekend in his apartment, and he felt like he was going insane. He requested a meeting with Bill Carter, and asked him if they were really planning to keep him in Washington for a full year before reassigning him. He felt he was being punished for doing too good a job undercover in Colombia and getting so deeply involved, which had been essential to the success of his mission there. He had already been punished enough by Raul.

"Why don't you sit back and enjoy it while you're here?" Bill Carter responded. "There are a lot of things to do in Washington. You haven't taken any vacation time. Isn't there somewhere you want to go?" he asked pleasantly, as Marshall looked at him intently.

"Yes. Anywhere in Central or South America. Back to work. I have nothing to do here." Bill had noticed and heard from others that Marshall had made no friends since he'd returned. He considered it a temporary assignment. He was a perfect chameleon when undercover, but had no idea how to be himself anymore. The only "himself" he knew was the right-hand man of one of the biggest drug dealers in South America. Being Special Agent Marshall Everett was now totally foreign to him. He had let his hair grow back to a buzz cut after he shaved it when he left Bogotá. Beards were discouraged at the Pentagon. He didn't even recognize the man he saw when he looked in the mirror without his long hair and beard, and his military surplus wardrobe.

He felt like he was living a lie every day, coming to work at a job he hated, with people he didn't care about or even want to know. What did he have in common with them? The men like him were all out in the field doing what he wanted to do, trying to break the chain of command and interrupt the activities of drug cartels. That at least seemed like important work. He was wasting his time at the desk job he'd been given, and even his superiors had to admit that his finely honed skills weren't being used.

"Let's see where you are by the end of the year," Bill Carter said, trying to fob him off, but he had no foreign undercover assignment in mind for him for the moment. They didn't want him going back to wreak vengeance of a personal nature. He had to maintain a cool head and neutral point of view at all times. Bill wasn't fully convinced Marshall was capable of that anymore. He had lost too much and paid too high a price for the work that he loved. He wasn't objective, and wanted to engage in a vendetta his superiors didn't want him waging in the name of the DEA.

They were having a hard time evaluating him and figuring out where to send him that would make sense both for him and for the DEA, without jeopardizing himself or operations they had in progress. He had made no friends in Washington, and wasn't dating yet either. He hadn't gotten over the woman and child he had lost. Nothing in his current profile encouraged them to send him undercover again, but everyone agreed he was wasted where he was, and Marshall knew it too. He got more discouraged every day. He had already decided that if they didn't give him a new undercover assignment within the next year, he would leave the agency, but he had no idea what he would do then. All he knew how to do was what he had done for the DEA.

Bill Carter mentioned it over lunch with Jack Washington, his opposite number at the Secret Service, who was an old friend. They often asked each other's advice over knotty problems they were dealing with at work, although they were loyal to their respective agencies and the people who worked for them.

"I've got a guy who's rotting on the vine at a desk job in the Pentagon," Bill told his Secret Service friend. "He's an incredibly talented undercover guy. We had him in Ecuador and Colombia for six years, and he got in too deep. There was a leak that made the decision easy, so we didn't blow the whole operation and get everyone killed. But I think we took him out too late. We only brought half of him home. His body is in Washington, but his heart and mind are still in the jungle south of Bogotá. He had a woman there—our target killed her hours after he left. And I'm watching this guy turn into a zombie. He's brilliant at what he does, but we all agree, he's still among the walking wounded, although he doesn't know it. I don't know what the devil to do with him." It had been bothering him for months. They were wasting Marshall's talent.

"That's the trouble with you guys, you send them off to lead a supposedly real life in a false situation, they get to believe it, and they don't know who they are by the time you get them out. I've seen some really great guys get broken in mind and spirit that way. It's the nature of what you do, but it takes a hell of a toll on your boys, like military intelligence in a war zone. Those guys never come back whole."

"Some do," Bill said staunchly, but Jack Washington wasn't buying it. He'd seen the damage too often before. They were the casualties of the drug wars.

"Our guys risk their lives every day, but they've got their feet firmly planted on terra firma. They know who they are, who they're working for, and who they're defending. They don't go nuts trying to become something else, in a different culture, language, and country. Can you send him somewhere a little tamer?"

"I really don't have anything for him right now. He's been requesting Mexico, but I'm not convinced he'd be safe there either. And the psych team at his debriefing said he needed a year at home. The trouble is, this isn't home to him anymore. Home is a jungle camp with one of the biggest drug cartels in Colombia."

"That's what I mean," Jack said knowingly, and Bill couldn't say that he was wrong. He just hated to admit how badly they damaged their men sometimes. But it was inevitable with the kind of work they did. Both men knew it was true.

"So what do I do with him?" Bill said, looking worried. He felt responsible for Marshall, and what his undercover assignments had done to him. He wanted to help him now. "He's a terrific agent. One of our best. He belongs in the field. His psych reports are fine—they just think he needs time to acclimate to the United States again, but it's not happening for him. It's written all over him. He deserves a better break than this. I get the feeling he might quit, because of the desk job, which would really be too bad. He's one of the most dedicated, talented guys I've got. He's got instincts like no one else I've ever met."

"I could use more of those," Jack said with a smile. "My guys get burned out too. Guarding ex-presidents can get pretty dull. Thank God, they don't get a lot of chances to show off their stuff. Your boys in the field get to use all their wits and everything they've got every day. Their lives depend on it." And then he thought of something as he said it and looked at Bill quizzically. "You said you were afraid he'd quit. Do you think he'd quit the DEA and come over to us? I have two vacancies on the presidential detail. We had a guy die of a heart attack two weeks ago, at thirty-nine. Perfect health, no cardiac history, and he dropped dead jogging before he came to work. And one of my best guys is going on family leave because his wife has cancer and he wants to stay home and take care of her and the kids. I know we don't cross-hire, but if I like this guy, what if you put him on a leave of absence and he came to me, for six months or a year?

It sounds like he's got the skills, and it might be more interesting for him than the Spanish desk at the DEA, analyzing reports for you. With his background, this guy is more of a doer than an analyst.

"What do you think? You know the guy—how polished is he? Would he hold up to White House protocol? It's a far cry from the jungles of Colombia. Has he got what I need?" He had a dozen other men he could use, but something about the story Bill had told him intrigued him, particularly if it was short term to fill in for his man on family leave. And then he could go back to the DEA and go undercover again.

Jack knew that if he hired from among Secret Service ranks for the presidential detail, no one would want to give up their spot, when his agent came back from leave. The presidential detail was considered a plum job by everyone in the Secret Service. There were risks, but nothing as dangerous as what Marshall had done for the DEA. Jack knew that those boys lived on the adrenaline rush of risking their lives every day. Marshall would certainly be capable of handling the presidential detail, if he wanted to and was willing.

"Why don't you send him over to me and I'll take a look? If you put him on sabbatical, I might be able to 'borrow' him from you for six or nine months. If I like him, I can ask the president what he thinks. We've done stranger things, and it might be a blessing for everyone. It would get him out from behind that desk, which might preserve him for you, rather than his just quitting because he hates it. Talk to him about it and see what he says."

They changed the topic of conversation then to other things: a scandal in the Senate, some changes in structure in the Justice Department, and a new appointee to the Superior Court bench, which had taken everyone by surprise. The new president was young and had some very different ideas that not everyone liked. There was always something to talk about in Washington. Both men liked their jobs and the responsibilities that went with them. And when they left each other after lunch, Jack reminded Bill again to talk to his agent about taking a sabbatical to be on loan to the Secret Service. Bill promised that he would, but didn't have time to do so until the next day. He called Marshall into his office. He walked in with a hopeful look.

"Good news? You're sending me back to the field?" Marshall looked like a kid at Christmas, as though he were still hoping for Santa Claus to show up. Bill hated to disappoint him.

"Not the way you mean," he said immediately. He didn't want to mislead him, and Marshall's face fell the moment Bill said it. "I had lunch with a great friend of mine yesterday. He's at the Secret Service, and he was telling me about the problems they're having. They just lost two guys on the presidential detail."

"I read about the one who had a heart attack two weeks ago. What happened to the other one?"

"His wife is sick. He's going on family leave. We don't usually cross over with the Secret Service, as you know, but my friend came up with an interesting idea. If you take a sabbatical from the DEA, he might be able to 'borrow' you for a while, until their man comes back. How would you feel about being on the presidential detail?" Marshall's face clouded for a minute. This was not what he had in mind at all. He hated his job on the Spanish desk, but as he saw it, standing around the halls of the White House, or at official dinner parties, was not his idea of hard work either. He wanted to go back into the field, live on adrenaline every day, and serve a useful purpose fighting the really bad guys. He had joined the DEA to make a difference in the world. As part of the presidential detail, failing a bomb or a direct assault on the president, he thought he would be as useless as he was now at the desk job at the Pentagon.

"I don't know," Marshall said honestly. "It's not what I was trained for. I want to go back to work, doing what I know how to do. I'm not a babysitter, or a desk man. I want to be up and running, in the field."

"And you will be again," Bill reassured him, "just not yet. You need to let some time pass. People know you now. We don't want to send you back to be slaughtered. We need to wait until the air clears a little. It was getting way too hot for you there when you left. Something like the presidential detail might be a nice middle ground in the meantime. Those guys earn their money too. They're not sissies. Would you like to meet my friend at the Secret Service?" Marshall nodded cautiously, but he still wasn't sure. It didn't sound like it was for him.

When he went to visit Jack Washington three days later, Marshall found him incredibly charismatic and convincing. He made the job sound just as exciting as what Marshall had been doing for the last six years, although Marshall wasn't sure that was true. Jack tried to make it seem very appealing, and he kept reminding Marshall of how bored he was on the Spanish desk, which made it an easier sell.

"You could actually take me on loan to the Secret Service?" He didn't want to leave the DEA permanently, which Jack said he understood. And Jack was impressed by what he saw when they met. Marshall was smart and was quick to get everything Jack implied. He looked presentable and was a very bright young guy.

"Pulling a few strings, I think I could borrow you from the DEA," Jack said cautiously. He had never done it before with a DEA agent, but he wanted to try.

"Let me be clear with you," Marshall said. "It's not what I want to do, and if they offer me an undercover spot anywhere in South America, I'm going to leap on it. But you're right, it's better than the Spanish desk. What do we need to do to clear me for the presidential detail?"

"Why don't you send me your CV, and I'll have a couple of earnest conversations with the right people about how much I need you. I can bill this as a rare opportunity to get our hands on a DEA guy. We did something similar with a CIA man a few years ago, and an FBI special agent about ten years ago. It happens, although it doesn't happen often. But sometimes it's worth the paperwork and the challenge, if it's the right fit."

"I'd like to do it. It would get me out of the office," Marshall said, beginning to warm to the idea. "If I have to stay there for another five months or longer, I'll go crazy. I might even quit. I've thought about it." Jack wasn't surprised, and Bill had suspected it too, and didn't want to lose him.

"Well, don't do that," Jack said calmly. "Maybe this will solve the problem, for both of us. Send me your CV, and I'll go to bat for you in the right places. Sometimes you just have to be creative." Marshall nodded, suddenly intrigued by the idea, although he hadn't been very excited about it at the outset. Marshall wanted action, he thrived on it, and had been longing for it since his return.

He didn't hear from Jack again until late October. Jack had spoken to Bill first, and had gotten the approval he needed, from the highest source. They had run a check on Marshall, and liked everything they'd heard. And if Marshall agreed, Jack wanted Bill to draw up the agreement to give Marshall a sabbatical, and then he could come to work at the White House. It was a prestigious job, and when Jack told Marshall about it in greater detail, he was excited about it. He knew the job wouldn't be as interesting as what he'd done undercover, but it was a lot better than the desk job he was desperate to get away from, and it was a highly prized assignment.

Once the paperwork for the transfer came through approved, Jack called him to start work on Monday. They had already filled the other position of the agent who had died with someone from within the ranks of the Secret Service. Marshall was going to be the exception, covering the man on family leave with the sick wife, and he wondered if his co-workers on the presidential detail would resent him for getting special clearance for the assignment. If so, he thought that he could handle it.

Marshall was nervous the first day on the job. He wasn't sure what to expect. Once he got there, he was given a run-through of his duties and a tour of the area where he'd be working, including the Oval Office and the private quarters. When an aide showed him around, they could only go so far in the private quarters because the first lady and the children were having dinner. The president had flown to New York on Air Force One to give a speech at the UN that night, and the first lady had stayed home. The person giving them the tour explained that the first lady often ate with the children, when she didn't have to attend an official function. She liked being with her kids, who were six and nine. Family was very important to this presidency, and the president was often seen playing with his children on the weekend. It gave a slightly more relaxed feeling to the current administration and the White House as a home. His daughter had even sneaked down to see a state dinner, and had been photographed peeking through the banisters of the grand staircase. The photograph had been adorable, the senior member of the Secret Service said, although Marshall didn't remember seeing it. He had had very little contact with children in his life, both undercover and in real life. His baby with Paloma would have been the first.

He was told to report for his first shift. He had worn the dark suit that he had bought for work, and had arrived early for the tour and orientation. And when he left the DEA for his "sabbatical," Bill wished him well and said he hoped he'd enjoy the temporary mission, although not so much that he'd abandon the DEA for good. Bill promised to speak to him from time to time to see how it was going, and made it clear that if Marshall still wanted to go back to South America as an undercover agent, they still wanted him. Marshall assured him that he would, and that he had every intention of doing his best on the presidential detail in the meantime.

"Make us proud," Bill Carter had said.

"I will, sir," Marshall assured him with a smile and left.

On his first morning, he was assigned to stand in a specific spot outside the Oval Office, and to follow the president if he moved. Three other Secret Service agents were near at hand. He wasn't expected to emerge until lunchtime, at which point he would eat in the family residence dining room, and he had a full afternoon of meetings in the Oval Office as well. Marshall's supervisor told him that the president was staying put and had important conferences by phone and in person set up for the entire day, some with foreign heads of state.

Marshall had been standing in the same spot for two hours, looking like a statue in a suit with "spaghetti" in his ear, which was slang for the earpiece and wire they wore to stay in constant communication by radio. Marshall's earpiece was turned on and he was fiercely bored as he tried not to fall asleep on his feet. Several pretty women whizzed past him, carrying papers, files, and iPads. He was staring at his shoes for an instant when he saw two small feet appear in front of his, in sparkly pink shoes with bows on them. And the moment he spotted them, he looked up to see a little girl with her blond hair in pigtails, missing her front teeth. She was looking up at him very seriously, and she was wearing a gray skirt and a pink sweater. She looked incredibly cute, and was giving Marshall a thorough once-over. She was even prettier than she was in pictures, and she had huge blue eyes that met his squarely. He was startled by the intense, direct look, and surprised to see the president's six-year-old daughter alone, unescorted.

"I've never seen you before," she said matter-of-factly. "Did you just get here?"

"Yes, I started here today," he said, as he would have to an adult asking the same question. He wasn't sure how to talk to her, and hadn't expected her to interrogate him.

"Do you like it?" she asked politely, and he nodded, trying not to grin in amusement. She was like a funny little elf. He hadn't expected to meet her or have a conversation with her.

"Yes, very much," he answered. "Everyone's been very nice," he said, wondering if she always wandered around the White House alone, and why she wasn't in school.

"My name's Amelia. He's my dad." She pointed to the Oval Office, and Marshall nodded. "Have you met my daddy yet?"

"Well, actually, not yet. He's been busy all morning."

She nodded as though that was expected, and then answered his unspoken question. "I usually am too, but they have chicken pops at my school, and my mom doesn't want me to get it. They give you spots and make you itch. Did you ever get them?"

"I think so. I can't remember," he said seriously,

continuing the exchange with his new friend in the pink shoes.

"Well, I don't have them, so you won't get them from me. My brother had them last year, but I didn't get them then either, so my mom doesn't want me to get them now. Martha, who takes care of us, has the flu. My mom is getting her hair done, so I came down to visit. What are you going to be for Halloween?" The question took him by surprise, and he started laughing.

"I don't know. I hadn't thought about it." He hadn't worn a Halloween costume in twenty years.

"You should," she said solemnly. "It's tomorrow."

"What are you going to be?" he asked her, enjoying talking to her. She was very bright and funny, and it made a boring morning of standing outside the Oval Office already more entertaining than his desk job.

"I was going to be Cinderella, but the shoes are hard to walk in and I might fall down, so I'm going to be a mouse. I can wear my ballet shoes for that, and a tutu," she added, looking pleased, and Marshall smiled.

"A mouse in a tutu sounds like a great idea."

"My brother is going to be a vampire, and Daddy bought him fake blood. My mom says it's going to make a mess everywhere," she said, and giggled. The notion of the president of the United States going out to buy his son fake blood for his vampire costume sounded remarkably normal to him. It was a far cry from what he had been doing for the past six years, and reminded him of what other people did, who had family lives and kids. And with that, the door to the Oval Office opened, and suddenly the president was standing there and looked surprised to see his daughter chatting with the Secret Service man assigned to the door. He glanced at Marshall and smiled, and then down at his daughter with a quizzical look.

"What are you doing down here by yourself, young lady?"

"Martha's sick, and Mommy's getting her hair done. I told him about the fake blood you got for Brad. He's not going to be anything." She indicated Marshall as she said it. "He forgot it was Halloween tomorrow. I told him about my mouse."

"I think it's almost time for lunch, and Mom is going to wonder where you are. Did you tell her you were coming down here?" He sounded like any other father as he asked, and Amelia looked instantly sheepish.

"She's busy." And Amelia loved sneaking off to visit him. She did so whenever she could.

"I'll take you back up." And then he turned to Marshall with a friendly expression. "Thank you for entertaining my daughter. She has lots of friends at the White House," he said. And she loved turning up at his office. He disappeared to the private elevator, and Amelia turned and waved to Marshall before she got in and called back down the hall to him before the door closed.

"I'll come show you my costume tomorrow!" she promised, and he waved as she and her father disappeared.

"She's cute, isn't she?" one of the president's assistants said, as she hurried past him with an armload of books. "They both are, she and Brad. He's got nice kids. They come down here all the time. It's one of the perks of the job." He hadn't been enthused about working for the Secret Service, it sounded boring to him, though not as much as what he'd been doing at the Pentagon. But he hadn't expected the family atmosphere created by the president's children. Much to his own surprise, he was looking forward to seeing Amelia all dressed up as a mouse. He wondered if the kids came trick-or-treating to the office. It made it feel as though he were part of a family and not just a job, having met Amelia, and he liked it. It added another dimension to his work to see how human they were.

The president came back ten minutes later and shook Marshall's hand. "I hope Amelia didn't give you the third degree. She loves to make new friends."

"Not at all. She was telling me about her Halloween costume and the fake blood for your son."

"I suspect we'll be seeing a lot of it tomorrow. Mostly on his mother's new white couch, and I'll be in the doghouse. Amelia thought I should come to work in costume tomorrow," he bantered with the new Secret Service man, sizing him up as he did. He liked the fact that he had been friendly to his daughter and Amelia said he was nice. He looked pleasant to him. "I thought Superman might be appropriate, but I'm not sure how the press would feel about a president in tights." They both laughed about what he said, and a moment later the president went back to the Oval Office, to meet with a head of state from the Middle East. Marshall had already been briefed that the British prime minister was coming to meet with the president the next day, though presumably not in costume. And the vision of the president in a Superman costume made Marshall laugh. It had lightened the tension of his first morning in a new job, particularly one like this. This was light-years away from what he normally did, working undercover for the DEA. And Marshall didn't see the president again until the end of the day.

Phillip Armstrong came out of the Oval Office at seven o'clock, said goodnight to everyone, and smiled at Marshall. "Decent first day on the job?" he asked him. He liked the look of Marshall, and had spotted him first thing, even before the meeting with Amelia, and Marshall nodded with a smile.

"Very good first day, sir. Thank you. And I enjoyed meeting your daughter."

"Who were you assigned to before this?" Probably

60 Danielle Steel

a past president, or someone similar, the president assumed.

"I'm actually on temporary leave from the DEA. I've been undercover in South America for six years. I've been at the Pentagon for the last eight months between assignments, and they sent me over here, on loan to you." Marshall smiled.

"This must seem very dull to you," the president said, raising an eyebrow, impressed by his work history. The undercover DEA boys were a hardcore elite, and lived an entirely different life in hardship conditions, at constant risk.

"No, sir. Just different. The Pentagon is a lot quieter than this." There had been a lot of activity around him all day. He was more of a passive but alert observer, unless the president went somewhere, which he hadn't. He had been busy in the Oval Office since early morning, except when he escorted his daughter upstairs.

"Well, welcome to the White House. I hope you'll enjoy it. We're happy to have you as part of the team," the president said warmly, and then went to speak to one of his secretaries, got in the private elevator immediately afterward, and went upstairs. Phillip Armstrong seemed like a quiet, wholesome family man, and he'd been pleasant to Marshall and made him feel at home on his first day. He was a likable man, and the polls said that the majority of Americans liked him as well.

When Marshall left the White House after his

first day of work, it had been a good day. He wasn't hunting down bad guys or trying to outsmart them, or arranging for transport of tons of cocaine to Africa, the Caribbean, or the United States. Today had seemed like a normal day at work, although he was working at the White House, and chatting with the president of the United States, and Marshall was beginning to think that maybe it wouldn't be so bad, for a while anyway. And he liked meeting the little girl. He smiled to himself as he drove home to his furnished apartment in Georgetown, and tonight it actually felt like home to him, despite the bare walls and sparse decor. And as he looked around, he realized that he needed to do something to warm it up a little. He felt as though he were seeing his apartment with new eyes. And for the first time since leaving Colombia and learning of Paloma's and the baby's deaths, he felt alive again. A little girl in braids with sparkly pink shoes had touched his heart and made it a good day.

Chapter 4

The next day at the White House was far more active than the first. Marshall was part of a detail of six Secret Service men who accompanied the president by helicopter to a meeting held at Camp David, with the British prime minister. They stayed there through lunch, and then the president spoke in Congress, and it was midafternoon by the time they got back to the White House. It had been an interesting day, and the British prime minister and his aides had been very pleasant to them all. The Secret Service men and their British counterparts had chatted and had a few good laughs. And there was something exciting about the people they met on the job. Marshall had had a chance to talk to the other Secret Service men, while they waited through lunch. They appeared to have a relaxed, easygoing style about them, but were always on the alert. One of them had been in the job for more than twenty years, but the others were closer to Marshall's age. They were intrigued when he said he was DEA, and was recently back from six years in the field in South America, which they knew meant he must have been assigned to the drug cartels, which instantly won their respect.

"This must be a hell of a change," one of the younger men said admiringly. "I thought about DEA, but I got married right out of college, and you can't have a wife and family and do that kind of work." Marshall thought instantly of Paloma and their baby and nodded. "You're lucky you got out in one piece. You hear bad stories." Yes, of the woman you love and the baby she's carrying being murdered as a reprisal, Marshall thought and didn't say it.

"Yeah, there are bad stories," Marshall conceded but didn't volunteer any information about himself. He was used to concealing who he really was, as a person, even now. "You don't think about that when you're there. You do what you have to do. But what you're doing here is just as important, more so. You're protecting the president of the United States, that's an important job. I was just following drug runners, and trying to make a dent in the cartels." They all knew it was a nearly impossible job, but Marshall had done some damage to their operation. Not enough by his standards, but according to his superiors and the reports written about him, his impact had been huge, especially with the information he had shared when he came out. Raul would be hurting for a long time. Marshall said nothing about it to the other men.

"Did you have to leave because someone blew your cover?" one of them asked, curious about him and the job.

"There was a leak," he said simply. "I had to get out fast." His eyes told nothing about how painful his departure had been, or what he'd left behind.

"That's a tough way to live. You must be glad to be home." Marshall sighed in answer. The truth was, he wasn't. He longed for his old life, and he considered the time in Washington temporary. That was the only thing that kept him going—the belief that one day he'd go back to undercover missions.

"It's different" was all Marshall said, and it reminded his new colleagues that the guys who did undercover work were addicted to it.

"Your Spanish must be amazing," another Secret Service man said with quiet respect, and Marshall laughed. They had all noticed how modest and discreet he was.

"Better than my English sometimes. I hadn't spoken English in six years. You become someone else, and forget who you really are, or used to be. It all seems pretty strange at first, and after a while it's the only life you know." He still read South American newspapers more often than North American, and watched Spanish TV, but he didn't say it, at the risk of sounding weird.

"Are you finished with the DEA?" the other Secret Service man asked with interest.

"I hope not," Marshall said quietly. "It suits me. You've got more room to move around, and do some damage where it counts. Maybe I'm addicted to the adrenaline rush." They all knew that a lot of operatives got killed working in the field for the DEA, even in the States.

"You get that rush in this line of work occasionally too. I always think how bad the boys must have felt when Kennedy was shot. They were doing all they could, but sometimes shit happens . . . you do everything right, and get screwed anyway."

"Undercover work is like that too. You never know the outcome till it's over, if you'll make it or get killed." They nodded, in silent agreement, and then the meeting with the British prime minister broke up, and they moved on to Congress with the president and had no time to talk. But it had been an interesting exchange, and gave the others a glimpse into who Marshall was. He didn't talk much about himself, and was still trying to get oriented to his new line of work, but they could see how serious and conscientious he was about it.

He didn't relax his guard all day until the president was back in the Oval Office, and Amelia appeared in her mouse costume with the pink ballet shoes and tutu, at four o'clock. Someone had painted mouse whiskers on her face. She was beaming and bouncing as she threaded her way through the desks, and darted in and out of offices, and came up to Marshall with a big toothless smile. She was carrying a plastic Halloween pumpkin already half filled with candy, and several of the secretaries had come prepared and dropped some miniature candy bars into her pumpkin. Marshall was sorry he had nothing to give her. He hadn't thought to buy candy for the kids. And minutes after she got there, her brother appeared, a serious, handsome boy, in his vampire costume, with the fake blood dripping from his mouth. He was wearing plastic vampire teeth, and politely shook Marshall's hand.

"This is my brother, Brad," Amelia introduced them.

"Marshall Everett," Marshall said as he shook the boy's hand. "Great blood," he said admiringly, and the nine-year-old smiled ghoulishly. Marshall could just imagine the damage the fake blood had done upstairs, some of it was dripping from his face.

"Are you two going trick-or-treating?" Marshall asked. Amelia looked instantly disappointed and sighed.

"Daddy won't let us. And we'd have to take Secret Service with us, which is no fun. We can only trick-or-treat here in the house." The house being the White House, but several of the employees had already contributed to their candy stash. "But I was in the parade at school," Amelia said proudly, as her brother knocked on the door of the Oval Office, and a familiar voice invited them in. They stayed in the office with their father for half an hour, and when they emerged, the president was with them, and had vampire blood on his shirt, and a spot on his tie. He looked at Marshall ruefully, and Marshall grinned.

"I see the vampire attacked you, sir."

"Be careful he doesn't get you too," the president warned him, as Brad guffawed, and one of the secretaries handed them each a candy bar with a smile as she walked by.

"We're going to the kitchen next," Amelia announced. She was more outgoing and chattier than her brother, who seemed shy to Marshall. Amelia had friends everywhere, and she acted as though she had known Marshall for years, and had enlisted him as one of her many friends. They ran off shortly after, with their trick-or-treat pumpkins nearly full, and the president went back to work, as Marshall and the three other men on duty outside his office stood guard.

"They're sweet kids," one of the other men commented. "This can't be an easy life for them." But they barely knew any different life. Their father had been in office for almost two years, so Amelia had been four when they moved in, and Brad seven. And the president had been in the Senate for eight years before that, so this was the only life they knew and would for a while. He was a shoo-in for the next election if the polls held up, which meant that Amelia would be twelve when they left the White

House, and Brad would be in high school. It was an interesting place to grow up, and a golden life, however normally their father treated them.

The following day, Marshall met the first lady for the first time. She was a taller, even prettier version of Amelia, and as shy as Brad. The children were a combination of their parents, and Marshall could easily imagine Amelia as president one day, mouse costume, braids, and all. Their mother was an intelligent, gentle woman, who had been an attorney and graduated from Yale top of her class. She and the president had gone to law school together, and she had given up her career when he ran for the Senate shortly after they married. She was a devoted wife, and had espoused many charitable causes, trying to improve the lot of the indigent, and was a staunch supporter of all the poverty programs, particularly those that focused on children. She avoided all controversy and sensitive issues, took no aggressive political positions, and was a model wife. She was the perfect partner for the president of the United States, and she had learned French and Spanish when he became president, and she was currently studying Chinese. She was forty-two years old, four years younger than her husband. She was beautiful, had a great figure, played tennis, was an expert skier, and worked out with a trainer every day at six A.M. And the country loved her. Melissa Armstrong's gentle shyness, in spite of her remarkable intelligence, made her especially appealing. Her husband always credited her with the elections he had won. There was something vaguely Kennedy-esque about them, but in a modern, more modest way. They weren't showy, they were the real thing, and far more popular and beloved than any presidential family in recent years.

The day after Halloween, Marshall met her at a state dinner, and he was impressed by how striking she was in a sleek black evening dress, which covered one shoulder and left the other bare. She spotted him immediately as someone new, and made a point of saying hello to him between greeting guests.

"Amelia told me about you," she said warmly, with the shy smile she was famous for, and he was instantly reminded of Princess Di when she was young. She had the same kind of blond good looks, in a wholesome all-American way.

"You have a fantastic little girl," Marshall complimented her, "and a very handsome son, despite the vampire blood."

She rolled her eyes as he said it, and groaned. "You should see our new white couch." The president had predicted that but bought the blood anyway, to please his son. He often tried to make up to them for the restrictive lives they led. There was no hiding the fact that they lived in the White House, and there were many "normal" activities they couldn't do. It didn't bother Amelia but often upset Brad. He had recently joined the boys' soccer team at his school, but half a dozen Secret Service men went to his practices and games, inevitably.

The first lady turned to her duties then, but her contact with Marshall had been brief and warm, and the president made a quick friendly remark to him that night too. For the first time in his career, Marshall felt as though he were being inducted into a family and not just a job. It made him enjoy his work far more than he had expected to. And the state dinner that night was an elegant affair for a hundred and forty people, given in honor of the Japanese crown prince and his wife. It was a spectacular evening, typical of the social events given by this administration. In just a few days, Marshall had gotten a taste of what they were about, from Halloween to state dinners, to meetings at Camp David, and the only time the job was stressful was when the president was on the move. Then every man with him had to be on the alert and ready to protect him at every instant. The president had a relaxed, easy style, which sometimes made it even harder to shield him from potential attacks. He was more than willing to shake a hand, or stop somewhere he wasn't planning to, which made the Secret Service men's job even more difficult than it already was.

President Armstrong did just that in Marshall's second week, when he insisted on stopping at a department store to buy something for his wife, and rushed into the store unannounced, surrounded by

Secret Service men, with Marshall in the lead. Melissa had mentioned something the night before, which he wanted to buy her as a surprise, and he wanted to buy it himself. He was almost instantly thronged by astonished shoppers who wanted to shake his hand, while the store security tried to help as best they could. Two of the Secret Service men finally convinced him to wait outside in the car, while they completed the purchase of the bag Melissa had wanted, to go with the suit she was planning to wear for Thanksgiving. And the president was delighted with getting it for her, while the Secret Service men heaved a collective sigh of relief when they got him back in the car.

"He scares the shit out of me when he does that," the senior agent in charge said to Marshall once they had delivered the president safely to his next appointment. "I age ten years every time he makes one of those random stops. He does it with the kids all the time. He doesn't realize how dangerous it is." Their surprise visit to the department store had made Marshall nervous too, as his eyes had darted everywhere, checking the crowd for suspicious people and activity. But stops like that were less dangerous than the ones where he was expected, when a deranged person, or even a terrorist group, could make a plan. But the unplanned stops and outings weren't easy for them either, and it was something the president loved to do, to maintain an illusion of normalcy in their lives. The first lady was always more sensible and easier to reason with, and concerned for her children's safety. President Armstrong loved spontaneity, and was famous for it, and rarely did as he was told, which kept them on their toes.

The president and his family spent Thanksgiving at Camp David, with relatives they had invited to join them there, and Marshall worked all four days and was happy to do so. Most of the other men had families or someone they wanted to spend the holiday with. Marshall didn't, and preferred being on the job to sitting alone in his apartment, so he covered for one of them every day, and they were grateful to him. They were surprised he didn't have plans of his own, but with no family after six years undercover in South America, there was no one he wanted to be with.

It turned out that being a part of the first family's holiday, even from a distance, was enjoyable for him, more so than he'd expected. He wasn't just a robot standing by. He kicked a football around with Brad, and had several conversations with Amelia, and both the president and the first lady thanked him for his kindness to their children, and warned him not to let them take advantage of him, or Amelia talk his ear off. They had a new black Lab who was full of energy, and Marshall played with him as well. It was the happiest Thanksgiving he'd had in years, and he liked the men he was working with. They had a good rapport, were a cohesive team, and were very serious about their job.

When Bill Carter checked on him with his superiors, they said Marshall was doing well and had integrated beautifully, especially with the first family, and the president had specifically requested him several times, particularly during weekends because he was so nice to the kids.

"I'm not so sure we're going to give him back to you in a year," his supervisor in the Secret Service said to Bill. "Maybe he won't even want to go back to work in the field."

"Don't count on it," Bill Carter said, knowing the breed too well, "it's in his blood. But I'm glad he's doing well. He had a tough reentry, and I was worried about him. Some bad things came down when we got him out. It sounds like he's coming around. Sometimes these guys never get over what we put them through," Bill said, feeling guilty for a minute. He had seen it happen too many times before, men who never recovered their lives when they came back, and couldn't forget the people they left behind. He had been afraid that Marshall would be one of those—he had seemed dead for a while. But his time close to the president and first lady, and particularly their children, was bringing him back to life. Bill was pleased to hear it, and happy to know he was doing well, and as efficient as always in the job. He was a dedicated agent at whatever he did.

Marshall was on duty over Christmas, at his own request, and went skiing with the first family in

Aspen after that, and personally skied with Brad, while Melissa taught Amelia herself. She had been a champion racer in her youth, and Amelia took to the slopes with ease. Only the president skied very little and stayed in the house most of the time—he had too much else to do—but he had asked Marshall to ski with Brad, as one of the younger agents on the detail. Brad loved hanging out with him, and sometimes when joking with him, Marshall spoke to him in Spanish, and Brad always laughed at that. The first lady overheard him one day, and addressed him in nearly flawless Spanish, which surprised him. And they conversed for a few minutes in Spanish. She asked where he had learned it, and he said he'd lived in South America for six years, and then she remembered his work history with the DEA. She was curious about his experiences undercover, but was hesitant to ask him about them. Only Brad hounded him to tell him stories, once he heard about it from the other agents, but Marshall never would. Brad said he wanted to work for the CIA one day, and Marshall always teased him that the DEA was better. He had an easy rapport with both kids, and enormous respect for their parents, how good they were with their children, and kind to their employees. And he was sorry to leave Aspen, where he had enjoyed the skiing and the relaxed time with Melissa and the kids.

Once back in Washington, he was on the job with the president again. Marshall still had no social life of his own, and didn't want one. He showed no interest in the women he met at the office. The one thing he knew after losing Paloma and their baby, and years earlier his parents, was that he never wanted to love anyone and lose them again. His work was enough for him.

They had a busy winter and spring, with state dinners, political meetings, a trip to Europe, another to Asia, another trip to Australia, appearances in Texas, California, and other states, and a brief stay in Oklahoma when a series of tornadoes devastated the state and the president went to observe the damage. It startled Marshall to realize that he had been back from Colombia for fifteen months, by the time things settled down in May, and he had been assigned to the president for seven months.

Amelia made him a birthday card herself and gave him a cupcake with a candle in it when he turned thirty. And Brad gave him a football autographed by Aaron Rodgers, which had been given to him and was one of his prize possessions. Marshall was hesitant to accept it, but Brad insisted he wanted him to have it, and Marshall promised to put it in a place of honor in his apartment, which still looked stark and sterile. He kept meaning to fix it up, but now he had no time. And Georgetown still didn't feel like home. The last place that had felt like home to him was his hut in Raul's camp, but that was because of who was there.

He thought of Paloma a little less often now, although she still haunted him, with her heavy round belly. And in the back of his mind, he still wanted to hunt Raul down and kill him one day. He had heard through his DEA sources that his operation had been severely hampered, and he was back in Colombia by then, in a different location. The DEA had an operative in his camp, working at a low level, but no one had been able to infiltrate into the operation to the degree that Marshall had. Raul was even more careful now, and had learned a painful lesson when he realized that Marshall had betrayed him, and outsmarted him for three years. But Raul had won in the end, when he killed Paloma, and struck at the heart of everything that mattered to Marshall.

In July, Marshall got a call from Bill Carter to tell him the news. They had enough information to move on Raul's camp again. They had effected a devastating raid, and Raul had been killed, along with two of his brothers. Bill wanted Marshall to know, and thought he'd be relieved. But all Marshall felt was emptiness, like a giant hole in his stomach or his heart. He was surprised to discover that his death didn't matter. Paloma was dead, whether Raul was dead or alive. Their child had never been born, and a beautiful young woman he had loved had been snuffed out. It felt right that Raul was dead now too, but it didn't change anything. It was all in the past.

The next day Marshall was thinking about them,

staring into space, and remembering Raul and Paloma and the life they had shared. It seemed like only yesterday and yet was so long ago. He was at a compound the president had rented for the month on Long Island, and Marshall was standing guard outside the house, when he felt someone tug at his sleeve, and he looked down and saw Amelia. He had been a million miles away, and she was wearing her bathing suit and gazed up at him with worried eyes.

"Are you sad?" she asked him directly. He was sad about Paloma and the baby, but had a sense of justice about Raul, none of which he could explain to the little girl, but she had seen the far-off expression in his eyes in an unguarded moment as he drifted in time and space to the camp in Colombia where he had had a life for three years as Pablo Echeverría. A part of him would always be that man. And now Pablo was as dead as they were.

"Of course not," Marshall said, smiling at her. "So when are we going swimming in the ocean?" He had promised to take her that afternoon. Brad had gone fishing with his father on a friend's boat, and Marshall had been assigned to stay at the house with Amelia and her mother. He didn't mind at all.

"You looked sad," Amelia insisted, watching his face intently, but he seemed fine now. "I want to look for shells on the beach, and build a sandcastle with you."

"Okay, let's go," he said, communicating with

other agents in the detail on the radio he wore. They needed three agents on the beach, and one to replace him at the house. And a few minutes later he and Martha, the children's nanny, headed to the beach, with shovels, pails, and molds to make the castle, and by the time the first lady joined them, Marshall had built a very creditable castle, and they had a bucket full of shells. The first lady looked pleased. She hadn't been feeling well recently, and seemed to be resting a lot, and there had been rumors about her health. Everyone was concerned. She was wearing a bathing suit that day, with a white cover-up over it, through which he could see her shape, and suddenly he noticed that there was a familiar bulge that he had last seen when Paloma was pregnant, and he realized that the first lady was expecting another child, although there had been no announcement yet, but he had just seen it for himself. She looked four or five months pregnant and had done a masterful job of concealing it until then. He didn't say anything, but she saw that he had observed it, and she smiled.

"We thought it best to keep this quiet as long as we could, to keep it out of the press. We're going to tell the kids this weekend," she said as Amelia ran down to the water's edge with Martha and her bucket.

"Congratulations," Marshall said quietly, and thought of Paloma again. At forty-two, given the stresses of the life Melissa led, he suspected it might not be such an easy thing, and he wondered how Amelia and her brother would take the news. Amelia was the star and the baby in the family for now, and might not welcome the competition. But two days later, Amelia told Marshall herself.

"We're having a baby," she announced matter-of-factly, as they built another castle on the beach. "I want a girl. If it's a boy, I think we should send it back. My mom says I can help take care of her." She didn't seem upset about it all—they had obviously handled the announcement well. She had turned seven and liked the idea of being a big sister. He was surprised to find he was looking forward to it too, although the memory was bittersweet for him. He and Amelia played games trying to pick out names for it, and he teased her by reminding her it might be a boy, at which she always made a face.

The following week the news was announced in the press. The president and first lady were expecting a baby in November, shortly before Thanksgiving, and the first lady was going to curtail some of her activities in the coming months. Marshall thought they were wonderful parents and was happy for them. The president seemed very pleased.

By the time they moved back to Washington at the end of August, Melissa was six months pregnant, and it was very evident. It gave a touching, human quality to the first family, and Phillip's popularity went up in the polls again. He was a sure win for the next election the following year. The decisions he had made in the last three years had been sound, the country was doing better than it had in a while, and felt secure with Phillip Armstrong at its helm.

The kids went back to school in September, and Marshall met with Bill Carter to discuss the end of his leave from the DEA in a month. He looked healthy and well in mind and body, and he appeared to have thrived during his eleven months protecting the president. Bill Carter had a strong feeling he wasn't coming back to the DEA, which he suspected would be better for him than the life he had led before. He had paid a high price for that life.

"So what do you want to do? You know you can resign from us, and become Secret Service. This was a good chance for you to decide if you want to work for the Secret Service full time. You gave us the best you had to give for a long time." He didn't want Marshall to feel guilty about quitting and moving on, and he was doing so well with the Secret Service that it seemed a shame to leave. But Bill was stunned by his response.

"I want to come back," Marshall said quietly. "It's what I was trained to do. I've had a great time for the last year, and I guess I needed the break more than I realized. I love the Armstrongs—they're a fantastic family. But my heart is with the DEA."

"You still want undercover?" Bill Carter stared at him. What he had just heard was hard to believe.

"It's where I can do the most good. This is a great job, but all my skills, training, and experience are for the DEA," he said simply. He'd been thinking about it a lot.

"They're crazy about you, Marshall. Every report you've gotten is gold star. And he's a shoo-in for the next election. You've got five sure years working for a president you like."

"I know, but that's not where I belong. I don't want to waste six years of everything I learned in Ecuador and Colombia. Raul may be dead, but there are waves of others to take his place. We have work to do down there. It's where I serve my country best. I want to come back. And I don't care where you send me, as long as it's Central or South America. That's who I am. I know I can't go back to Colombia or Ecuador, but Mexico is getting hotter by the day, and in the right setup, I think you could use me there. All my work for Raul in Mexico was done through third parties. No one will recognize me there." He was totally clear on what he wanted. "I have six more weeks left in my commitment to the Secret Service. I can push it till the end of the year if you want. But they don't need me, and the DEA does. Lots of Secret Service agents want the job I have now. I want another assignment in the field, no matter how rough it is. It's time. I'm getting soft sitting around at state dinners and playing with the kids. I'm thirty years old, I have no attachments here. I know this is right for me."

Bill Carter couldn't disagree, but he was surprised anyway. Marshall seemed so happy working with the Secret Service, and they were thrilled with him, although in some ways he was overqualified for the job, and they knew it. They didn't need any of his drug enforcement and undercover experience for what they did. And he wanted to use all his skills again.

"Give us a little time to find you the right spot." There was a huge operation that had been growing exponentially in Panama, even bigger than Raul's, where Bill thought they could place him. And Mexico was an option, just as Marshall said. It was a decision that would have to be made by committee, and the assignment, whether in Panama or Mexico, would be even more dangerous than the ones he'd had before. But Bill realized now more than ever that Marshall was one of those men who thrived on the danger and the challenge. When Bill told Marshall's superiors at the Secret Service, they were disappointed, but the agent he had replaced on family leave was ready to come back, so it would work out. His wife had done well on chemo and was in remission, and he could resume his duties on the White House detail. The first family was fond of him too.

By the first of October, word had gotten out that Marshall was returning to the DEA before the end of the year, to go back to field work. They had promised to tell him where in the next few weeks.

And they were due to ship him out in November or December. The president told him how sorry he was to hear it, but said that he admired him for his courage and the kind of work he wanted to do. Brad wanted to hear all of the gory details of his next assignment, none of which Marshall knew yet, and would never have told him. The first lady made him promise to come and see the baby. They had learned it was a girl, and Amelia was thrilled, but she was crushed to hear that Marshall was leaving, and told him that was really mean and stupid of him. She had cried when her mother told her.

"I've got to go fight the bad guys again," he explained to her, "to keep you and your brother and new sister safe. That's what I do."

"Why can't someone else fight the bad guys and you stay here?"

"Because I'm better at it," he said, teasing her, but in many ways, it was true. "I'll visit you," he said, although he knew it wouldn't be soon, and he didn't want to mislead her, "whenever I am in Washington. Besides, you're going to be busy with your baby sister. You won't miss me at all." But he knew just how much he would miss her. He had come to love both children in the past eleven months, and had a deep affection and respect for their parents. And he knew he would be sad to leave.

The children were getting ready for Halloween again in his last weeks on the White House detail. This year Amelia had decided to be the witch in

The Wizard of Oz with a green face, and Brad was going to be an astronaut in a spacesuit that NASA had sent him, made specially for him in his size. He was very excited about it. Amelia had already practiced walking around the White House several times with her face covered in green face paint. It was a bittersweet memory, remembering he had met them exactly a year before, at Halloween.

Their mother was eight months pregnant by then, and said she was going as the Great Pumpkin this year. They were all excited about the baby, and in good spirits when the president agreed to dedicate the opening of a children's hospital in Virginia and bring the children with him. Melissa said she was very tired, but agreed to go anyway. The hospital was important to her because it was going to serve indigent children from all over the country who needed surgeries their parents couldn't afford. She had spent two years pushing the project, and the president had given it his support, so the whole family was going, and Marshall was assigned to the detail. The ceremony was scheduled for Saturday so the children could attend without missing school, and Amelia was going to cut the ribbon at the dedication. They were looking forward to it, and Marshall had a lump in his throat when he boarded the helicopter, knowing that this would be one of his last official functions with them. He had no illusions about it. He knew he would miss them terribly, particularly the children.

The helicopter landed on schedule, and a limousine was waiting to take them to the hospital. They had a full complement of Secret Service, with Marshall in the lead. He gave Melissa a hand out of the helicopter and helped her into the limousine. She was moving slowly, and she reminded him constantly of Paloma in the last days of her pregnancy, when it seemed as though her belly could stretch no further. The baby was due in three weeks, she was obviously uncomfortable, and she had been a good sport to come that day.

A large reception committee was waiting for them at the hospital, and a crowd of onlookers who had come to see the first family, and particularly the children. Amelia could hardly wait to cut the ribbon. The president moved through the crowd shaking hands, as the Secret Service pressed around him. By previous arrangement, Marshall had hung back to stand near Melissa, and there were additional agents with her and the kids.

They were given a tour of the hospital, and then came back outside, for Amelia to cut the ribbon. She was hopping up and down, she was so excited, and she stood in front of her mother during innumerable speeches, as Marshall watched the crowd, out of habit and reflex more than any real concern. It was a benign event, but he examined all the faces around them. And then suddenly in slow motion, he saw a man step forward and lift a high-powered rifle to his shoulder, take aim at the president,

and in the flash of an instant shift it to Melissa, as
Marshall shouted a warning. Three Secret Service
men threw the president to the ground and covered him with their bodies, and Marshall leaped
toward Melissa, knocking her to the ground as
Amelia screamed. All hell broke loose by then. Secret Service men were everywhere. The shooter was
grabbed by two of them, the president was still on
the ground with two Secret Service men on top of
him, the crowd was running away screaming, and
Melissa was groaning. She had hit her head when
she hit the ground. Brad was tackled in the arms of
a Secret Service man, and Marshall was on top of
Amelia. He had pulled her down and grabbed her,
but he had heard a bullet whiz past them, and as
he looked down at her beneath him, he could see
blood everywhere, it was all over her face and his
hands. He had no idea where she had been hit, but
he knew she had been. He tried to pick her up and
run to safety with her, but he couldn't. His left arm
wouldn't pick her up, and she looked at him with
terrified eyes, not even crying.

"Am I going to die?" she asked him in a hoarse
whisper. Her mother was on her knees by then, trying to cradle her daughter as Marshall told her not
to move her, and to lie down. She was injured herself and deathly pale.

"Don't move, baby," he said to Amelia, as he laid
her down gently, as police and Secret Service rushed
to help them, with the president right behind them,

surrounded by agents protecting him. They put her on a stretcher and took her into the hospital, with Melissa running beside them, looking dazed, the president supporting her, and Brad running with them. A battalion of Secret Service and police had surrounded them. Doctors came from everywhere, and all eyes focused on Amelia and the blood on her face. Everyone but Secret Service and the first family were cleared from the room, as they took Amelia's clothes off and examined her face and body. A bullet had barely grazed the side of her head, there was no point of entry, and no serious damage. It was a superficial wound, only because Marshall had yanked her away so quickly and saved her. Another inch or two, and she would have been shot in the head and killed. When Melissa realized what had nearly happened to her daughter, she fainted on the spot, and doctors were brought in to examine her too. Phillip was afraid she would go into labor. He and his son had sustained no damage. Amelia was treated for shock and possible infection for the wound. They put a bandage on her head after shaving and cleaning the area, but the wound was only a flesh wound and a very small one. Marshall had never taken his eyes off her from the moment they entered the hospital, and as the president turned to thank him, Amelia smiled at Marshall.

"You saved me, Marsh," Amelia said, and Marshall smiled with tears of relief running down his cheeks.

Melissa was conscious again by then, and they had determined that she had sustained a mild concussion when she fell to the ground, and they were going to do a sonogram to check on the baby, but it was moving, and they already found a heartbeat. A potential tragedy had been averted thanks to Marshall, his quick reflexes, unfailing instincts, and reactions. The president turned to put an arm on his shoulder to thank him with a deeply moved expression, and as he did, he saw his own hand covered with blood and the arm of Marshall's suit soaked dark in it. It was running down his arm and pooling on the floor. He hadn't even felt it.

The bullet that had grazed Amelia's head had hit Marshall's left shoulder. His arm hung at his side useless, and blood was gushing from the wound as doctors rushed to him, at a shout from the president. His head had been swimming, but all he had thought of was saving Amelia and Melissa's baby. He didn't want to happen to her what had happened to Paloma. He didn't want any of them to die.

The room was spinning as they lowered Marshall into a wheelchair, cut away his jacket and shirt, and put him on a gurney minutes later. The bullet was still lodged in his shoulder, and suddenly he didn't know where he was. Marshall looked up and saw Raul's face as they rolled him away, he was speaking Spanish, and he kept calling out the name Paloma. The other Secret Service men were crowded around, and arrangements were made to get the first family out of a back entrance and driven away to the helicopter as quickly as possible, to be treated and checked further in Washington. There was pandemonium outside the hospital as people begged to know if any of them had been killed. Vans of reporters and TV cameras had already arrived on the scene, and the shooter had long since left with the police.

"Is Marshall going to die, Daddy?" Amelia asked with a look of panic, as tears rolled down her cheeks. "He saved my life, he got shot because of me." He had taken the bullet that had grazed her and could easily have killed her or Brad, or hit Melissa's belly. Instead, as he reacted instantly to save them, it had hit him.

The president looked somber as he answered. "No, baby, he's not going to die. But he was very brave." His rapid actions had saved Phillip Armstrong's family, and he was deeply grateful that no one had been killed that day.

They were shepherded into the helicopter and brought back to the White House, where they were examined again. Melissa and the baby were mercifully unhurt, Phillip and Brad untouched, and Amelia's head wound remarkably clean. Melissa had a headache from the bump on her head when she'd fallen, but other than that she was fine. Only Marshall had been injured, and when Phillip inquired of the Secret Service men around him, during the next hours, he was told that Marshall was stable and still in surgery, to remove the bullet in his shoulder. He got the same answer for the next five hours, every time he asked, and was deeply concerned about him. He called and spoke to one of the doctors himself, and was told that they were trying to save the use of his left arm, as there had been considerable nerve damage, from a bullet that had been slashed to cause greater destruction on impact. It had done its job well.

Two of the Secret Service men had stayed with him at the hospital, and four others showed up shortly after. The senior agent on the scene called their superior, who called Bill Carter, who drove out to Virginia immediately and together the seven men waited for Marshall to emerge from surgery. There was no question in anyone's mind, he had saved Melissa and Amelia Armstrong. The surgeons who came out to talk to them during the surgery told them that they were performing microsurgery to save the use of Marshall's left arm. The bullet had done incredible damage, and at one point during the surgery, he had nearly died from the loss of blood.

At eight o'clock that night, all three surgeons came to tell Bill and the others that Marshall had survived, but the nerve damage was too extensive— he would never regain the use of his left arm. There was silence among the seven men who listened, and they knew what it would mean to Marshall, and what it would have meant to any of them. His career in the Secret Service and the DEA was over. He was irreparably impaired. He might regain some minimal function in his left arm over time, but not enough to operate as an undercover field agent in the DEA, or as a Secret Service agent. He had saved three lives, Melissa's, Amelia's, and the baby's, and had given up the use of his left arm to do it. It was what he had dedicated his life to do, and they all knew that he wouldn't have changed it. But they also knew that Marshall Everett's life, as he had known it, and all that he had lived for until that moment, was forever altered. It was a death sentence for the way he wanted to live his life. Bill Carter sat silently, wondering if he would survive it. Marshall would never work in the field or in any active role again.

Chapter 5

The president had Marshall transferred to Walter Reed Hospital by helicopter, as soon as he was well enough to be moved. As they had suspected initially, the final verdict was that his left shoulder and arm had suffered irreparable damage. The president had had three specialists called in, and all concurred with the surgeons' prognosis. He would never regain full use of his left arm, or possibly any at all. They were going to keep him in the hospital for several weeks to watch his progress, and also to begin rehab and physical therapy as soon as possible, so the arm didn't atrophy too quickly. He would have to work hard to maintain his recovery, and not have it affect his balance. His left arm hung now like a dead weight at his left side. And as he lay in bed at the hospital, Marshall knew what that meant. It was easy to figure out, but hard to understand. He had risked his life for six years of brutally dangerous undercover work and emerged unscathed. And in the last two weeks of his year in the Secret Service, at a ribbon-cutting ceremony at a hospital, his career had ended while trying to save a woman, an unborn baby, and a little girl. He didn't regret for an instant his instinctive act of courage, but the irony of it didn't escape him. Six years in the South American jungles, hunting drug dealers, hadn't killed him, but a ribbon-cutting ceremony had. Life as he had known it was forever changed. He could never again be a DEA agent, or even perform the Secret Service job he had considered tame. All he could have was a desk job, which he didn't want.

The president visited him to thank him personally for what he'd done, but it was so soon after surgery, Marshall hardly remembered. And Melissa and Amelia came to see him as soon as he was well enough to have visitors. Melissa brought tears to his eyes when she told him that they were giving the baby his name as a middle name, because he had saved her life. It was some small consolation for the baby who had died because of him, when Raul shot Paloma once he knew who Marshall was. He wondered if he was meant to atone for it in this way. And Amelia came to visit in her Halloween costume, complete with green face so he could see it. She had kissed him on the cheek, and got some of her face paint on him, but he didn't mind. And, to make her feel better, he said it was okay about his arm.

"Are you mad at me about your arm?" she asked him softly, looking worried, as her mother gently rubbed her hands over her huge belly.

"Of course not. I'd have been a lot madder if you had died. I couldn't let that happen to you," he said gently. He had been willing to take a bullet for her, or any member of her family. That was why he was there, and he had done his job. The surgeons had told him he could lead a normal life, and do anything that didn't require the use of two hands, like being an agent of the DEA or protecting the president of the United States, or playing the violin or the piano, or working undercover. And he knew that a desk job at the Pentagon would kill him. He was born to prowl the jungle and try to outwit the bad guys who ran the drug cartels, and risk his life. He had no idea what he would do now, but surely nothing he had ever done or cared about. It was going to be an enormous adjustment. But as they kept reminding him, at least he was alive. He just didn't know why.

"Thank you for saving my life," Amelia said with her green face, "and my mom's, and the baby's. Will you come and visit us? My dad says you can't go to South America now."

"No, I can't," Marshall confirmed, trying not to sound upset about it, but Phillip and Melissa knew that he was. Inevitably. At thirty, his career was over, and he had been a hero, even right up to the last day. His instincts had saved them from tragedy.

"I'm glad," Amelia said stubbornly, "because now the bad guys can't kill you, and maybe they would have. My dad says you were really lucky before, and maybe you wouldn't have been so lucky this time." Marshall knew that he would rather have died than lead a hampered life. They had told him that there were innumerable things he could learn to do with one arm—drive, ski, play tennis, do sports, work on his computer—and he was right-handed, but he was far too distinctive to send back out into the field now, a one-armed undercover agent. He wouldn't be able to load a gun fast enough, or defend himself against a drug dealer in a confrontation. He was going to get an honorable discharge from the DEA, based on disability, with an enhanced pension for life, for service above and beyond the call of duty, defending the president's life. The president had personally ordered the enhanced pension. It was a more than honorable end to his career, but an end nonetheless. He could start a business now, buy a house, or live more than comfortably on his pension for the rest of his life. And he had earned hazardous duty pay for all his years undercover, and had saved most of it. But he had no idea what to do with himself now. The rest of his life lay before him like a terrifying wasteland. It was a lot to absorb. But each time he looked at Amelia and Melissa, he was glad he had done it. He hadn't made a choice, he had just done it by instinct as part of his job. He would have made no other choice, and he felt

as though he were paying back his debt to the universe for the innocent people who had died because
of him.

The week after her visit to the hospital, Amelia
called to tell him that her mother had had the baby.
It had come a week early, but the baby was fine,
and Amelia had been to the hospital to see her and
loved her. She couldn't wait for Marshall to see her
too. He lay in his bed after her call, thinking about
them. They had everything that he had sacrificed
and never really wanted when he was younger, until
Paloma: children, a family, stability, a home. And
he had been willing to give that up again, and now
his whole life had been changed. He felt suddenly
very old, thinking of himself with one arm. And he
felt stupid for feeling sorry for himself, but without
the career he had loved, at times he wished he were
dead. As part of his rehab, they insisted on psycho-
therapy, and they wanted to give him career counseling, which he refused. What could he do now
with his training? Hire himself out as a one-armed
hit man? Bill Carter reminded him that there was
a lot he could do at the DEA if he wanted to, at
a desk, processing information, and using his language skills and thorough knowledge of the drug
cartels, but sitting at a desk was of no interest to
him. A lot of retired DEA, CIA, and FBI guys got
into the security business in some form, but that
didn't interest him either. It was all too easy. He was
thirty years old, not fifty, and the last year, although

he loved the first family, had been much too quiet for him, until the last day. It was what he had been trained for, but not the end he had expected—a bullet that ended not his life but his career.

At their insistence, Marshall spent Thanksgiving with the Armstrongs, and he held Daphne Marshall Armstrong in his one good arm. She stared up at him with a look of surprise. She looked just like Amelia and her mother, and was a tiny delicate blonde. She was three weeks old by then, and he couldn't help thinking that his baby with Paloma would have looked something like her, since Paloma had been as fair as Melissa. But it was all history now. Everything in his life felt like history, and all the excitement in his life was behind him.

He spent Christmas alone in his apartment, trying to figure out what to do with the rest of his life, and got drunk on red wine, after a stiff scotch. He knew that that was another option—he could turn into a drunk and do nothing at all. There were times when the idea appealed to him, and Bill Carter noticed that when he took him to lunch, to see how he was doing, Marshall had two tequila Bloody Marys before lunch. There were lots of guys who left the DEA with a disability, or Justice, or the CIA or FBI, but they all had to find a way to make their lives work after that, without turning into drunks or giving up on life. Bill gave him a lecture about it, and Marshall pretended to listen but really didn't care. He urged Marshall to get out and be with people, which Marshall thought was easy for him to say since he still had a job. And dating seemed even more improbable. He hadn't been out with a woman since he left Colombia and Paloma was killed, almost two years ago, and he didn't know if he ever would again. He couldn't imagine any woman he would ever love as much. And now with a dead left arm, he only felt like half a man, or a seriously damaged one, and dating was the farthest thing from his mind. He had decided he was better off alone, and had no desire to see anyone at all, even the Secret Service agents he had worked with, and come to like. He felt like an object of pity, seeing them now.

In January, still isolated, he learned that he was to be decorated for his act of heroism. The ceremony was scheduled for the end of the month. He was to receive the Public Safety Officer Medal of Valor, for extraordinary valor above and beyond the call of duty. It was similar to the Congressional Medal of Honor. All the men he knew at the DEA and the Secret Service were going to be there, and the first family.

The president decorated him with a moving speech in the East Room, and then Marshall's eyes filled with tears when the president had Amelia pin the medal on him. He hadn't expected that, and there was thunderous applause, and a reception afterward. The medal was gilt and blue enamel with a five-pointed star on a red, white, and blue ribbon. It meant more to Marshall than he had thought it would. It turned out to be one of the highlights of his life, along with the baby he had saved, who now bore his name. But it didn't solve the problem of what to do next. He still had considerable pain in his shoulder, and he was doing exercises to strengthen his left arm. He could raise his forearm a few inches now, which was helpful for minor tasks, but he couldn't grip a ball in his left hand, or do anything useful with it. And his left arm hung dead at his side. He had become remarkably adept at doing everything with one arm, including driving a car.

And without a job, he had nothing to do with his nights. He didn't want to hang out with the Secret Service men or other agents he knew, who talked about work all the time. He had nothing to add. He drove to New England for a few days, and went skiing in Vermont, and managed relatively well. And when he came back, he was cruising the Internet one night, and found himself on a site offering apartment and house rentals in Europe. He had nothing else to do, so he drifted through their listings, for villas in Tuscany, a palazzo in Venice, a summer home in the south of France, a farmhouse in Provence, and several apartments in Paris. There were also several quaint-looking cottages in the Cotswolds that didn't appeal to him at all, knowing the climate there. And he didn't know why, but he stopped at the listing of apartments in Paris, and was surprised at how inexpensive they were. He wasn't really interested in them, but after a few glasses of wine, anything seemed intriguing to him at night, including the mating habits of lions, or a variety of insects, and he'd spent an entire night, after too much to drink, learning about UFOs. His nights were long and sad.

And for some reason that made no sense, there was an apartment in Paris that sounded good to him. He looked at the photographs that had been posted, it was furnished and looked airy and sunny. It was in the sixteenth arrondisement, on a side street off Avenue Foch, according to the map, close to the Arc de Triomphe, and a park called Bagatelle. It was a fairly fancy residential neighborhood.

"What the hell would I do in Paris?" he said out loud to himself. But what would he do anywhere else? His fluent Spanish was of no use in France. But Paris seemed like a good place to sit around and drink and feel sorry for himself for a few months. The apartment was available for six months to a year. It had a living room, a large sunny bedroom, and a small kitchen with a dining area. There was an elevator, and a terrace with a narrow view of the Eiffel Tower, which was shown lit up at night. He thought it would be a good way to get lost. It wasn't South America, where he would long for his old life, or Spain, which would seem like second

best to the Spanish-speaking countries he knew in
South America that had a whole different flavor.
England was too dreary in the winter, but he had
been to Paris once and liked it, and he could travel
from there to other countries around Europe, like
Italy, or ski in Switzerland. He was tired of the Secret Service guys he had worked with calling him
out of pity, asking him how he felt and what he
was doing. Telling them he felt like shit and wasn't
doing anything never seemed like the right answer,
and he was tired of lying to them and saying he was
fine. He wasn't fine, but he didn't want to tell them
the truth. And the decoration and medal he'd gotten had begun to seem like a poor trade for his left
arm. He was feeling sorry for himself, and he knew
it, but maybe doing so in Paris was far enough
away not to matter. At least it would be a change
of scene, and if he hated it, he could come home.
He had to give up his apartment anyway, because
it belonged to the DEA. They had extended his
time there while he was on the presidential detail
with the Secret Service, and again after he'd been
injured, but he knew that sooner or later, he'd have
to find his own place. So why not move to Paris for
a few months while he figured out what to do and
where to go next?

He e-mailed the listing of the apartment in Paris,
and got a response the next day. The rent was actually less than stated in the ad, they had just lowered the price, and it was something he could easily

afford. And feeling a little crazy for doing it, he agreed to a starting date in two weeks. He rented it for six months, with an option to renew for another six. The owner said he was moving to Brussels but wanted to keep his Paris apartment. The owner warned him that it was perfect for one person and was feasible though tight for a couple, since it had few closets, like most Paris apartments. But it was impossible with a child. The owner said his furniture was mostly leather, in good condition, and he wanted to keep it that way. The apartment had a masculine feel to it, since the owner was a man, which had made it seem appealing. It wasn't fussy, overcrowded, or feminine.

"No worries," Marshall e-mailed him, "I don't have either one. No wife, no child."

"You can have a dog," he e-mailed back.

"Don't have a dog either."

"I'll put it in the lease," he offered, "in case you change your mind. It's close to the park, good for a dog."

Marshall agreed to wire the money, and three days later the deal was done. He had an apartment in Paris, and he notified the DEA that he was leaving the Georgetown apartment at the end of the month. And he e-mailed Bill Carter to say that he was going away for a few months. Bill e-mailed back that he thought it was a great idea, and was startled when Marshall said he was going to Paris. Bill hoped it would do him good. He knew the challenges Marshall was facing, and felt sorry for him. They all did, which was why Marshall wanted to go away, as far as he could. He was tired of people pitying him. He was doing enough of that himself.

It only took him days to pack up the apartment, and he listed whatever he wanted to get rid of on craigslist. He had just posted the listing when he found himself looking at the notices about dogs. There were puppies of all shapes and sizes, and he had no idea why he was bothering to look, when a listing caught his eye that sounded so ridiculous that he read it in detail with a grin. It was posted under adoptions, and was a one-year-old blood-hound named Stanley, for whom the owner wanted to find a good home. Marshall went to the owner's website and saw a photograph of him. He was a seriously depressed-looking dog, a large black-and-ginger-colored bloodhound with a mournful face and a thousand wrinkles. And feeling as crazy as he had when he decided to move to Paris, he called the owner's number to talk to him.

"Why are you giving him up? Did he kill some-one?"

"He's just too big. I live in an apartment in Georgetown. I really don't have room for him. It's not fair to the dog. And my girlfriend is allergic to dogs." Marshall almost suggested he give her up, but didn't want to be rude.

"Is he housebroken?"

"Totally," his owner said proudly. "He's fantastic,

but he gets depressed being left alone all day. He likes company."

"He looks depressed," Marshall commented, but there was something about the dog that appealed to him, even his ridiculous name for a dog, Stanley. He sounded like a man, not a dog. "Can I meet him?"

"Sure. Where do you live?"

"In Georgetown for another ten days. I'm moving to Paris, to an apartment next to a park. Does he speak French?"

"No," Stanley's owner said seriously, "but he plays dead."

They discovered that they lived a few blocks from each other and agreed to meet the next day. And Marshall felt foolish, but he was excited all day. It felt like he was going on a blind date, not going to meet a dog.

They met at the appointed hour, on a street corner, and Stanley looked at Marshall with suspicion. He sat down and stared at him, and then offered him his paw. He had the most mournful face Marshall had ever seen, except possibly his own. And after shaking Marshall's hand, he rolled over and played dead for a treat. They went on a short walk, and the dog seemed very well behaved, and even slightly skittish around other dogs. He was an enormous dog, but was terrified when a Yorkie barked at him.

"He's kind of a sissy," his owner admitted, but

he walked politely on the leash. "He's had all his
shots, and he has a chip in case he gets lost, and a
tattoo on his stomach. He's pedigreed, but I don't
want money for him. I just want to know he has a
good home. What do you do?" He had noticed the
limp left arm, and Marshall was tempted to say he
was a right-handed pitcher for the Yankees. He was
still uncomfortable about explaining the arm, and
didn't want to.

"I'm retired," he said simply.

"Lucky you," the young man said enviously,
imagining unlimited wealth or a lucky deal. He
was about the same age as Marshall, and seemed
nervous and stressed.

"Not really. I worked for the DEA, the Drug Enforcement Administration. I retired recently, so I'm
going to spend six months or a year in France."

Stanley's owner didn't ask if the arm was why he
had retired, but guessed that might be the case.

"I don't know if I can take a dog to France. I assume I can, with a health certificate."

"Yeah, and I think you need a chip, but since he
has one, it's not a problem. The French are pretty
dog-friendly. My mom lived there for a year. She
had a French bulldog and took it everywhere, even
to restaurants, although Stanley is too big." He was
practically the size of a Great Dane, but Marshall
liked the idea of a big dog, and he loved Stanley's
face, and he seemed good-natured and would be
company on long, lonely nights.

"I'll take him," Marshall suddenly said out of the blue, feeling as though he'd been possessed by aliens. He had rented an apartment in Paris and was adopting a gigantic bloodhound, all in less than a week. Maybe he was losing his mind.

"Are you sure?" The owner looked a little stunned, but no more so than Marshall.

"Yes, I am," Marshall said clearly, wondering what had possessed him. Maybe it was some kind of psychosis that happened with an injury and the loss of a career. He felt a little nuts. "How do you think he'll manage traveling cargo on the plane?" He was faintly worried about it, and didn't want to do anything that would hurt the dog.

"He's never flown before, to be honest," his owner said cautiously, "but you can get a sedative from a vet. I'll give you the name of mine. You can take him in the cabin with you, if you say he's a service dog."

"I don't think I can pass for blind," Marshall said seriously. Crazy maybe, but not blind.

"They use service dogs for epileptics now, to warn them before a seizure. For depression, and a lot of other things." He glanced at Marshall's limp left arm as he said it, and Marshall wondered if that would work. It would be worth trying, if the dog was well behaved on the plane. Stanley looked pretty calm, and was sitting on the sidewalk again, watching passersby.

"I'll give it a shot, and take the sedative with

me, in case they don't buy it." They exchanged information, and Marshall offered to pay him, but Stanley's owner declined. He promised to deliver him the next day with all his papers, and Marshall agreed. His owner said he wanted a last night with him to say goodbye, which sounded sad, but Stanley looked depressed anyway. He wagged his tail as Marshall patted him and said, "See you tomorrow."

And true to his word, Stanley's owner showed up with him at Marshall's apartment the next afternoon. His pedigree was in order, and all his vaccination certificates. He had gotten a health certificate and proof of his chip from the vet so Marshall could take him into France. He had a bottle of sedatives, in case Stanley needed them for the trip, since Marshall had decided to say he was a service dog, as the owner had suggested, so he could keep him in the cabin. Stanley sniffed his way around the apartment in true bloodhound style. And despite his somber face, he seemed happy and wagged his tail.

"He's really a great dog," his soon-to-be-ex-owner said, and looked like he was about to cry. He gave the dog a last loving pat, thanked Marshall, wished him luck, and slipped out the door, as Marshall sat staring at his new dog.

"Well, Stanley, I hope you like Paris," he said seriously. He had always wanted a dog, but couldn't have one because of his work. And now he had

Stanley, and an apartment in Paris. It felt like an adventure, and he was ready for it.

The following week, he went to say goodbye to the Armstrongs, and he brought the dog. The children loved him, and Amelia said he was the funniest-looking dog she'd ever seen. And she gave Marshall a big hug when he left, and so did Brad. And he got a last look at the baby, asleep in Melissa's arms after being nursed.

"Take good care of my namesake," he said, and kissed Melissa on the cheek.

"Keep in touch, Marsh," the president said warmly. "Let us know where you are."

"I will," Marshall promised, feeling sad to say goodbye.

The Armstrong children had added warmth and joy to his life. And now it would be just him and a dog in Paris. He didn't know a soul there. But he had made no close friends in Washington anyway—only the Armstrongs. So he had nothing to leave behind.

The plane trip to Paris went better than Marshall had hoped. He was traveling in business class, and with a matter-of-fact expression, he told the woman at the Air France desk that Stanley was a service dog.

"For what purpose?" she asked as she filled out the form.

"He cuts my meat," Marshall said seriously, indicating his arm, and she nodded without really listening and jotted down "service dog" on the form. Half an hour later Marshall was on the plane, and Stanley lay down at his feet and went to sleep. The person sitting next to him looked surprised, but didn't seem to mind.

He took the night flight and arrived in Paris at noon the next day with two suitcases and his dog. The cab driver dropped them off at 22 rue Bugeaud, near a small, elegant hotel called the St. James. They rode up in the elevator of his building to the fifth floor. The guardian gave Marshall the keys that were waiting for him in an envelope. The apartment was as cozy and well kept and bright as it had looked in the pictures. It was a gray February day, but the apartment was filled with light, and it started snowing as Marshall set his bags down in the bedroom. He hadn't realized it until that moment, but it was exactly two years to the day since he'd left Bogotá, heartbroken and heartsick over leaving Paloma and their baby, the same day that she died. And now with one good arm and a dog, in a Paris apartment, knowing no one in the city, Marshall felt as though his new life had started at last. He could finally put all the old ghosts to rest, and begin to live again.

Ariana

Chapter 6

Robert Gregory had always had everything he could have wanted and needed in life: Family money to back him up. An education at the best schools, Princeton undergraduate, and the eating club he had chosen, Ivy. Harvard Business School after that. A wife he adored, and a daughter his life revolved around from the moment she was born. And the successful career he had expected. The one great tragedy that had befallen him was when his wife Laura died of a brain tumor only a year ago. They had been to all the best doctors in the country, and neither his money nor his love could save her. He had been devastated by her death, and he turned to his daughter, Ariana, constantly for comfort. And he focused all his love and attention on her now. She loved her father too, and tried to fill the void her mother had left.

The only thing lacking in Robert's life, as he began

winding down in his career, was a dream he had had as a young man. He had always wanted to be an ambassador, to either Britain or France. His father had had the same wish before him, and it had never been fulfilled. And as Robert Gregory watched the presidential campaign unfold, of a man he could truly support wholeheartedly, Phillip Armstrong, the dream of becoming ambassador took hold of him again. To that end, and out of genuine respect for the man he hoped would be president, Robert contributed vast amounts of money to his campaign. He was sure that ultimately, after Armstrong won the election, it would get him the ambassadorship to Britain or France, and he said as much to Ariana several times during the campaign. His hope was the only thing that distracted him from his deep mourning for his late wife.

"Daddy, for heaven's sake, what do you want to be an ambassador for? It would be such a headache! That's the last thing you need." Ariana wasn't enthused about it, especially now that he was widowed. At nearly seventy, he had had a demanding career for more than four decades, and Ariana thought it would be too stressful for him, especially after all his agony and grief over her mother, which had been so hard on him. He had had a heart scare a few years before, and a successful angioplasty, and she didn't like the idea of his taking on more. Her father was all she had, her only living relative in the world now. And at twenty-two, she had no desire to live in England or France, and wouldn't have let him go alone.

She had graduated from Barnard at Columbia six months before. She hadn't wanted to go to Princeton like her father, although he had pushed hard. And now she had the job she wanted, as assistant to the editor of a prestigious online fashion magazine. She had always wanted a career in fashion, and now she had it. She loved going to fashion events, and learning about new trends and important designers. Her long-term ambition was to become editor of **Vogue** magazine one day. Ariana had loved fashion almost since the day she was born, and she had the same simple natural style as her mother, who had shared her love of fashion with her. Laura Gregory had been elegant and gracious, and Ariana was a more exuberant, younger version of her mother. Her father kept photographs of his beautiful late wife everywhere.

Ariana had the same flawless blond looks, long legs, and blue eyes. Laura had been twenty years younger than Ariana's father and had died much too young. He had worshipped her from the moment they met, just as he did their daughter now. Ariana thought his longing for an ambassadorship was silly, and probably wouldn't be good for his health. She wanted to stay in New York. She loved her friends and her job. She had just gotten her first apartment, in Tribeca, as a graduation present from her father, and she was having a ball. She had friends over almost every night. She didn't have a serious boyfriend, but she had lots of dates. She was living a life that was the dream of every twenty-two-year-old girl, and many older.

Her doting father lived to make life easy, happy, and safe for her. He had gotten the apartment in a building with a doorman, so she had twenty-four-hour security. The one thing he always insisted on was that she was safe. He wanted her to use a car service at night when she went out, and not take cabs. He insisted she live in a great building, in a good neighborhood, and had granted her every wish all her life. And now he was in pursuit of what he wanted. And Ariana was attentive to him with her mother gone. She had dinner with her father once or twice a week, and called him every day, knowing how much he missed her mother.

He met with Phillip Armstrong several times during the campaign, at fund-raisers, and reminded him that he wanted to be ambassador to Britain or France, if Armstrong won. The presidential candidate never promised to grant Robert his wish, but he said that he would consider it and do his best. He had other equally big donors to his campaign, and there were other considerations, as to who would fulfill the post best. He had integrity and was an honest man, which only made Robert respect him all the more.

Ariana wasn't worried even when Armstrong won. Her father was invited to the inauguration, and he asked her to join him for the ball that night. It was an exciting moment for her too. She met the president and his wife, and Melissa Armstrong was kind and delightful to her. It was obvious that Phillip Armstrong held her father in high esteem. On their way back to New York, her father practically gloated, he was so excited, certain that he would get the appointment as ambassador to either country soon. Ariana didn't want to discourage him, but she wasn't as sure. Her father wasn't young, had less-than-perfect health, no longer had a wife to act as hostess, and had no experience as a career diplomat, although she knew that many of those posts were given according to campaign contributions. Her father was like a little kid about it, and she didn't want to rain on his parade.

When nothing had happened two months after the inauguration, she figured she was home free. She was having fun with her new job and didn't want to go anywhere, even London or Paris, although she would have tried to get a job in fashion there. But she liked her job in New York. It was the most exciting time in her life, and in March, she met a boy she really liked. He was in law school at NYU, twenty-six years old, and they were having a great time together.

She felt sorry for her father when ambassadors were appointed to both Britain and France. The one being sent to London was actually a friend of her father's, which made it even harder for him to swal-

low. At least he didn't know, and had never heard
of, the man who had been appointed to France. He
was from L.A. She was relieved that she had nothing to worry about after that, her life in New York
was secure. Until May, when her father asked her
to come to dinner one night, and he looked serious
when she arrived. She was instantly worried that he
had another problem with his health. She was constantly concerned about him now that her mother
was gone. Her worst fear in life was that something
would happen to him. She loved him every bit as
much as he loved her, and she had always idolized
him. One of the worst times in her life was when
he had the angioplasty, but he'd been fine ever
since.

She sat down to dinner with him in the dining
room at his Fifth Avenue apartment, overlooking
Central Park. He claimed that it was tomblike now
without her mother, and she tried to have dinner
with him as often as she could. She invited him
to visit her too, but he didn't like coming down
to SoHo and Tribeca, even though she lived there
now. He liked it better when she came home, as she
had that night.

"I spoke to President Armstrong today. He called
me," he said quietly, and Ariana looked surprised.

"Why did he call you, Daddy?" She knew that
the two ambassadorships he wanted were gone, so
it couldn't be that.

"He offered me an ambassadorship," Robert Gregory said as their soup was served, but he didn't look happy about it.

"He did? To where?" She suddenly wondered if the president was going to offer her father something like Rome or Madrid, which she thought were career posts. Or something really scary like Ghana, or Nepal, or someplace else she didn't want to go.

Her father hesitated for a minute before he answered her. He'd been thinking about it all day. "Argentina," he said somberly. "We'd be in Buenos Aires, which everyone seems to love, but it's a lot different for a two-week vacation than three or four years. I don't think it's a good idea. The country's been in terrible trouble for years, they're dead broke. And they may be wonderful people, but I can't solve their problems for them. It would be a lot of pressure on me, and it's only a stone's throw away from all those countries that are dangerous, with revolutionaries, kidnappings for ransom, and the drug cartels. It's just a headache we don't need."

"I totally agree," Ariana said politely, relieved that he wouldn't consider it. "So you told him no?"

"I tried to, and he asked me to think about it. He said we'd absolutely love it once we got there, he said everyone does, and the reason it took so long to offer me the appointment is because they practically had to pry the last ambassador out with a crowbar. He didn't want to leave because he was so happy there."

"Maybe he had a girlfriend down there," Ariana said tongue in cheek, trying to make light of it to her father. She had no desire whatsoever to live in Argentina for four years, or even three. Especially now that Paris and London had passed him by, she wanted to stay in New York and assumed he did too. "But you're going to say no, Daddy, right?" She wanted reassurance from him, and she could see he wasn't sure.

"I don't know. Maybe it doesn't matter where we are. The experience might be wonderful, for both of us. Being ambassador is really a great honor, and Argentina could be fun for you too. I hear the people are absolutely terrific and very hospitable, the city looks like Paris, and the social life is fabulous. He said the embassy needs a woman's touch and some decorating, but that would be fun for you."

"I don't want to go anywhere, and least of all Argentina," she said with a feeling of panic. "We don't speak the language and we don't know anybody there." She was trying to think of everything she could to discourage him, but she could tell she wasn't getting anywhere. The president had done much too good a job of selling it to him.

"As ambassador, we'd meet everyone. And you speak enough Spanish to get by," he encouraged her.

"No, I don't, I took two years in high school. I can get you to the post office and the train station and that's it."

"What do you think, Ari?" he asked her, sitting back in his chair. He hadn't touched his soup, nor had she. She couldn't eat. "Should we try it? You only live once. We might regret it forever if we turn this down." He might, but she knew she wouldn't. And he was making it clear that he'd expect her to go with him. She felt anxious listening to him talk about it.

"Daddy, what if you get sick?" She was justifiably worried, given his problems before, and she didn't want to go through another heart episode with him on foreign turf.

"I'm fine. I had a checkup a month ago, and everything is great. I don't know, it probably sounds foolish to you, but I would love to be an ambassador somewhere before I die." She could see the dream still in his eyes.

"You're not dying, and you'd better not. And you said you were only interested in going to England or France." She was panicking as she listened to him, and could sense she wasn't winning the argument. She didn't want to step into her mother's shoes and move to Argentina with him. She wanted her own life.

"It might be fun. Everybody loves Argentina. Maybe you would too." He tried to convince her, as her heart sank.

There were tears in her eyes when she turned to her father. "That's such a long time. Three years, maybe four. What if we hate it there? We'll be stuck for all that time. I'd be twenty-six years old when we came back. I'll have missed all that time to get ahead at my job." To her, twenty-six felt like ninety.

"But this is an experience you might never have otherwise." It was clear that the president had swayed him with whatever he had said, and for that moment in time Ariana hated Phillip Armstrong for selling her father on an ambassadorship in Argentina. She fell silent for a while, not knowing what else to say to express her reluctance and concerns, and they both ate their soup. "I just wanted to let you know that I'm thinking about it, so it doesn't come as a surprise." That sounded even worse to her.

"Daddy," she said honestly, "I don't want to go." It was as clear as she could make it, and he looked very worried by what she said.

"I wouldn't feel comfortable leaving you here alone. And I'd need you there, Ariana. I can't do this alone without your mom." He looked imploringly at her, which made her feel guilty. It was a sacrifice she didn't want to make, and she thought it was unfair of him to try and push her. But whether he did or not, she felt responsible for him. She had promised her mother that she would take care of him. But moving to Argentina was more than she had bargained for. What scared her was that once her father made a decision, that was it. And it sounded like he was getting there fast. She was near tears by the end of dinner, and left immediately afterward to meet up with friends at the Waverly Tavern downtown. Her new boyfriend was among the group, and he could see how upset she was, although he didn't know her well.

"Something wrong?" he asked as he put an arm around her and kissed her.

"My father got offered an ambassadorship in Argentina today."

"That sounds like fun," he said enthusiastically. "You can go visit him and learn the tango," he said, trying to lighten the mood. She didn't tell him that her father wanted her to move there as well. She wouldn't be "visiting," she'd be living there. But she didn't want to tell him that and spoil their romance, before her father made the decision.

Her father called her the next day. The decision had been made. He had just spoken to the president and had accepted the post, and he had to be in Buenos Aires in four weeks. Ariana burst into tears the minute he told her, and he tried to assure her how interesting and exciting it would be, how much she'd love it, and she would be like an ambassadress herself. She loved her father, but he was high-handed at times, and always convinced that he was right. But this time he wasn't, for her.

"I don't want to be an ambassadress," she said fiercely. "I'm twenty-two years old. I have a life and a job here. I'm not going with you, Daddy. I don't care what you say. This doesn't work for me."

"Ariana, you're all I have," he said sternly. "I'm

not leaving you here. I would worry about you too much."

"It's safer than Argentina. They kidnap people there." She just threw it out for good measure, but he had already discussed it with the president.

"We'll have bodyguards at all times. And no foreigner has been kidnapped there in years. We have nothing to worry about," he reassured her, and a moment later she hung up. She went to discuss it with him again that night, and got nowhere, and she went back to her apartment furious with him. But the reality was that he was a seventy-year-old man, who had already had some serious health problems, had lost his wife a year before, and he was her father. She didn't feel right about letting him go alone. She thought about it for a long time and by the next morning decided it was a sacrifice she had to make, for him. The last thing she wanted to do was go to Argentina and give up her job in New York, but maybe he was right. Maybe she'd enjoy it and be glad she'd done it. Given how determined he was to go, she felt she had no choice.

It nearly broke her heart to give up her job at the online magazine that she'd enjoyed so much. Her editor couldn't have been nicer and told her that there would always be another assistant's job when she came back, and the editor suggested she do a blog from Buenos Aires. It was harder telling her new boyfriend Ian that she was moving to Buenos Aires with her father, but he was a lot less upset than she'd hoped he would be, which told her that he considered her a passing thing. He gave her a big hug and told her to stay in touch, and maybe he'd visit her there sometime.

Her father told her to do as much shopping as she wanted, since she'd need lots of pretty clothes when they entertained, which was small consolation for the life she was giving up. She was depressed about it until they left New York, and she knew it would be winter there when they arrived in June. They had shipped some things ahead, and she had eight suitcases with her when they took the flight to Buenos Aires. She was painfully quiet on the trip, flying first class with her father. She couldn't begin to imagine their new life, and he was grateful that she hadn't put up much of a fight, although he knew she was unhappy about it. She had made it plain, and he had promised to make it up to her in every way he could. He wanted her to have a fabulous time.

They moved into the Four Seasons Hotel in Buenos Aires until the embassy was ready. They had already been warned before they arrived that the embassy needed some "help." Ariana and her father went to see it the next day, it was on Posadas in the Recoleta district. It was a spectacular building with beautiful frescoes, moldings, and fireplaces, and what it required was furniture, lots of it, to fill the empty rooms. Beautiful curtains were already there, and her father's new secretary gave Ariana a list of fine antique stores where she would find what they

needed and offered to go with her. Ariana could see
that she'd be busy for a while, getting the embassy
ready for her father, and she was touched by their
warm reception by all his staff, who were equally
helpful to her. Both of his secretaries came to the
hotel with them, one to work with each of them.
And the younger of the two handed Ariana a stack
of invitations from well-known hostesses in Buenos
Aires, and almost every embassy in town. Everyone
wanted to give a dinner for them, a luncheon, or a
ball, and present them to everyone. Local hostesses
were vying for the honor of entertaining them first.
They had enough invitations to be out every night
for the next month.

"Oh my God," Ariana said, looking overwhelmed
as she sifted through them, but she had been part
of her father's social life for the past year since her
mother's death, and knew she had to be now, host-
ing dinners with him at the embassy, and going to
social events with him. It was why she had come.
Eugenia, the young woman who was assisting her,
was only a few years older than she, beautifully
dressed with perfectly groomed hair, and small dia-
monds at her ears, and came from an aristocratic
family. And she was already explaining the most
important local families to her, and the various ambassadors and their wives. The social life in Buenos
Aires appeared to be extremely busy, and Eugenia
pointed out that they would have to entertain a
great deal.

The next morning, Ariana was at the antique stores with Eugenia, and her father had given her carte blanche to buy everything they needed for the embassy. He could easily afford it, and Ariana was shocked at how low the prices were, compared to New York, for beautiful antiques, many of which had come from France originally. But many of the old families were in desperate need of money, and several of them were selling off their belongings for next to nothing. Ariana almost felt guilty buying them for so little. By lunchtime, she had bought enough pieces to fill several rooms, and two beautiful Aubusson carpets in pale pink tones, and light blue.

Eugenia spoke perfect English and had gone to college in the States, and she promised to find a teacher so Ariana could brush up on her Spanish. Now that she was here, Ariana was ready to do whatever she had to, to make things easier for her father and play her role well. She was being a good sport about it, and wanted to make him proud of her. She wanted the embassy to look beautiful, and their dinners to be the most elegant in Buenos Aires.

They went to a black-tie dinner that night at the French embassy. The food was fabulous, and the women were exquisitely dressed in evening gowns. Everyone was warm and welcoming to her and her father. There were liveried servants behind every guest, and dancing afterward, and Ariana had never seen such beautiful crystal and china in her life.

It was like going back to another era, when everything was elegant and luxurious, and people were beautifully mannered and lived a life that no longer existed in other parts of the world. People loved going out here, and entertaining exquisitely.

The French embassy was matched only by the dinner they attended the following night at the British embassy, followed by the Italians, the Germans, the Spanish. They were out literally every night, and met all the most aristocratic and important people in town, who then took turns entertaining them at their lavish homes. And even if they had less money than previously, they had armies of help and beautiful homes, entertained fabulously, and were fashionably dressed. The women were the prettiest Ariana and her father had ever seen, the men handsome and dashing. There were many Germans, Italians, and Irish, and even those born in Argentina had foreign names, as so many people had come from Europe to settle there in past generations. It was a city that never slept, entertained constantly, and danced all night. And every handsome man in town was dying to dance with Ariana and teach her the tango, while her father stood proudly by and watched, smoking Cuban cigars with the other men. But there Ariana drew the line. She took one gently out of his hand, kissed his cheek, and whispered, "No cigars," mindful of his health and the problems he'd had. She knew her mother would have done the same.

The local hostesses were just as enchanted with her father as the men were with her. Beautiful women flirted with him at every dinner party, and were delighted to dance with him. They were the most sought-after couple in town, and even Ariana had to admit after the first two weeks that it was fun. She was meeting young people she liked, girls who were fun to talk to who invited her to their homes, and boys who flirted with her and were very handsome and well dressed. It was hard not to be seduced by the charms and beauty of the city, which everyone was dying to show her. She had never felt so welcome or had so much attention lavished on her in her life. She wanted to write a blog about it for the online magazine in New York where she'd been working. But she was so busy decorating and furnishing the embassy and going out at night that she never had time.

And as the antiques she'd bought were delivered, the embassy began to take shape. She put it together as quickly as she could, with what she purchased and what was at hand. Six weeks after Ariana and her father arrived, they gave a beautiful party to thank everyone for their hospitality and for the many invitations to both of them. And her father was very proud of the evening Ariana had organized. She had even hired a wonderful band with the help of her new friends.

By the end of August, both Gregorys were feeling at home. Robert was thoroughly enjoying his job as ambassador, liked the people he was dealing with, and was learning the ropes from the career diplomats on hand. He was having a ball and liked the challenge of learning about the country. And Ariana had a wide circle of friends who invited her constantly for dinners and lunches, to watch the boys play polo, and to go to their clubs. She was invited out every night, with and without her father, and in September she admitted to her father that he'd been right, and she was glad she had come. Her Spanish was improving, and she loved their home and her new friends.

"I never thought it would be like this. Everyone says it's like Paris used to be," Ariana said to her father. He was happy that she was happy there. She went to Punta del Este, in Uruguay, for the weekend with some of her new friends. It was the favorite beach resort of the rich and aristocratic Argentines, and she had a wonderful weekend. Her father made her take two bodyguards with her, just to be safe, but she felt silly with them. She didn't need them at all, and went out without them, with her friends. Some of them had bodyguards too, but they never used them at Punta del Este, only when they went to their country homes in the more provincial regions, where bandits tended to roam and held people up on the roads.

Ariana's father surprised her on a weekend in October. He said that they'd been invited away for the weekend by friends. It was a family Ariana particularly liked, with three daughters close to her age, and two handsome older sons. It was a constant party at their house. And even more so at their country home, their **finca,** two hours outside of Buenos Aires, where many of their new friends had homes they went to on the weekend. And on Saturday, after lunch, her father and their hosts took a little drive. There was a beautiful property adjacent to theirs, which her father wanted to see, and as soon as they got out of the cars, he told her he had rented it.

The family who owned it had moved to the States, and were happy to rent the property to them for several years. It was impeccably maintained and the house was empty, although there were seven servants living there. It was another home for her to decorate, and Ariana could instantly visualize the weekend parties they would give there with their friends. There were a dozen bedrooms in the main house, several smaller guest houses, and separate quarters for the help. Ariana's friends were as excited as she was, to have them as neighbors, and the following week she began shopping to fill the house so they could use it as soon as possible.

By Christmas, which was the Argentine summer, she had turned the rented house into a wonderland of elegant comforts and delights, with beautiful French antiques and pastel colors, and airy comfortable bedrooms with canopied beds. Her father had hired half a dozen more people to serve them, and they took the embassy chef with them when they went. They gave their first weekend party there on New Year's Eve. They had twenty guests in the house, and all their neighbors came, and they danced until six in the morning, and then had breakfast on the terrace, and everyone went home at eight, to sleep all day. It was a decadent, opulent, thoroughly addictive life, and it was hard to believe they had already been in Argentina for six months. The time had flown, and Ariana's Spanish was close to perfect by then. And she kept Eugenia busy with her decorating, entertaining, shopping, and going out with friends. There was always something new to see and do and buy, and people to meet, visitors arriving from the States whom Ariana had to plan embassy dinners for. She had never been so busy in her life. At twenty-three she was one of the most sought-after young women in Buenos Aires, with her elegant blond good looks and classic aristocratic style, perfect manners, and easy laughter. She was fun to be with, and she was turning into one of the most expert hostesses in town. Everyone adored her and her father.

She planned another weekend party in mid-January, two weeks after her now legendary first weekend at their **finca** over New Year's. Those who hadn't visited the **finca** yet wanted to see how she'd decorated it, and to spend the weekend there. She invited a dozen young couples, and had just started dating one of her close friend's older brothers, and they were all planning to be there. Her father said he had to stay in Buenos Aires to catch up on some work, and he wanted to give the young people a chance to have some fun on their own. He reminded Ariana to take both bodyguards with her, since the road to their **finca** was notoriously peppered with the bandits people talked about, but with the bodyguards she'd be safe. And in the end, she took only one, since the other had a bad case of the flu, and she felt mean dragging him along. And she took the embassy chef in the car with her, to cook for the large group. She left the sous-chef in the city for her father, and she was busy making lists and doing table seating as they drove out of town. The chef fell asleep in the backseat, and she stayed busy for most of the two-hour trip to their new country home.

She was excited about the weekend and liked all of the group she'd invited. They had been driving for nearly two hours and were almost there, when the car came to a sharp stop with a jolt. She looked up from her notepad, and saw that an old military truck was blocking the road. A half-dozen men were standing behind it in front of her father's car, and she could see more men in the back of the truck. She glanced at the bodyguard to see if he was concerned. The doors were locked, and she wondered if he would drive around them, or wait for them to move on. The men in a motley array of military gear walked slowly toward them as Ariana realized that all of them were holding guns. The bodyguard at the wheel of the car didn't move and remained calm.

"Felipe, are we okay?" He nodded, and the chef was still snoring in the backseat, unaware that they had stopped. "Should we try to drive through?" She looked worried, and the driver was watching the armed men intently but seemed unafraid.

"They'll shoot out the tires," he said quietly. Two of the men moved next to the driver's window and gestured to him to roll down the window, which he didn't do, and without hesitating, the man standing in front of the car pointed his pistol at the driver's head, and shot him through the windshield. Felipe fell forward against the steering wheel as blood gushed everywhere, and Ariana screamed. Another man broke the window in her door, pulled up the lock, and yanked her out of the car before she knew what had happened to her, and they rapidly slipped a hood over her head, picked her up, and threw her into the back of the truck. They paid no attention to the chef in the backseat, who had woken up when Felipe was shot, and had seen Ariana be pulled out of the car and carried away with the hood over her head. Her arms were flailing, and she was trying to fight off the man who was carrying her, but they had dumped her in the truck and jumped in after her, and they were gone within minutes. The cook stared in shocked horror and watched the truck drive into the bushes at the side of the road and disappear. It all happened so quickly, and there was nothing he could have done. He had counted at least eight men around the car and more in the truck. All were bearded and wore helmets, and some had been wearing ski masks to conceal their faces. They were a faceless mass as they took Ariana. The cook sat shaking in the car for another five minutes, and then got out and pushed Felipe's body into the passenger's seat. The driver's seat was drenched with blood, and he drove the rest of the way to the **finca,** shaking so violently he could barely drive, and the moment he got to the property, he ran out screaming at the top of his lungs, as people came running to see what had happened. With the car door open, they could see Felipe's body, and blood everywhere, and sobbing hysterically, he told the staff and two guests who had already arrived what had happened to Ariana. Ariana's guests screamed when they saw Felipe's body in the car, and the crying cook covered with blood.

They called the local police. It was an hour before they came, and the cook described what had happened. They asked if her father the ambassador had been called, and no one had called him yet. What had happened was not an unusual occurrence—it had happened on that road before, but not recently to someone as important as Ariana. This was a serious matter, and the policemen who had come to the house called their local chief of police, who called the chief of police of Buenos Aires. The daughter of the American ambassador had been kidnapped, and her father had to be told.

The chief of police of Buenos Aires went to the embassy himself and asked to see the ambassador. He was asked to wait for a few minutes, and Robert Gregory came to meet him where he was waiting, and instantly thought that an American citizen in Buenos Aires had committed a serious crime. He held out a hand formally, as the chief of police nearly trembled at the prospect of telling this man the news. He was an important man.

"Excellency," he said, still standing as he had when Robert came into the room, "it is my sad duty to inform you that your daughter has been kidnapped while traveling to your **finca.** The driver was killed, and an employee in the backseat was unharmed. Your daughter was not injured and she was alive when they took her. We will comb the countryside, and do everything in our power to get her back. I give you the promise of our government that we will do everything to return her to you unharmed."

The room swam around Robert Gregory as he listened to the words. There was a terrible unreality to them. What the chief of police was saying was not possible. It couldn't be real. They couldn't have taken Ariana. He had sent her with a bodyguard, who was supposed to keep her safe. People went to their weekend homes all the time from Buenos Aires. Why had they taken her?

"Do you know who took her?" he said in a choked voice, taking a vial of pills from his pocket. They were nitroglycerin, and he had a terrible pain in his chest. He had had a pain like it once before. He slipped a pill under his tongue, and sat down, looking at the chief of police in shock and terror.

"We do not know yet," the police chief said honestly, "but I will drive there myself. We will mobilize a search for her immediately. I believe it has already begun. Do you wish to go with me, sir?"

"Yes." Robert nodded, feeling as though he were moving underwater. He had to get to her. He had to find her. They had to save her from whoever had taken her. He followed the chief of police blindly out of the embassy and got in his car. The chief had a driver and another man with him, and the men spoke softly as they drove to the **finca,** along the same route Ariana and Felipe had traveled. Robert Gregory said not a word on the way. He was in shock.

The local police were waiting for them at the house, after the chief of police of Buenos Aires had sent word that he was on the way. The cook who had watched it all from the backseat told his story more calmly this time. And the police told Robert that they had no idea yet who had taken her. There were so many groups of bandits along the roads, it was impossible to know. And they felt certain that a demand for ransom would come shortly, which would give them an idea who had her. But until then, they just had to wait.

"I'll pay them whatever they want," Robert said in a shaking voice. His face had been gray and his hands trembling since he'd heard the news. It was like a very, very bad movie.

"We will put it on the news immediately," the police chief said, "in case anyone sees her anywhere. We need a photograph of her."

"If you send someone to the embassy, they'll give you whatever you need." Robert was slumped in a chair, and one of Ariana's friends was trying to comfort him, to no avail. He looked suddenly very old and very sick. The others had started to arrive by then, had been told the story, and could still see the inside of the car covered with blood. Police were everywhere, and Ariana's friends were crying, knowing that often stories like this had a terrible end, and even paying ransom to bandits like this didn't always mean you got the person back. Or you got the body back, after they'd been killed.

Both chiefs of police stayed with Robert Gregory for over an hour, trying to reassure him that the entire government of Argentina would do everything in their power to get his daughter back. And as Robert looked at them, rivers of tears ran down his cheeks.

"Please," he said, looking desperate, "please . . . she's all I have. . . ."

Chapter 7

The man who dragged Ariana out of the car and carried her had done it so quickly that she hardly had time to react. She tried to fight with him and free herself, but he had her in a viselike grip, and before she could get any power into it, he had thrown her onto the floor of the truck, and two men put their full weight on her with their boots, so she couldn't move an inch. She had a hood over her head that made it hard to breathe, and they tied her wrists and legs with rough ropes that cut into her skin. She had been wearing a light summer dress, which was already filthy from the floor of the truck and their boots. She could hear rough Spanish spoken and tried to listen to what they were saying. They were speaking some kind of dialect, and the heavy hood, made from a rough blanket, muffled their words. She had no idea where they were taking her or who they were. They were talk-

ing about a man named Jorge, and were calling
her "La Rica," the rich one, when they referred to
her. She was sure that they just assumed they had
picked up some girl from a rich family, and had no
idea they had taken the daughter of the American
ambassador. She wondered if it would make a difference or only make things worse. She could guess
that she'd been kidnapped for ransom, and not as a
political prisoner.

She was trying to fight back panic, with the men's
boots pressing her down, the ropes cutting into
her hands and legs, and the suffocating hood over
her face. They were driving over rough terrain,
and her head kept bumping on the floor of the truck
as they bounced along at a steady speed. She nearly
passed out a couple of times, and would have cried,
but she didn't dare. All she wanted was to come
out of this alive, and she was trying to keep her
wits about her, and hear what they said. One of the
men kicked her with the toe of his boot a couple of
times, and she let out a sharp sound, and was sure
he had broken a rib. She wondered what her father
was doing by then, and if he already knew, and if
a search for her had begun yet. She was praying
police would stop them, but no one did. She had
never been as frightened in her life and was fighting to stay calm. She knew panic wouldn't help her,
and she was trying to be brave.

It had been noon when they left Buenos Aires,
and they'd been on the road for almost two hours

when she was dragged from the car, but she had no sense what time it was now. She could feel her heart pounding for most of the trip. And it felt like many hours later when the truck finally stopped, and she could hear men's voices shouting inside and outside the truck, and the sound of people running, and then she was lifted up and dropped hard on the ground. It knocked the wind out of her, and she couldn't make a sound. She just lay there unable to move with the ropes binding her, her head throbbing. One of the men pushed her hard with his boot, and she heard the name Jorge again. And she could feel that she had lost her shoes in the truck.

She heard a sound of gunfire then nearby, and wondered if they were going to shoot her like Felipe, but through a haze of fear and pain, she realized that she was more valuable to them alive. She was desperately thirsty by then, and had dirt from the hood in her mouth, and could still barely breathe from the thickness of it, but suddenly there was silence all around her, and she could hear one man's voice shouting orders.

His Spanish was different from theirs. It was a Spanish she recognized, like that of the people she knew, and he was telling them to put her in the box. She had no idea what that meant, and then felt herself lifted off the ground again, and carried a short distance, and then dumped into a constrained space. They had to push her to fit her into it. She heard a sound of a heavy lid being dropped on top of the space where she lay. She could hardly breathe, and it was hot. She could move no part of her and wondered if she would die there. And then slowly, in the heat and the misery and the pain of the ropes and her rib, she had an overwhelming urge to sleep. All she wanted was release from the terror and the pain. She drifted in and out of consciousness as she lay in the darkness with the hood still over her head, barely able to breathe, and then—she had no idea when, a long time later—she heard voices, and the top of the box being removed again, and felt cool air. It woke her up, and she was sorry that it had. She just wanted to drift away in sleep.

She could hear men shouting again, and then one voice next to her, giving orders. It was the same voice she'd heard before. Then the ropes on her wrists and legs were cut. She could feel the knife slide past her skin, and she was released from her bonds, but she couldn't move. Her whole body was frozen into place and stiff. The voice told them to take her out and stand her up, and as soon as they did, she fell to the ground—her legs were too weak and stiff to hold her up. As she lay on the ground, she was too terrified to move. The same voice told them to take her inside, and she could hear heavy footsteps on gravel, as someone carried her. She just hung there like a broken doll, and then she was dumped into a chair, as the group of footsteps re- treated again. She was no longer bound, but didn't move, with the hood still over her head. The only part of her moving was her heart pounding in her chest. She sat very still, wondering if she was waiting to be killed. She could sense someone close to her and hear his breathing, and she didn't know if he had a gun pointed at her head. And then, ever so slowly, she felt the hood removed and closed her eyes, afraid of what she'd see.

"Don't be afraid," a voice said softly next to her, but she didn't believe a word he said, and she kept her eyes closed. "I'm not going to hurt you. I want you alive," he said quietly in what sounded like an educated voice to her. He spoke to her in Spanish, which made her wonder again if he knew who she was, or if he cared. If he had kidnapped her for ransom, anyone would do, and being an ambassador's daughter would only increase the price on her head. "My God, you're a pretty one," he said, looking at her. Her face was dirty, and her dress filthy and torn. She was barefoot with marks from the ropes, but he hadn't expected to see her blond beauty or the young aristocratic face. "Don't be afraid," he said again, "you can open your eyes. I won't hurt you." She found that hard to believe, given everything they'd done to her so far.

But something in his voice told her he was their leader. And slowly, she opened her eyes and looked at him. She found herself staring at a man with a deep tan, and a long, narrow, chiseled face. He had electric blue eyes, jet-black hair, and a cleft chin, and he hadn't shaved in several days. He was wearing a green military jacket, fatigue pants, and military boots. But he had an aura of power about him, and a pistol in his belt. She hadn't said a word to him so far, as their eyes met, and he reached out and touched her face. There was a bruise on her cheek from where she fell when they had dropped her on the floor of the truck, and nasty cuts on her wrists and legs from the ropes.

"I'm sorry they did that to you," he said gently, as though he were allied with her. "They're savages, they don't know the difference between a lady and one of their pigs." She didn't smile at him, and her eyes never left his face. "Can you walk?" he asked her quietly, and she didn't answer. She had no idea if she could. Her legs had pins and needles, and every inch of her body ached. It was dark by then, and there was a gentle breeze. The air felt cool. She had the feeling they were in the foothills or the mountains, but she had no idea where. All she could see was that they were in a tent.

He helped her out of the chair then, and she wondered where he was taking her, if he was going to rape her, or kill her, or torture her. She still hadn't said a word.

He led her out of his tent, and she found herself walking stiffly along beside him. She knew there was no point trying to run away. She couldn't have gotten far on her stiff legs, and one of them might have shot her. He walked her to a little hut then, and pointed to it. She realized it was an outhouse, and he waited outside until she was finished, and took her back to his tent. He poured her a glass of water, and handed it to her. She didn't thank him. She had nothing to say, and was still too shaken to find her words.

"Are you hungry? Do you want food?" She shook her head and drank the glass of water. Her whole mouth was parched, and the water felt good going down. "What's your name?" She didn't answer him, and he asked her again. She didn't want to anger him, so she finally spoke in a voice that came out as a hoarse croak after everything she'd been through that day.

"Ariana," she said softly.

"Beautiful name, for a beautiful girl. Your family will want you back soon. As soon as they pay us, we'll take you home. I'm sorry to do this to you, but we need the money. Trust me, it's for a good cause." A cause that led them to kill people, and kidnap women for ransom. She distrusted everything he said, even though he was being kind to her. "I won't let the men hurt you again." He ran a gentle finger over the bruise on her cheek again. He sat talking to her for a while then about things needing to change, and said sometimes the only way to catch people's attention was to do things they didn't like. He made it sound like he was fighting a holy war for the good of the people. It would have sounded like ranting, except that some of what he said made sense. He talked about the poverty and how the whole country was being run into the ground. And in some ways, she knew it was true. "Your people need to change their ways," he said, looking deep into her eyes. It told her that he had no idea who she was, or that he had actually taken an ambassador's daughter and kidnapped her for ransom. He continued talking for some time, and then he signaled to one of his men, and told him to take her away. "Carefully, this time," he reminded him. And she heard him tell two of his men to put her back in the box. They reached for the hood, and he yanked it away from them with a smile at her, as though reminding her that he would let nothing bad happen to her. "No ropes," he said to them as they led her away. "Just put the lid on the box."

They pushed her and forced her back into the box—she had to pull her legs up to fit into it—and then they lowered the lid back on it again. Without the hood, she could see that there were air holes in the lid, and in the corner a little tube that gave her some more air. She lay in the darkness, trying not to panic, and finally, praying that her father would rescue her soon, she fell asleep.

She woke the next morning to the sound of their dragging the lid off the box again. They pulled her roughly to her feet and took her back to their leader's tent. He was sitting at a table, writing in a journal, as Ariana blinked in the bright sun. "One day, the world will read my words, and understand what we're all about, and know that we were right." He looked her over again, and handed her a stack of clothes. There was an army shirt and a man's T-shirt, a pair of rough cotton pants, and a pair of boots that looked like they might be almost the right size. She went to the outhouse to put them on, and saw that her dress was torn in a dozen places, and there were bruises all over her. And she could feel that her long blond hair was a tangled mass. She smelled of sweat and terror, but the men smelled no better, except for their leader. She could see that he had shaved. "We'll take you down to the river later," he said quietly, "so you can bathe." He told them to bring her something to eat, and they brought her some indistinguishable meat and a plate of rice. He poured her a cup of coffee and handed it to her. He still hadn't heard her speak except to say her name.

"How soon are you going to send me back?" she asked him after she ate the meat and rice. She didn't want to, but she was starving. She hadn't eaten since before she was kidnapped. It was the first time she had spoken to him, and he looked surprised.

"As soon as they pay. Where are you from?" He could tell that her Spanish wasn't Argentine, although she spoke Spanish well. "You're American?" It had never dawned on him that she might not be one of them, but suddenly he looked pleased. She nodded in answer to his question. "That's even better. Now our message will be heard by the entire world."

"You can't teach anyone lessons by killing people, and using violence to spread your words," she was bold enough to say to him, and he smiled.

"Sometimes violence is the only way people will listen. You have to get their attention first. What are you doing in Argentina?"

"I live here," she said simply, afraid that knowing she was the ambassador's daughter would make things worse for her. They had heard none of the radio broadcasts announcing that the American ambassador's daughter had been kidnapped.

"You're a rich American," he said, his eyes angry for a minute, and then he calmed down. "Don't you ever question how you live, how many people are starving while you eat, how many people die for you every day?"

"And if I die for them, it won't help them. Killing people won't change anything."

"This is a holy war, Ariana, a war for the starving, dying people that rich people like you use and throw away." She didn't answer him, and a little while later, he walked her through the forest to a river, and stood watching her while she bathed. She turned her back to him, and came out of the river feeling clean and refreshed. He walked her back to his men, who put her back in the coffinlike box again, and she lay sweltering there all day.

She nearly fainted when he finally came himself to get her out that night. His men were always the ones to punish her, and he was always the one to rescue her, order her taken out of the box, feed her, and give her cool water. And when they returned to his tent, as she stumbled along beside him, dizzy from the heat all day, she saw his journal on the table again. He handed her a glass of cool water, and she emptied it, as he waved her to a chair.

"When you come to trust me, I won't put you in the box anymore." She wanted to tell him she trusted him so he wouldn't put her back in it.

"I want to go home," she said sadly, looking at him. He seemed like someone she could reason with. He wasn't a goon like the others. He told her that night that he had gone to school in Spain, and studied with the Jesuits, and he had come back to Argentina to free his people and change the world. He saw himself as the champion of the underdog and the savior of the poor. He justified that he had to kidnap rich people to further his cause and fancied himself some kind of Robin Hood. He talked to her for a while and then put her back in the box and told her how sorry he was to do it. It was the second night she had spent in his camp. And as his men put the lid back on the box, she hoped her father was okay. She was trying to be brave, but she lay in the box that night and sobbed.

Her father had gone back to Buenos Aires, where the chief of police continued to assure him that they would find his daughter soon. No request for ransom had been made. Her photograph was everywhere on TV, and Ariana's kidnapping had made world news. President Armstrong had called him that afternoon, deeply grieved by the terrible news, and he promised the help of the CIA. He said they were already on the way, and six agents flew in that night, and asked to see Robert immediately. The embassy chef was interrogated again and told them everything he knew. He described the men who had taken her, the truck, and everything they'd done. They didn't learn anything new.

"It could be one of several groups. One of the drug cartels could have sent someone over from Colombia, to seek revenge on the United States for the damage we've done them, but honestly, they've got bigger fish to fry than to kidnap an ambassador's daughter. To put it bluntly, they're businessmen and have more sense than that. And you've never been involved in a fight with them. They have no reason to hurt you," Sam Adams, the head CIA man, told Robert after hearing what the chef had to say. "It could be just a group of local bandits, but you'd probably have heard from them by now. The operation sounds a lot smoother than something they'd do.

"There's another possibility. There's a revolutionary called Jorge, who thinks he's going to change the world. He thinks he's a modern-day Che Guevara. He's kidnapped a number of people. He moves his camp around in the foothills of the Andes Mountains, and he's looking for ways to bring his message to the world. An ambassador's daughter might be just the vehicle he wants to spread the message. His men may not even have known who they were taking, but now that he has her, he may try to hang on to her for a while. Most of the other local small-time groups want their money faster than this." They were taking their time asking for the ransom.

"Do you know where his camp is?" Robert asked him. His face had been the color of concrete for the past two days.

"We've tracked him a number of times, but he moves too fast. He has a small group of followers, and they don't stay anywhere for long. We're asking around the area, to see if anyone will talk. The locals are afraid of him. He's not doing business dealing drugs, so although we know about him, we've left him alone. It takes too much manpower to keep track of him. And revolutionaries aren't our problem. Drug dealers are. He's not a drug dealer. He's more of a holy man, preaching against 'corruption' and the sins of the rich."

"Who kidnaps women, and kills others. He doesn't sound holy to me," Robert said, angry again. He had bounced between rage and terror for two days.

"He's not. He just thinks he is," Sam Adams said in a dry voice. They had brought in a special task force to try and find Ariana, but so far they had turned up nothing. It was going to take time. Sam just hoped they kept her alive, and didn't kill her as an example of capitalist corruption. He didn't try explaining it to her father, and they were working closely with the Argentine government and the police. They were doing the best they could, but it was difficult because their **finca** was close to rough mountainous terrain filled with jungles and forests where anyone could hide.

The search for Ariana went on for days, with no sign of anything that turned up. And still no request for ransom had been made.

Several days after her capture, Jorge left the camp for a day, and they put her in the box to swelter in the heat of the day. No one knew where he'd gone. But when he came back and rescued her from the box, he knew who she was. He had gone to the city, to see if there was word of a missing American woman. Her photograph was in every newspaper and on TV. He smiled when he saw her. She was a prize of a magnitude he had never expected.

"So, you're an ambassador's daughter," he said with a broad smile. "Your government will do anything to get you back. Advise me, Ariana. You set the price. How much should I ask?"

"Whatever you think is right. The government won't pay to get me back. I'm only important to my father and no one else," she said quietly, and set down an empty glass. He was the only one who fed her and gave her water. The others gave her nothing and left her in the coffin until he got back. "And my father can only pay so much."

"He must love you very much," Jorge said, toying with her. "How much do you think he loves you? Is he a businessman?" She nodded. "How many people do you think have died at his hands?"

"No one has ever died because of my father," she said solemnly. "He's an honest man."

"That's what my brother says about himself. He's high up in the government. But he's a rich man. Rich men are never honest. One day he'll carry our message. He is already starting to help us. He knows I'm right. One day he'll take over our sick, dying government and make it healthy again, and turn it over to the people who deserve to be in power, and will finally care for the feeble and sick, and feed the poor." She could tell that he believed what he said, and she would have been more impressed by his message if she weren't his prisoner. "Ariana, what are you worth to your father? Ten million? Twenty million? Only five?"

"I don't know," she said quietly, wishing that he would set the ransom and ask for it, so she could go home.

"Your photograph is all over the TV in Buenos Aires. You must be worth a lot." As he said it, he called out to one of his men, and told him to bring her a plate of food. And in the flash of an instant, she realized that dressed in the same military garb, she looked like one of them. If their camp was raided, while the authorities looked for her, they might kill her. She was trapped between two worlds. And he was rapidly becoming both her captor and her savior, since all bounty came from him. But she was not confused. He had kidnapped her, and now he was setting the price on her head. She knew her father would pay whatever it took, his entire fortune if he had to. He would bring her home at any price.

Two members of the Argentine government came to visit Robert Gregory at the embassy that night. One was a quiet, soft-spoken younger man, who promised all the help his government could provide them. The other was an older, slick-looking politician who smelled heavily of cologne, was wearing an expensive suit, and wanted to convince the American ambassador that he had done all he could to facilitate the search for his daughter. He reeked of corruption even more than his perfume. The younger man had had Communist leanings in his youth but had seen the light and was powerful in the government. According to Sam Adams, he had aspirations of running the country one day. He was a man of the people who had done well, and he spoke with deep compassion for the ambassador's pain, and vowed his help as well. Robert didn't trust either of them, and said as much to Sam when they left.

"Julio Marcos is full of hot air, and as ineffective as he looks. Luis Muñoz could be dangerous one day. He has powerful connections, he's smart and ambitious, and some people think he will go far. I think they were both just trying to impress you with what good guys they are. I'm not sure that either of them will really try to help us." Sam had much more faith in the CIA and their own informants than in the local government, which was famous for its inadequate assistance in cases like this. Robert didn't disagree with him. Every embassy in the diplomatic community had offered their help as well, and seemed more sincere. Robert was putting all his faith in the CIA agents who hadn't left his side since Ariana had disappeared.

The nightmare went on relentlessly with no word from the kidnappers, and Robert was afraid Ariana was dead. It was a possibility, but the CIA were combing the countryside and the foothills and hoping that wasn't the case. But no one had seen Ariana, or was aware of a group like the one the police described. The CIA were still convinced it was Jorge who had kidnapped her, and that they were hiding in the forest in the foothills of the mountains, but they had found no trace of him yet.

And then finally, two weeks after she'd been taken, an untraceable number in Buenos Aires called a local television station, and asked for twenty million U.S. dollars, in unmarked bills, in cash. The drop-off was to be determined later, but they had set the amount. And when the CIA and local authorities finally traced the call, they found that it had come from a pay phone in a government building. The call could have been placed by anyone. But at least now they had set the amount, and Robert could take action to free his daughter and meet their demand for ransom. It gave him hope that she was still alive.

Jorge moved his camp deeper into the forest two days before the ransom call was made. This time Jorge sat beside her himself in the truck. She wore no hood, and they didn't tie her up. He had become her protector, and kept her with him at all times in their new camp. There was no place for her to run—she would have been lost in the forest instantly, and died trying to get out. Her only hope of salvation was staying close to him.

"You know I'm right," he said to her that night, as he handed her her dinner of rice and beans. He was eating the same meal as she did, and afterward took a cigar from a battered aluminum box sitting on the table. He kept his journals in it too, and told her it was an aviator's box he had found in the jungle, after a small plane crashed, running drugs from Ecuador. "We took the drugs, and buried the pilot and the remains of the plane. I've used the box ever since. The money from the drugs gave us what we needed to start our movement. We lived on it for a long time."

"And now you support it by kidnapping women for ransom," she said with a look of disapproval.

He laughed at what she said. "You remind me of my mother when you look like that. She was a good woman, and brave like you. My father was a rich man, and beat her every night. She was a poor girl from a mountain village. He fell in love with her when she was fifteen, and treated her badly for the rest of his life. I killed him when I was fourteen. He had come home one night drunk and had beaten her, and I hit him for that night and all the times he had done it before. He fell backward and hit his head. I never regretted it. He thought he could do whatever he wanted to her because he had money. My mother had a good life after he died. She died a few years later, but she finally had the life she deserved at the end. My brother was a policeman then. He filled out a report that a robber had entered the house and pushed my father. He deserved to die, just like the rest of his kind." Jorge had had a vendetta against the rich all his life. "My mother sent me to school in Spain then, after he died. I came home when she got sick. She was too young to die," he said, looking sad.

"Who got what was left of the money?" she asked, curious about him. He was a complex man. "Did she have anything left?"

"My brother," he said simply. "He used it to become an important man. He helps us now whenever he can. Quietly, so he's not in danger. We need him where he is. He knows that I'm right. And when the time is right, he'll step out of the shadows. Our day will come." He lit his cigar again, and offered her a puff. But she declined. She was curious about who his brother was, but didn't dare to ask. If she knew too much, he might kill her before the ransom got paid. "And now, with the money your father pays us, we can fund our movement for a long time. Until we're ready to come forward. My brother says it won't be long, the government is so weak, it's ready to fall on its own. There are people all over the country, waiting to join forces with us. I've been building the foundation for the last ten years, while the rest of you live well. I've been willing to sacrifice everything I have for what I believe. How many people do you know who can say that?"

"Not many," she had to admit.

"Even one?" he asked, as they sat in the flickering candlelight.

"Maybe not." There was something mesmerizing about him. Even though his actions were so wrong, she was beginning to wonder if his motives for his cause were sincere.

"One day you'll know that I'm right," he said, convinced of it. "Maybe you won't even want to go back, and will wait for our time with us." To Ariana, it was still a horrifying thought—she wanted

to go home, and she was worried about her father—
but at least she felt safe now at Jorge's side. No one
had hurt her since she arrived, and he treated her
well.

He let her sleep on a cot in his tent that night.
Their camp was so deep in the forest, he knew she
wouldn't try to escape. There was nowhere to go.
And his men were sleeping in other tents. As always, he was alone. And he had his own cot, and
had another one put in his tent for her. And as she
lay on it, drifting off to sleep, she saw him writing
in his journal, holding his cigar in one hand. He
had a beautiful face as she watched him in the candlelight, almost like Jesus. The thought occurred
to her, as she fell asleep, that maybe he was a holy
man after all.

Once the demand for ransom had been made,
Robert Gregory got busy organizing the transfer of
funds, with the help of the CIA. One of the career
diplomats had been running the embassy since Ariana had been taken. Robert could no longer do it.
And he was taking the nitroglycerin now every day.
The embassy doctor was worried about his heart,
and he was worried about Ariana. After two more
weeks they still hadn't received instructions about
where to pay the money.

• • •

Jorge took Ariana swimming in a stream every day. The water was cold, and he watched her as she turned her back to him, and one day, he swam over to her and held her in his arms. They were both naked, and she didn't stop him. He turned her slowly around to face him, admiring the beauty of her body under the clear water, and she was mesmerized by his blue eyes and the angles of his face, and then he kissed her, and she could feel his passion rising up against her, and suddenly all she wanted was for him to hold her and to keep her safe forever. There was something so simple and primal about the life she lived with him, and they made love under the water with all the passion he had felt for her since the first time he had seen her. He was infinitely gentle with her and told her that he loved her, and she believed him. She had come to feel that what he believed wasn't wrong, even if his methods were. He was a solitary warrior swimming against the currents, and life had never seemed as simple or as pure as it did at that moment, and afterward she was breathless in his arms, and told him she loved him too. Her survival depended on it, their life together in the forest was reduced to basics. He was a man and took care of her, defended and protected her. He told her he would never let anything bad happen to her, and she believed him. The fact that he was holding her for ransom no longer seemed important. She wanted to be there with him.

They made love again that night, and after she

fell asleep, he went back to his journals. He wrote her a love letter filled with all he felt for her, and all he hoped they would share one day, in a different world, a better world, that he would make for her. He told her she had become his inspiration, and that their lives were fused as one now. She cried in the morning when she read it. He was the only thing that was real to her. Her father was fading from memory, and everything he stood for seemed so wrong now. Only what Jorge said to her made sense.

They walked in the forest together that afternoon, bathed in the stream, and made love again. And suddenly all she wanted was to be with him. He was the embodiment of love and tenderness, and the world she had known before him had disappeared. All that was left was her life in the forest with him. She no longer cared if her father paid the ransom, and Jorge laughed when she said it that night when they made love by candlelight in his tent.

"You may not care, but I do, Ariana. We have thousands of people depending on us all over Argentina. I have a responsibility to them, and your father will help us feed them. He is funding a sacred cause. All we have to do is work out a safe way to transfer the money." He didn't tell her his brother would help. It somehow made the ransom seem even reasonable. But all she wanted now was to be with him. And he wrote a love letter every night before he went to sleep, after he wrote in his journals. She found the love letters from him every day when she woke up and read them avidly. No one had ever shown her such an outpouring of love. They took all their meals together, separate from the men. They shared a simple life. Ariana had been with him for six weeks, and it seemed like an entire lifetime to both of them.

The instructions as to how the ransom was to be paid came to the embassy this time. The money was to be divided in cash in small amounts, and dropped off at points all over Argentina, each of them in a secure way, that would make it difficult if not impossible to trace. Even the CIA was stumped by their system, which was overly simplistic but had the potential to work and was far more difficult to trace or intercept than a single drop-off.

"They must have thousands of people ready to make pick-ups, and find a way to get it to them. The problem is it'll take months for them to collect the entire ransom. They're obviously not in a hurry. It could take four, five, or even six months to get the whole twenty million to them." Jorge had been extremely cunning in how he planned it, and Sam Adams didn't like it at all. Jorge was a clever devil.

"And what happens to Ariana in the meantime?" her father asked, looking terrified again. "She could already be dead for all we know."

"That's not how he operates, from our experience with him. He would keep her alive as his prisoner, to use as leverage." Sam didn't tell him that they had rescued one kidnapping victim who'd been kept in a box with a breathing tube for eight months, but the man had survived and been returned after they paid the ransom. There were other instances where that wasn't the case, but they had no reason to believe that Jorge had killed Ariana. He didn't say it to her father, but Sam thought her youth and beauty were in her favor. And for now, they just had to believe she was still alive, and start making the payments. Sam suggested a system of accelerated payments, which would deliver the full amount within two months, and Robert approved.

For the next month, they used every drop-off they were given. Ariana had been gone for almost three months by then, and her attachment to Jorge was growing every day. It increased dramatically when she began to suspect that she was pregnant. She didn't say anything to him until she was almost certain, and then she whispered it to him one night as she lay in his arms. It was their ultimate gift to each other. And Jorge was thrilled. This was just the bond to her he wanted. Ariana thought it had happened the first time they made love, since she hadn't had a period since. At first she thought it was from the trauma, but her breasts had gotten fuller, and her waist was thickening. Jorge said it only made her more beautiful to him, and he was even more careful with her now, and looked at her adoringly. He never left her side for a moment. She was too valuable to him to let anything happen to her.

The day Ariana told Jorge she was pregnant was the day the British and Israeli ambassadors came to the embassy in Buenos Aires, to meet with Robert and the CIA task force that was working to find Ariana. The British suggested an intense reconnaissance flight using infrared units over the forest where the CIA thought Jorge might be hiding. And the Israeli ambassador offered commandos to move in for a rescue mission if they had any sign at all that he was there.

Robert looked at Sam with eyes filled with hope as he listened to them. "Can we at least try it?"

Sam was skeptical about their success, but agreed it might be worth a try, even if a long shot.

"We've got nothing to lose if it doesn't work, and they can't see anything," Sam said. They had tried everything else by then, but they had everything to lose if they attempted a raid, bungled it, and Jorge killed her.

"Except my daughter," Robert Gregory said darkly. But a whole new task force was set up for their combined efforts, and the ballroom of the embassy became the command post for the entire project. With the British and Israelis, combined with the CIA, there were forty men working on it night and day.

The first and second reconnaissance missions came up with nothing. But the third one, flying farther south, saw flickering dim lights in the forest. Almost nothing showed on the film they had taken, but the head man sent by Israeli intelligence swore it was a camp, albeit a small one, and Sam told them that Jorge always kept his operation small but spread out. The British ambassador, who was ex–army intelligence, was sure that he could see a tent on the film, but no one else agreed. But the faint lights allowed them to pinpoint a location. It was deep in the forest, and when Sam conferred with the others, they agreed it would be difficult to get into, but the Israelis thought that they could do it.

The plan they suggested was that when they got close enough to the camp they had identified on the map, if they were right, they would start a ring of fire that would engulf the camp. It was a brutal way to flush them out, but it would cause enough chaos and distraction to rescue Ariana, if she was there. Their objective was to rescue Ariana, however they had to do it, and leave no survivors behind. Jorge was of no value to them—he had no information they wanted. He was known to be a small-scale revolutionary with distorted religious ideas, and the country would be better off without him. The Argentine government gave them the green light for the plan as well, since Jorge was the kind of problem that could cause a major disruption in later years, if his following grew. The Argentine advisers to the task force were more than willing to sacrifice him. And the decision was made in the utmost secrecy. The CIA were willing to take full responsibility for killing him, and no one would ever know except the task force. The only survivor the combined forces wanted out of that camp was Ariana—the rest could die in the forest for all they cared. There was no value in keeping her kidnappers alive.

They set a date to put the plan in action three days hence. They ran one more reconnaissance mission the next day and came up with the same flickering lights, and this time confirmation of at least one and possibly two tents. And by that night and the next day, the Israelis were ready to go. They were getting support from the British and the CIA, and had the local government's tacit albeit unofficial approval. They had identified a place in the forest, not far from where the lights were, where they could lower a helicopter, have it hover, and get the commandos and Ariana out after they raided the camp. It was going to be delicate, and everyone involved, including Ariana's father, was aware of how wrong it could go, and the consequences if it did. But they were all uncomfortable about letting the ransom drop-offs stretch out over another month. Too much could go wrong in the meantime, and by the time they finished paying the ransom, Ariana could be long dead. They all agreed it was time to get her out. The whole mission was kept top secret, in the Argentine government as well. They wanted as few people aware of it as possible, to prevent any leaks and anyone warning Jorge, if he had sympathizers among their ranks.

They had decided to make their move at night, using infrared devices, and the entire task force set up camp far enough away from the forest so as not to attract attention, but close enough for the helicopter to land once they got her out, if they did. The men involved in the mission wore similar garb to Jorge's group of bandits, so no one would notice them locally.

The Israeli commandos set off on schedule. There were twelve of them, equipped with all the gear they needed for their mission. It took them an hour to get to the camp on foot. They moved with the utmost stealth, imitating the sounds of the forest, advancing in total darkness but fully able to see with the infrared devices. And what they saw once they were in deep enough were the three tents of Jorge's camp. They sent the information back to the task force by text. And then they backed away far enough to begin to lay the fire ring, with hand signals they made to each other.

By then everyone in the camp was asleep. There was only light in one tent from a candle. Jorge had finished his journal entry for the night, and was writing his nightly love letter to Ariana. He placed it next to her cot, kissed her, blew out the candle, and slipped into the cot beside her. Ariana was sound asleep, as he held her. Just as he had written to her many times by now, he believed that she had been sent to him by spirit forces to allow him to complete his mission, like an angel, to bless his people.

Within half an hour, the circle of fire had been lit. The commandos were wearing asbestos suits so they could go in and get her and pull her out. They had identified their escape route. The only thing they weren't sure of was which tent she was in. They were certain that the largest one belonged to Jorge, but they had no idea where Ariana was being kept, nor under what conditions—if she was manacled, or tied up in some way. They were prepared for almost anything. The first tent caught fire from the blaze, and half a dozen men came running out naked. One of them was wearing clothes that were on fire. They had slept as their tent turned into a blaze, and there was no way for them to escape through the ring of fire blazing around them. They were trapped, and the burning men screamed to the others, as their tent caught fire too. And then they saw a man and a woman come running out from the larger tent—the fire hadn't reached it yet. There was a rapid exchange between the man and the woman, as he handed her a box of some kind and rushed to help his men.

Ariana ran back to their tent for an instant and

put Jorge's love letters in the box. She had been keeping them tied with a piece of fabric in her pillow. She quickly put the letters in the metal box Jorge had handed her, and ran back outside. She could hear the men shouting and screaming in the fire, and saw Jorge dart among them, helping those he could. One commando signaled to another then and pointed to Ariana. It could only be her—they were sure there would be no other women in the camp. And all the men in the camp were distracted by the blaze and not watching her. And without a sound, three of the Israeli commandos plunged through the ring of fire and grabbed her, wrapped her in an asbestos blanket, and carried her out. She fought them and was screaming for Jorge, while she clutched the metal box to her and wouldn't let go.

She had no idea who the men were, and they couldn't have told her. With their fire masks covering their faces, they couldn't speak to reassure her or identify themselves. They pointed to a distant part of the forest, as she tried to fight them. She kept screaming Jorge's name, and he couldn't hear her. He was fighting the fire with his men, and before any of them knew what happened, she was gone, being carried to safety by the commandos, as she tried to fight free. She pulled out of the asbestos blanket for an instant, just in time to see a burning tree fall on their camp and crush Jorge. His entire body was on fire, and she thought she could hear

him calling her name. She struggled fiercely, but
the men holding her wouldn't let go. The last Ariana saw of Jorge was his body lying under the tree,
and the entire camp in flames, as she clutched his
box to her chest.

She was glad she had put his love letters in it for
safety when they fled the tent.

She had no idea what was happening as one of
the Israelis raced through the forest with her, holding her in a viselike grip so she couldn't run back to
the camp, which it was clear she wanted to do. And
the others followed closely. No one had seen them
come or go, and they had no doubt that all the men
in the camp were trying to fight the blaze or dead
by now. They carried Ariana to the clearing, who
fought them with all her strength. All she wanted
was to go back, and as the helicopter came down
out of nowhere and hovered, they threw her in, and
climbed in after her. The helicopter was gone again
in less than a minute, and from the air they saw the
blaze spreading through the forest. But the mission
was successful—they had rescued her. The senior
officer in command took off his fire mask then, as
did the others, and they rapidly explained who they
were.

"We're here to help you, Miss Gregory. We're part
of a task force sent by the British and Israeli govern-
ments, the CIA, and your father." But all she could
do was scream and shake her head. She looked deranged, with wild hair and flashing eyes. Someone

had given her a jacket to put on when she fought free of the asbestos blanket. She had come out of their tent naked and had no clothes.

"No . . . no . . . Take me back . . . you don't understand." She pounded on one of them and pushed him away. "Take me back. . . ."

"You're safe now, Ariana," the second-in-command said gently, wondering what they had done to her in the past three months. She looked like they had driven her mad. But what they didn't know was that she had just watched her lover and the father of her unborn baby die.

"You killed Jorge!" She was screaming at them. "He's a holy man!" And then they understood, as she clutched the metal box to her chest with his journals and letters in it. It was all she had left. They saw then too that she had slight burns on her hands, and twenty minutes later, after flying over the forest, they set down in their camp, where the others were waiting for them. And the moment they saw Ariana come out of the helicopter, one of the British agents radioed Sam at the embassy, where he was waiting for news of her with her father. Robert had been taking nitroglycerin all night, and the stress of waiting to hear if she was alive was driving him over the edge.

"We've got her" was all the commander said. He didn't know more than that yet. "We'll have her back to you in a few hours. We need to assess what kind of shape she's in and if we need to take her to a hospital." As soon as he signed off, Sam turned to Robert, and patted his hand with tears in his eyes.

"They have her. Your girl is coming home." Robert burst into tears then, and hugged Sam as he sobbed.

"Oh my God, I thought she was dead."

"She'll be home in a few hours. They're assessing her now." But what Sam didn't know, and wouldn't have told Robert anyway, was that she was sobbing and distraught, and begging them to take her back, although she knew there was no point. She had seen Jorge killed by the falling tree. The man she loved and the father of her baby was dead. Jorge had been the first to die in the fire. And she stared at the men who had saved her with empty, broken eyes. One of them finally got her to put down the old metal box and helped her get into clothes. She looked like a madwoman, as they handed her water and she drank, her hair tangled around her head, her eyes looking at them as though she didn't understand. They could see that it was going to be a long way back for her to return to a normal life. They had seen it before, with people who had been kidnapped for long periods of time and been turned around by their captors until they no longer knew what they believed or who they were. They could tell that Jorge had done a good job on her.

The combined task force made a quiet decision, standing away from her, out of earshot, to take her to the hospital and not to the embassy. She was in no condition to go home. She was confused, distraught, and traumatized, she was hysterical, and nothing they said calmed her down. One of the CIA men on the scene called Sam at the embassy and let him know the plan, to admit her to a hospital that night. They had already made arrangements for it, in case she was hurt.

"Is she injured?" Sam asked quietly, after he left Robert for a moment.

"Physically, she looks fine, except for some minor burns on her hands," the agent answered, sounding tense. "We have some serious Stockholm Syndrome going on here. She wants to go back. She fought us like a cat."

"Shit. I don't think her father is expecting that. Maybe we can get her calm enough so he can see her." He was worried about Robert. He had already been through too much.

"She wants to go back to Jorge. She thinks he's a holy man. And he's going to pass for a martyr now. He's dead. A burning tree hit him before we left. She says she's carrying his child. I don't know if that's true or not."

"Wait till her father hears that. Let me know when you get to the hospital, and I'll bring him over for a few minutes." But when Sam went back to him, Robert's face was gray, and he was clutching his chest.

"She's all right, Robert. She's safe. Try to calm down."

"I think I'm having a heart attack," he said, grimacing with pain.

Sam went to call an ambulance, and they came five minutes later. The paramedics confirmed what he had said. He had been through too much in the past three months. Sam rode in the ambulance with him, and they defibrillated him on the way in. He was in excruciating pain, and they rushed him to a cardiac ICU unit as soon as he came in. A doctor came out to talk to Sam, and told him that they wanted to do an angiogram but he wasn't strong enough to survive it. They were doing everything they could. It was touch and go for the next few hours while they waited for Ariana to arrive. They flew to Buenos Aires in the helicopter rather than take her by car, and then they drove her to the hospital from the airport, where Sam met them.

The man in charge looked grim. "She says she doesn't want to see her father, that he's an evil man."

"Well, that's one piece of good news," Sam said tersely. "He had a heart attack two hours ago, and he's in cardiac ICU. She can't see him anyway."

There was a team of doctors waiting to assess Ariana's condition, and she cried piteously while they examined her. They took her box from her and promised to keep it safe when she screamed for it. She said she was having terrible pains, and the doctors noticed immediately that she was bleeding. A sonogram showed that she was having a miscarriage. They tried to explain it to her, and she only cried more. There was blood everywhere when they finally sedated her, and all she could do was mumble Jorge's name over and over again. They did a D & C on her that night when she was asleep. She had lost the fetus as soon as she came in, which everyone agreed was a mercy.

And they gave the metal box she'd been clutching to Sam, to send back to the embassy with one of the CIA men, to leave it for her there. The men who had come in with her had asked her what was in it, and she said Jorge's love letters to her. Sam opened the box and rifled through it—he never saw the journals under the letters—and approved the box being sent to the embassy for her. It was harmless, and he hoped she would throw it away one day. It was a souvenir of a terrible time.

Ariana was calmer in the morning when she woke up, and looked severely depressed. She remembered losing the baby the night before. They said she had been about six weeks pregnant, so it wasn't far along. And otherwise, physically, she was all right. They treated the burns on her hands, but they were only superficial. The main thing wrong with her was her mind. Sam and a psychiatrist tried to explain it to her as something that happened to people sometimes when they'd been kidnapped, that they begin to identify with their captors, and forget who they were and everything they believed in when they were taken hostage. Jorge had begun to seem like her protector and the only person she could trust.

"But what if he was right?" she said, after listening to them. "Think of all the poor people in the world. All he wanted to do was help them."

"You don't help poor people by kidnapping innocent women and holding them prisoner in the forest, for twenty million dollars ransom," Sam said clearly, looking her in the eye. She had said as much to Jorge herself in the beginning, and in time he had convinced her otherwise.

"He wanted to use that to feed the poor and liberate the oppressed," Ariana answered softly, ready to defend him. In her mind, he had ceased to be her oppressor, when he became the man she loved, after they made love.

"That's certainly a noble cause," Sam said quietly, "but he also had his men kill your driver, and Jorge and his men have killed people before. They're revolutionaries, Ariana. They want to overthrow the government and kill people like your father, who is a good man. He loves you, Ariana. Your father never hurt anyone. Jorge has hurt a lot of people." Including her. He had twisted her thinking beyond recognition.

"He killed his father," she said in a dead voice, "because he hurt Jorge's mother. He was protecting her."

"That doesn't make it right," Sam said sanely, and

she looked as though a small light had gone on. She was remembering what Jorge had said. Sam knew she would be confused for a long time. "You're going to need time to think about all this. You can't do it all at once. The one thing I do know is how much your father loves you. He's been worried sick about you for three months."

"Where is he?" Ariana suddenly looked frightened and concerned about him, as though she had just remembered who her father was.

Sam hesitated before he told her, but she had to know, even now, with her confused mind. "He had a heart attack last night. He's upstairs in cardiac ICU. They said he was resting comfortably this morning. He's been through a lot, and so have you," Sam said sympathetically. No one was to blame for all that had happened except the men who had kidnapped her. Surely not Robert Gregory or his daughter, no matter how confused she was about it now.

"Can I see him?" Ariana asked, and Sam nodded, and a few minutes later they took her upstairs in a wheelchair, and she wheeled herself up to his bed. Robert looked terrible, but better than he had the night before. Sam had thought he might die before he got him to the hospital, and Robert wasn't out of the woods yet. They were considering an angiogram that morning, if he was up to it.

He smiled and tears ran down his cheeks the moment he saw Ariana's face. He gently smoothed her hair. "Thank God, you're all right."

"I love you, Daddy," she said, and sounded like a little girl.

"I love you too, sweetheart. I was so worried for you. I'm so sorry it happened. I'm sorry we ever came here. You were right. I've already sent in my letter of resignation. As soon as I get out of here, we'll go home." She nodded, with tears in her eyes too. She was no longer sure where home was, in the forest with Jorge, here in Buenos Aires, or New York. She felt like Dorothy in **The Wizard of Oz.** All she wanted to do was go home, wherever it was. And she remembered all too vividly that Jorge was dead. But she still had his journals and love letters in the aviator's box. And she believed that everything he'd written and felt for her was real. But she remembered now that she loved her father too.

"Just try to rest," she told her father gently. "Don't worry about anything. I'm back." Her body was anyway, but she knew her mind was lost.

"Thank God," her father said, and closed his eyes. They had given him a sedative, and a few minutes later, he drifted off to sleep, grateful that she was safe and alive. Her return was the greatest gift of his life.

They did an angiogram on him that afternoon, and tried to do an angioplasty. Two of his arteries were blocked, but he started failing on the table, and his vital signs plummeted. They defibrillated him twice and brought him back, but there was nothing they could do. He wasn't strong enough to withstand the procedure, and he was fading fast when they brought him back to his room, where Ariana was waiting for him. He looked exhausted, and she kissed him gently on the cheek, and then sat next to him holding his hand. He stopped breathing a little while later, while she was watching him. She pressed the emergency button and a team ran in and tried to revive him. They tried for twenty minutes, while Ariana watched them, sobbing softly. She remembered now that her father was a good man, and not a bad one. And she knew just how much she loved him, and how much he had loved her.

But there was nothing they could do for him. His heart was too damaged, and he was too weak. They gave up their futile efforts to revive him, and left Ariana to sit with him for a while. In two days, she had lost two men she loved, and a baby. She had watched Jorge be killed the night before, and her father die from his months of worry about her. She felt as though she had killed him as she kissed him for the last time and left the room. Sam was waiting for her outside, and he took her to the embassy, where Eugenia was waiting to help her. The embassy was going to take care of the formalities of getting her father's body home. And Eugenia helped her pack everything she had in Buenos Aires. They had already emptied the **finca** after she'd been kidnapped.

President Armstrong called Ariana that night to

tell her how sorry he was about her father, and how relieved he was that she had been rescued and was all right.

"At least he had the comfort of knowing you were alive and safe before he died, and seeing you again. That must have meant the world to him," the president said, sounding deeply moved by everything that had happened. He promised to come to her father's funeral when they held it in New York, and two days later, Ariana boarded a plane to go home. Her father was on his way to New York in a casket on the same flight, and Ariana was still in shock. Embassy officials said she was too shaken up to talk to the press. She had called a few of her friends in Buenos Aires to say goodbye before she left, but she didn't have the time or heart to see any of them. She had thanked the British and Israeli ambassadors for their help in rescuing her, and two men who came as emissaries of the Argentine government to express their relief that she'd been rescued and extend their condolences about her father. Their visit was formal and brief. And she hugged Eugenia hard at the airport before she left. She had the box with Jorge's letters and journals in her carry-on and a bodyguard was traveling with her.

"Take care of yourself, Ariana," Eugenia said as she held her, and Ariana nodded, as tears slid down her face. She had nothing to go home to. The father who had loved and shielded her all her life was gone. And the man who had kidnapped her and said he loved her and turned her mind and life upside down was dead too. She knew she needed help sorting it all out, but she had no one to turn to, and nothing solid to hang on to except herself now. She had been in Argentina for ten months, and everything was confused now. Who were the good people, and who were the bad people? And who was she in all of it? Because of her, both Jorge and her father had died, one while she was rescued, and the other because she'd been kidnapped and he had worried so much about her. And the shock of the fire and the rescue had killed her baby too. She was responsible for three people dying, and wondered if she could ever forgive herself. She felt guilty for all of it, as the plane left Buenos Aires and she flew back to New York. She wanted to forget everything that had happened, but she knew she never would.

And the aviator's box with all of Jorge's secrets and his love letters to her was going home with her. As she thought of them, she could see him in the candlelight, writing, with a cigar in one hand, and his handsome face as he bent over his journals and the piercing blue eyes that had convinced her everything he said was true. Maybe nothing he had said to her was true. Maybe he didn't even love her. But she knew it would take her a lifetime to make up for the three people she felt she had killed. All she could hope now was that God would forgive her. She couldn't forgive herself, but maybe He would.

Chapter 8

Her father's three secretaries, still on sal-
ary while he was in Buenos Aires, helped Ariana
with all the arrangements in New York. They took
the largest "suite" at Frank Campbell's, the funeral
parlor on Madison Avenue, where people came
to pay their respects for two days. Ariana could
be there only for a short time, and then would go
back to her father's apartment, and try to sort everything out in her head. Nothing made sense. All
she knew now was that her father was dead and she
was alone. How it had happened, why they had
gone to Buenos Aires, and everything that had happened there were all a blur, a jumble of people and
parties and places that meant nothing to her now.
The only voice in her head was Jorge's. The aviator's box she had brought home with her was hidden in her closet. She didn't have the courage to
open it and read his journals and letters to her, but

she wanted to keep them safe, to read one day. She had come back to New York to become everything he hated, the spoiled rich girl she had been before she left, and that he had accused her of being and told her she had to change. She felt as though she was betraying him just by being there, even though this was her home. The only thing clear to her was that she loathed herself for the destruction she had caused, and the lives that had been lost because of her. It never occurred to her that it was all because of Jorge, and what he had done to her, and most of all to her mind. He had emptied it and refilled it with his twisted philosophies and revolutionary ideas. She recognized nothing in her own head—it was like a closet in a hotel room that belonged to someone else. Only she had to live there now, with someone else's thoughts, none of which fit who she had been before. Now she felt like a ghost, with no future and no past.

Her father's funeral was exquisitely painful, and they laid him to rest in the family mausoleum with her mother. She left him there on a windy, chilly April day. Everyone he'd ever done business with came to the funeral, and many to the apartment afterward, his friends, associates, people who just liked and respected him, people he had grown up with, and her old friends out of sympathy for her. And as promised, President Armstrong came, which caused such a huge security problem and traffic jam outside, as the Secret Service stopped traffic and escorted him in, that Ariana was relieved that he wasn't coming to the apartment afterward. He kissed her cheek and hugged her, and told her how sorry he was about everything that had happened. He looked as guilty as she felt. And finally, when everyone left, she was alone, and felt lost.

Sam Adams had come to the funeral too, and he stopped in to see her the next day, to see how she was doing. She sat numbly in their living room with nothing to say. And as she looked at him, her eyes were blank. He could see that she still had a long rocky road ahead of her, and was not surprised. The CIA had recommended several therapists to her in New York, experienced with kidnapping victims.

"What are you going to do now, Ariana?" he asked with a look of deep concern. They had spent almost three months rescuing her, but he knew only too well that only part of her had returned, and a piece of her had died and would never be the same again, particularly now, without her father's help to reestablish who she was. Jorge had burned some of her history and essence to ashes, and there was nothing to replace that now with her father gone too. She felt as though parts of her had disappeared, lost forever. And all the empty places were filled to the brim with guilt. It was a hard way to live, and Sam was seriously worried she might take her own life.

"I don't know," she said, staring into space. They had given up her apartment in Tribeca when they

left ten months before, and her father's apartment
felt tomblike to her now. His housekeeper fussed
over her just as she had since she was a child and
cried every time she saw her. She could tell that the
young woman who had returned from Argentina
was not the girl she had known and loved all her
life. Ariana had become someone else, a stranger
even to herself.

"You need to keep working with a therapist to
heal from all this," Sam said gently.

"I want to do some charity work," she said
vaguely, but she was in no condition to help anyone at the moment, he knew. She had to clear her
own head first.

"You have time to do that later. Why don't you
take the summer to relax and find your footing
again?"

As he said it, a thought came to her mind, of a
peaceful place she had once gone to with her father.
She remembered his saying that if he ever needed
to get away, it was where he would go. It was a safe
haven where she could hide, where no one could
see how guilty she was, and where no one would
judge her. She had blood on her hands now, and
she was sure that everyone could see it. And to
demonstrate that, she had washed her hands constantly ever since she'd gotten home, and they were
bright red.

He promised to keep in touch, and said he would
come back to see her again. He only hoped that the

disordered pieces of her mind would fall back into place in time, like a thousand-piece jigsaw puzzle, where most of it was sky. But the only sky he saw in Ariana's eyes now was very dark, as she thanked him for the visit. He left wondering if he would ever see her again and desperately sad for her.

After Sam left, Ariana sat staring into space for a long time, thinking of her father and Jorge. She thought about the box of Jorge's love letters in her closet, but didn't feel strong enough to read his words. All she could think of was the night he died, and the camp in flames. She didn't even remember the Israeli rescue and being carried out of the camp with her fists flailing. The trauma of that night had swept it from her mind, and everything after she saw the burning tree fall on Jorge was now a blank. Sam and others had told her the rest. For them it was all over now that she was home. For Ariana, the agony was just beginning. She had a whole life to live without two men she had loved.

Ariana went for a walk after Sam left the apartment, and everything around her looked the same. The same houses, same doormen, same shops on Madison Avenue. It still looked like winter in Central Park in late April, and as bleak as she felt. And she kept thinking now of the quiet monastery in the Berkshires that had come to mind a few hours before. She was suddenly desperate to go there, although she could no longer remember the name, but she remembered the town it was near. And after a sleepless night, she got up early the next morning, called the garage to have her father's car ready, wrote the housekeeper a note that she had gone away for the weekend, packed a bag with a few simple clothes in it, and left. And at the last minute, she ran back to her room, and took the aviator's box with her. She stuck it in her suitcase, for safekeeping, afraid it would disappear. It was her link to everything that had just happened to her, and her only proof in her own mind that it had been real. And she needed to keep it with her.

She left the city and drove north for three hours, and more than once she felt breathless, particularly after she left New York. She was terrified she would look up and see a military vehicle blocking the road and she would be kidnapped again. The memory of it was still vivid. And more than once she had to stop, pull over, and catch her breath. It was the last memory of her recent life and who she had been then. And as she thought of it, she could see Felipe slumped over the steering wheel shot through the head. It brought into sharper focus that he had died for her sins too. According to Jorge, her greatest sin was that she was rich, and rich people were the cause of all the troubles in the world. Poor people died because of them, just like Felipe. It all made sense to her, and confirmed everything he had said. And the fact that he had wanted twenty million dollars of her father's money to help poor people made sense too. Poor people were the saints, and rich ones the sinners. And it only increased her hatred of herself, that he had instilled in her. But Jorge had promised to save her, and now he was dead.

She reached the small sleepy town in the Berkshires that she had entered into the GPS, and once there she stopped at a gas station and asked for the Carmelite convent that she remembered so well. She and her father had stopped there after a weekend with friends when she was younger. He had gone into the chapel and lit a candle, as he always did, and she remembered the nuns being very nice to them. Her mother had stayed in the city, and she had enjoyed the time with him. Her father had always had a soft spot for Carmelites and said they were a remarkable group of women. They had surprised her by how warm and chatty they were, and well informed, although he had told her they were a cloistered order and silent most of the time. The old nun who had led them around had been lively and fun and clearly enjoyed their visit, and it had stuck in Ariana's mind. They were exactly what she needed now. She drove into their parking lot around two in the afternoon, and could hear the nuns singing in the chapel. She heaved a sigh of relief and laid her head back against the seat. For the first time in the days since she'd been back, she felt as though she had come home. The sign at the entrance to the convent said it was St. Gertrude's, and once she saw it, she remembered the name.

And just looking around her and listening to the nuns singing, she knew she was meant to be there.

She walked into the office of the convent, and a nun in their old-fashioned heavy wool habit, and open sandals, looked up with a warm smile.

"May I help you?" she asked, looking at Ariana with wise eyes. She was somewhere in her forties, and had the ageless smooth-faced look of many nuns. She was shielded from the stresses of the world.

"Yes," Ariana said softly, sinking into the chair on the other side of the desk, "I think you can. I came here once a long time ago with my father . . . about four or five years ago." The peaceful nun waited quietly to hear the rest. She heard remarkable stories from people who came to visit for a few minutes, or to stay for a while, or to become postulants and join the order. They were a resting place in the shifting sands and troubled times in the world.

"What can I do to help?" She could tell the beautiful blond girl in front of her hadn't come for a tour. She had the saddest eyes the nun had ever seen.

"I am responsible for the deaths of several men and a baby," Ariana said solemnly, adding Felipe to the list, as she thought of him in the car, and the men who had died in the fire when she was rescued from Jorge's camp.

The nun looked unimpressed. She had heard worse. And she was certain the young girl had not killed them herself. "I don't hear confessions," she said gently, "but we have a wonderful priest who will be here to say mass tonight. You could talk to him if you like." Ariana shook her head—she wanted to talk to her now that she was here. She needed to unburden herself and tell her why she had come. And she knew as she sat looking at the Carmelite that she had done the right thing. She needed to seek refuge here, and find forgiveness for what she'd done, if she ever could.

"I just came back from Argentina." Ariana stumbled through what she had to say. It was all so hard to explain. "My father died because of me . . . because he was so worried about me. . . . I was kidnapped in January . . . on the way to our country house. . . . They killed our driver, because of me . . . and Jorge saved me, he was a saint . . . but they killed him because of me. . . . He was just trying to feed the poor, and he needed the ransom money to do that . . . but they killed them all . . . all his men, and they took me away from the camp. And then my father died the next day . . . and I lost the baby. . . ." It all spewed out in a jumble, pouring out of her, as the Carmelite listened quietly, and nothing but compassion showed in her eyes. She could see how confused Ariana was, and could tell that her story was worse than most.

"You were kidnapped in Argentina?" the nun

asked quietly, trying to get the details straight and untangle the story. Ariana nodded. "For ransom, I believe." She nodded again. "How long have you been home?"

"About a week," Ariana said with burning eyes. "We just buried my father a few days ago. . . ." She tried not to think of the lonely mausoleum where she had left him. But at least he was with her mother, whom he had adored and missed so much since her death.

"And your mother? Was she in Argentina too?"

"No, she died almost two years ago, a year before we went to Buenos Aires." And suddenly as the nun listened to her, she remembered reading the story of the American ambassador to Argentina, whose daughter had been kidnapped, and found only recently. Her rescue had been a much smaller news item than her disappearance. But the nuns read the papers carefully, keeping up with the world, and she was almost certain they had prayed for her in January, when it first happened.

"We read about it," the nun said thoughtfully.

"Israeli commandos rescued me. That's when they killed Jorge and his men. They took me out of the camp and everything was burning. I lost the baby that night, and my father died the next day." There were tears running down her cheeks as she said it. She was breathless as she told the story, and the nun stood up and came around the desk to fold her into her arms and hold her.

"You didn't kill anyone. They died because of the mistakes they made, not because of anything you did. Even your father. It's very sad, but it wasn't your fault." She didn't mention the baby, and had no idea whose it was. All she wanted to do was comfort Ariana. "Would you like to stay for a few days and rest here? We'd be very happy to have you." She looked as though she meant it, and Ariana nodded.

"I think that's why I came here. When we visited, my father said he would come here if he ever wanted to get away. I don't know where I live now, who I am, or what I should do. I want to help the poor, as Jorge said, but I don't know how."

"There are many ways to do that. You have no sins to atone for. Others have sinned against you. The men who kidnapped you and kept you from your family." She could tell that Ariana's mind was disordered and she was confused. "Tell me your name." She couldn't remember it from the article she'd read, only that her father had been the ambassador to Argentina, and it seemed like Providence that she had come here. She wondered if their prayers had drawn her to them. And she wanted to tell the mother superior about her as quickly as she could.

"Ariana Gregory."

"Let me show you to a room, and you can stay with us for as long as you like." Ariana nodded like a child who had found her mother who was going to save her from all the terrible things that had happened to her, or tell her it was just a bad dream and she was safe. "When you settle in, we can go for a walk in the garden." She smiled broadly then. "The sisters will be so happy to have you. We're preparing the beds now to plant our summer vegetables next month. Do you like to garden?"

"I don't know how," Ariana admitted sheepishly. To her, like so many others, vegetables just appeared magically on her table, and she had no real idea how they grew.

"Well, we'll teach you. There's nothing more exciting than when carrots come up, or tomatoes . . . we grow some wonderful basil. Sister Luisa makes delicious pesto. Her family is Italian." She chatted easily as she walked Ariana up a flight of stone stairs, down a hall, and to a small room. They were rooms they kept for people on retreat, or other guests who just came to rest and pray. The room was small and bare. It was far from everything she knew and looked like a haven from all the terrifying and confusing memories she now carried with her. "Did you bring anything with you?" She nodded, thinking of her small bag in the car, with the aviator's box in it. She felt as though Jorge had given her a sacred mission, and she couldn't let him down, so she was keeping the box with her, like the Holy Grail.

"Why don't you put your things away, and change into comfortable shoes, and I'll tell Mother you're here." They went back down the stairs together, so

Ariana could get her bag out of the car, and the nun drifted off and disappeared through a door, to find the mother superior peeling potatoes in the kitchen. They shared the chores equally, and it was Mother Elizabeth's turn to peel potatoes. She always said it was a wonderful opportunity to pray, and her eyes lit up as soon as she saw Sister Mary approaching across the big kitchen. Mother Elizabeth had a look of joy and laughter in her eyes, and always seemed as though something wonderful had just happened.

"We have a visitor," Sister Mary said with a serious expression, still shaken by all she had just heard, although she hadn't shown it. "She's the daughter of the ambassador to Argentina, the one who was kidnapped in Argentina a few months ago. They rescued her ten days ago but her father died and now she's here. She sounds frightened and confused. I gave her a room, and she said she'd like to stay with us."

"Can she peel potatoes?" the mother superior asked with a grin, and Sister Mary smiled in answer.

"She doesn't look it."

"We'll teach her. I'm glad she's here. It will do her good, and us as well," the old nun said, unimpressed by what the younger nun had told her. The superior was a small wizened old woman with just a hint of an Irish accent. She had come from the old country at sixteen, and the following year had come to the monastery, and had been there ever

since. She was well into her seventies and, despite
being cloistered, was unusually wise to the ways of
the world. "This is a good place to be while she re-
covers. Does she have a mother?"

Sister Mary shook her head. "It sounds like she
has no one."

"Well, she has us for now. Take her out to the
garden. I'll come and see her when I finish these."
There was a mountain of peeled potatoes in the
huge pot next to her. And the choir singing had
stopped. Sister Mary knew that most of the nuns
would be working in the garden for the rest of the
afternoon. It would be a good place for Ariana to
meet them.

In her room, Ariana unpacked her suitcase and
put the aviator's box under the bed. She put on
running shoes for her visit to the garden and went
downstairs and found Sister Mary waiting for her.
They went through a back door into an enormous
walled garden that looked like the Garden of Eden.
It was full of neat planting beds where they would
plant tomatoes, corn, cucumbers, squash, lettuce,
and peas later on. And Sister Mary told her that
they grew herbs all year long. Half a dozen nuns
were quietly working, and they turned to smile
at Ariana when she and Sister Mary approached.
They had been silent and used their gardening as a
time of contemplation and prayer, but with a visitor in their midst they began speaking, as soon as

Sister Mary explained that she had come to stay with them.

"That is good news!" a young nun said with a broad grin. She looked about Ariana's age, and wore a different habit from the others. Sister Mary said she was a postulant, and had been with them for almost a year. She was due to become a novice when she'd been there for a full year. The others were in their thirties and forties. And one of them looked to be about sixty. She was heavy-set and looked jolly. "I can use some serious help with the tomatoes when we plant them," the young nun said, and rolled her eyes as the others laughed.

"Sister Paul is still trying to learn about the garden," Sister Mary explained.

"No, I'm not," she corrected. "I'm just trying not to kill it!" And as she said it, the mother superior came up behind them with a warm look and smiled at Ariana.

"Sister Paul is our prayerful challenge. We have to pray her vegetables back to life." They all laughed as she said it, and Ariana did too. They seemed to have a peaceful community, doing simple things, and enjoyed the life they led and one another.

The women chatted for a while and went back to work, preparing the soil with nutrients, and Ariana volunteered to help Sister Paul. The two young women liked talking to each other as they worked, and Mother Elizabeth signaled to Sister Mary to leave them together. By dinnertime, Ariana was exhausted, her hands were filthy from the earth, and she washed them for the first time all day, which was a change from her frantic guilty hand-washing in the days before she came. And Sister Marianne in the kitchen, a daunting old nun with a serious face, asked her to help shell the peas for their dinner that night. It was a first for Ariana, and she felt victorious with every pea that fell out of the pod into a bowl.

"Watch out, she's scary," Sister Paul had whispered to Ariana when she left her, but Ariana rapidly discovered that Sister Marianne only looked that way, and was full of praise if you did what you were told. Then Ariana helped set the table for the eighteen nuns who lived there, and sat down to dinner with them shortly after. Conversation was lively at the table because she was among them and she was the center of attention, although no one asked what had brought her to the convent, they knew better. They were just happy to have her with them. The priest came to hear confessions and serve mass after dinner, and he spoke to her for a little while, and offered to hear her confession. She told him in the darkness of the confessional that she was responsible for the deaths of many men, if you included her driver and the men in Jorge's camp who had died because of her, and a baby. She estimated that she had killed ten men, including her father and lover, and their unborn child. And she was stunned when the priest gave her only one Hail Mary as penance. Mother Elizabeth had already told him about her and who she was.

"That's all?" Ariana said about the meager penance, which seemed far too light to her. Although her parents were, she hadn't been a regular church-goer in several years, especially during college, but had started attending mass more regularly in Argentina, because her friends did, and she liked going to church with them. It was part of the culture, tradition, and social life there.

"That's all," the young priest confirmed when he came out of the confessional. "Just one Hail Mary, for **you.** I want you to forgive yourself, Ariana, and the pain you are putting yourself through now. You did not kill any of those people. They all died as a result of their own actions, not yours, except for your father. But he was not a young man, and it must have been his time, sad as that is for you. What you need to do is forgive yourself for these men who died, for what happened to you, which was not your fault but theirs, and even the baby you lost, whom God knows was never meant to be, conceived in and because of your captivity. The **only** person you need to pray for and forgive is you. You did nothing wrong." He said it in a strong, clear voice that startled her.

"Are you sure, Father?" she whispered, convinced that he was mistaken and being too forgiving.

"Absolutely, totally sure," he said firmly. "Use

your time here, and try to forget about all these things. The nuns at St. Gertrude's are wonderful people, and they're happy to have you."

It made her confess one more thing to him, which didn't surprise him either. It was all of a piece with the rest, and a result of the kidnapping and the months she had spent as a prisoner of a very disturbed man, who had twisted her mind with his own insane ideas.

"I've been thinking that maybe I should stay here. Maybe this is how I could dedicate my life to the poor." She was groping for some way to pay penance for what she considered her sins and he didn't.

"Join the order, you mean?"

"Yes. Maybe that's why I came here."

"Do you think you have a vocation?"

"I don't know. Maybe I do." She still thought Jorge was right and she needed to sacrifice her life to the poor, despite the fact that he had tried to extort twenty million dollars from her father, killed her driver, and kidnapped her, none of which were acts of virtue, which she still didn't see.

"Only you can know that," he said quietly, "and if you truly have a vocation, it will emerge. But I believe that God wants you to live your life as you were meant to, marry, have children, be in the world you grew up in, not give up your life to atone for crimes you didn't commit. You have much to give the world, Ariana, and at the right time, you will. In the meantime, spend your days here with the sisters, and try to find peace. That is your only mission for now." He was a wise man, despite his youth. He was only about ten years older than Ariana, but had grown up in a tough neighborhood in Boston. Still, what she had been through was beyond his realm of experience. It was hard to imagine, and it made the young priest angry just thinking about what Jorge had done to her. Ariana thought about what he'd said when she went back to her room. And after all her work in the garden, helping in the kitchen, spending time with the sisters, and talking to the priest, she slept like a baby, as she hadn't since before she'd been kidnapped.

Ariana spent the summer at St. Gertrude's in an atmosphere of peace and healing. She had planned to leave the convent in September, but when the time came, she didn't feel ready. It would be like leaving the womb. She still questioned herself about having a vocation, but Mother Elizabeth said the same thing as the young priest. As much as she would have enjoyed having Ariana among them, she felt that her place was still in the world for now, to do good where she could, not living a cloistered life. She had the strong feeling, even after praying about it, that Ariana was meant to go back to her own life and not stay with them. Mother Elizabeth had the sense that she wanted to join the order to punish herself, or to hide from the world, which was the wrong reason. She had committed no sins, and had been gravely injured by others. She just hoped that Ariana would recover from it one day. But she seemed to be healing at St. Gertrude's, and she stayed and spent Thanksgiving and planned to have Christmas with them, and put off leaving the convent until after New Year's.

She had dropped Sam Adams a note and let him know where she was, and he came to visit her there when he had business in New England in December. She looked healthy and well, and she was obviously happy living at the convent, but he could still see the pain in her eyes from everything she'd been through.

"How long are you planning to stay here?" he asked cautiously. He'd been beginning to wonder if she was planning to join the order, when he got a Christmas card from her, still at the same address at St. Gertrude's convent.

"I don't know," she said softly, looking hesitant. "I thought I'd leave in January, but I have nothing to go home to," she said sadly. The aviator's box was still under her bed. She still read Jorge's love letters but never his journals, which were too rambling and dogmatic for her. She had tried once or twice, but they were of no interest to her. His love letters still were. She was twenty-four years old, and the man who had kidnapped her for ransom and held her hostage for three months was the only man who had ever loved her. She had nothing to compare it to, to try and assess if it was real, which everyone else said it wasn't. Ariana still wasn't sure, and believed he had loved her deeply, whatever he had done to get her there. She expressed her belief again to Sam. It was obvious to him that eight months after her dramatic rescue, she was still heavily influenced by Jorge, in love with him, and defending what he'd done.

"I have an idea for you," Sam suggested. He had mentioned it months before, but she hadn't been open to it, and he hoped she'd be ready now. Sam could sense that she needed more professional help than the nuns. "There's a deprogrammer in Paris, who is one of the best in the world. There are a few others in the States, but he's so good, the CIA has quietly used him for years, with outstanding results."

"Do you think I need a deprogrammer?" she asked, looking shocked. She felt saner and more like herself than she had eight months before. She wasn't aware of how severely Jorge had manipulated her mind. And his beliefs were still firmly in her head. "I feel a lot better, and I'm happy here." She still thought about Jorge and everything he'd said, but no longer every moment of the day. But Sam could still see the confusion in her eyes.

"You're living like a nun," Sam said gently. "You're a twenty-four-year-old girl, paying penance for other people's sins. Wouldn't you like to be free?" She nodded and knew that what he said was true.

She felt that as long as she was living in the convent, she was making up for what she had done, which was becoming less and less clear with time. She felt she was guilty, but she was less sure now of what.

"What does he do?" she asked about the deprogrammer, frightened by the idea.

"You know, the usual," Sam said lightly, "he cuts off your head, fills it with sawdust and apple juice, and sets your toenails on fire." Her eyes flew open wide for an instant, and then she laughed and so did he. "Honestly, I'm not sure. I think he talks a lot, and he knows cults and political issues and the dynamics of being the prisoner of brilliant, twisted people, better than anyone in the world. The men and women we've sent there have come out of it in one piece, swearing that it saved their lives, especially the quality of their lives. It's not enough to just survive," which she had, but barely more than that. She was still punishing herself.

And living like a Carmelite nun at her age was not his idea of a life for her. Even Mother Elizabeth knew that and was gently trying to prod her out of the nest, but Ariana didn't want to go home to her father's empty apartment. There was no one there but the help. And she didn't want to go back to work at the online fashion magazine where she'd worked before they went to Buenos Aires. She felt disconnected from the frivolous fashion world now. Her life and her mind had changed too much to pick up the threads of her old life. And she had trouble concentrating now on anything but simple tasks. She didn't feel ready to work, although she wanted a job in time. She just didn't know what. And even after his death, she felt she should do something Jorge would have approved of. She was no longer an innocent young girl fresh out of college. She had been brutalized by a master and traumatized to the edge of sanity.

She was sane now, and appeared whole, but Sam knew there was still a big piece of her missing. And he hoped she would find it with the deprogrammer in Paris. He thought it was her only hope of ever having a normal life again. She didn't realize how hampered she still was.

"Would you like me to help you check it out? I can call him and see what kind of time he has available. He does private work for us, and the French military, and he's been busy ever since Iraq. But I'm sure he'd make time for you. And our office of relocation can probably help you find a temporary place to stay." He wanted to do everything he could to encourage her to take the leap and work with the deprogrammer who he was convinced could help her.

"I can do that for myself," she said, looking pensive, and then glanced into Sam's eyes with fear. "It sounds scary. What if he makes it worse and brings it all back?" There were some things she didn't want to remember, like the kidnap itself and early days of her captivity.

"He's never done that before," Sam reassured her. "None of our operatives ever said they felt worse." He didn't tell her that they had never sent a civilian there before, only CIA agents who had been held hostage for long periods of time, sometimes years, but the dynamics were the same. "I've met him. He's a good guy. He was a political prisoner in Libya for eleven years, being tortured every day, and he managed to survive that. He seems whole and normal, he has a wife and four kids. Now he helps others get their lives back, and he's incredibly good at it, the best."

"I have my life back," she said seriously, as he glanced around the visiting room at St. Gertrude's and met her eyes again.

"No, you don't," he said quietly. "I don't know whose life this is, but I don't think it's yours, Ariana. Don't you want your own? You're too young to give up now and live with 'good enough,' hiding for the rest of your life, from yourself and everyone else. You deserve the best. You've been through enough pain. Why not let him try to help you?"

"I'll think about it." She didn't sound convinced, and Sam felt as though his mission had failed when he left. Ariana told Mother Elizabeth about it that night.

"What a wonderful idea," she said with her usual

bright smile and knowing eyes, as though Ariana had just mentioned a shopping trip to New York or lunch with a friend.

"Do you think I need it?" Ariana asked, probing the wise old eyes.

"Possibly. Probably," she corrected herself. "Now is the time to do everything you can to heal from what you went through, before it sets in cement with time. It's all still fresh. I'd love to keep you here with us forever, but I think you're destined for a bigger life. You need to free yourself of the past now so you can fulfill your destiny," she said fairly. "You can always come back to us later if you make that choice. But you need to explore the world first." Ariana had been rescued only eight months before, and she had needed these peaceful months to give her time for the wounds to close, but the scars were still there and were very raw. They probably always would be, but the deprogrammer might help them be less ugly, and less damaging in the end. "It can't hurt, Ariana. And it's not prison camp. If it's not right for you, you can stop." Ariana hadn't thought of that. "Why not check it out? If it's good enough for agents in the CIA, who need to recover and go back to work at full strength, why wouldn't it be good enough for you? Sometimes you just have to jump in. You've been very brave about everything that happened. And you've had a good respite here and made great progress." She no longer had the broken, ravaged look she'd had when she came in.

"Now you need to finish the work." And then the wise old nun said something that shocked Ariana. She didn't know that the mother superior knew. "You can't drag that tin box around for the rest of your life, with everything that's in it. It's too heavy to carry. Don't you think?" She smiled brightly at her, but her eyes went right to Ariana's heart. Ariana nodded and said nothing, but Mother Elizabeth had made her point.

Ariana thought about it for two days, and then called Sam in Washington. He was surprised to hear from her. She had never called him, since her release.

"Okay, I'll try it," she said in a tense voice.

"Try what?" He sounded distracted and was concentrating on something else when she called. He had a number of difficult cases at the moment, but she was a priority for him.

"The deprogrammer in Paris. What's his name?" she said in a shaking voice.

"Yael Le Floch. He's from Brittany." He had been a commando in the French Special Forces, but he didn't tell her that. It sounded too hardcore, which he was, but brilliant at what he did. And he knew that Ariana needed everything he had. "I think that's great," he encouraged her. "I'll shoot him an e-mail right now."

The response came back less than an hour later, although it was late in France.

"He can start with you in two weeks. He's just

finishing a case now." He tried to work with one person at a time, although he had people he had trained, who did the same work, but when the CIA sent him a case, he always handled it himself. He had a deep respect for them.

"How long does it take?" Ariana asked, sounding nervous.

"As long as it takes," Sam said honestly. "That really depends on you, how open you are with him, and how fast it goes. I know from cases I've referred to him, it's hard to predict. It can be six weeks, or even a year. On average, my guess is probably a few months. But there are worse places to be than Paris while you work on your head. The other guy we use is on an army base in Mississippi. Something tells me you'll be happier in Paris with Yael." She laughed at what he said.

"Yeah, I guess you're right. Okay." She sighed deeply as though she were about to bungee-jump off a cliff and was praying the rope would hold. "Sign me up." It was the bravest thing she'd ever done, but suddenly she wanted to do it, and she went to tell Mother Elizabeth as soon as she hung up.

"I'm so proud of you." The mother superior beamed at her, as though she had just won the Nobel Prize. "I think it's going to be wonderful, and you'll be glad you did it. Send us a postcard from Paris. I haven't been since I was a little girl."

"I'm going to miss you so much," Ariana said,

throwing her arms around her. She felt as though she were leaving home, and now this was the only home she had. Her father's old apartment in New York was just an empty shell. The soul had gone out of it for her, when her father died.

"This is so exciting!" the old nun said, clapping her hands with motherly pride. She announced to the other nuns at dinner that Ariana was going to Paris to take a special class. And the other nuns oohed and aahed and told her how lucky she was. Ariana didn't feel lucky—she felt scared and was trying not to show it. But once Mother Elizabeth made the announcement, Ariana felt she had to follow through. She contacted Sheila, one of her father's secretaries, who had stayed on to oversee the apartment and the remainder of the estate, and asked her to help her find an apartment in Paris. She said she didn't care where, just somewhere in a decent neighborhood and not too big. All she needed was one bedroom, a living room, and a small kitchen, since she didn't really cook or eat a lot and didn't know anyone there. She felt like she was going back to school. Sam had told her that the house where Yael worked was in the Eighth Arrondissement, which was a combination of business and residential, and kind of a bland neighborhood.

Sheila got back to her the next day. She had a listing from a real estate broker in Paris of both furnished and unfurnished apartments. Ariana chose furnished since she was hoping not to stay too long, more like the six weeks Sam had described. Sheila offered Ariana several choices, including a small house in the Seventh, an apartment on the Île St. Louis that the broker had admitted was charming but inconvenient, a student apartment in the Marais, and two furnished apartments in the Sixteenth, one with a bedroom, and the other a studio on the ground floor, which her father's secretary didn't think would be safe, and Ariana agreed. Safety was more important to her now, and a studio might be too small. The broker had said that the house in the Seventh looked very chic, but it was on the Left Bank, which was farther away from Yael, so it would be a bigger trek every day, and it was more space than she needed.

"It sounds like the one in the Sixteenth would be the best. It's on the top floor, is supposedly sunny, and is close to a park." And all of the apartments were reasonably priced.

"Why don't you try that one?" Ariana said, with that breathtaking feeling that she was taking a huge leap of faith.

Sheila called her back an hour later. Everything was in place. She could have it for a year, with an option for a second year if she wanted, and with thirty days notice she could get out of it at any time. The owner of the apartment had moved to Holland and was keeping it as an investment. And everything was there, cooking utensils, linens. She could arrive with her suitcases and unpack. She didn't need a thing. "Oh," the secretary added—she was as efficient for Ariana as she had been for her father. She was a pleasant woman although Ariana wasn't close to her. She wasn't warm and fuzzy, but she was good at what she did. "And you can smoke and have a dog." Ariana laughed.

"I don't do either."

"Well, you never know. Maybe you'll become very French, and start smoking French cigarettes and buy a dog." Ariana had a sudden vision of herself with a French poodle with a fancy haircut, walking it with a Gauloise hanging out of her mouth. The image made her laugh.

"Thank you so much, Sheila. I really appreciate it."

"The money will be wired today, by the way, and I'll set up a checking account for you in Paris, in case you need it. What are you doing over there, by the way?"

"I'm taking a class." Sheila was happy to hear it. The months she had spent in a Carmelite monastery in the Berkshires sounded depressing for a girl of Ariana's age, but she had been through so much. Paris sounded a lot healthier, and she knew Ariana's father would have been pleased. He had always loved Paris, and had been there many times with Ariana and her mother.

"Will you need a car?" Sheila asked, thinking of everything, as she always did.

"No, I'll take the metro and cabs. I don't think I'll be there long, just a couple of months."

"Well, bon voyage," she said with a heavy American accent, "and have fun. Let me know if you need anything. Call anytime." Ariana had had her book a flight on February 1. She was starting with Yael the day after she arrived. She didn't want to waste any time, so she could get it over with as fast as she could. She was still uneasy about what he would do to her. It sounded mysterious and scary. She wondered if he used hypnosis, and how much of what had happened he expected her to relive. She really didn't want to talk about the relationship with Jorge with him. It was tender and private, and she wanted to keep it to herself. Some things were not fair game, in her mind anyway. She didn't know whether Yael would agree.

The nuns all cried when she left St. Gertrude's and so did Ariana. Sister Paul had written her a poem and knitted her a scarf. It had lots of dropped stitches in it, and Ariana laughed as she put it on. It was pink.

"I never did really learn how to knit," Sister Paul admitted, looking sheepish, and Ariana promised she'd wear it every day.

Mother Elizabeth had made her a small painting for her Paris apartment, of a bouquet of flowers. It was cheerful and bright, just like her. And she gave her a photograph of all the nuns, so she could remember how much they loved her, and she reminded her that she could come back anytime.

"Bring me back a beret!" dour Sister Marianne, who ran the kitchen, joked with her. She had come to love Ariana even though she had never seen anyone butcher a potato the way she did instead of peeling it. "I'll hang it on the kitchen wall. It'll give us a touch of class." She smiled at Ariana and then gave her a big hug. "God bless you, child, take care. We'll be praying for you every day." Tears were streaming down Ariana's cheeks as the car Sheila had hired for her drove her away. Ariana had had her father's car sent back to New York months before. She didn't need it there with the nuns. The car took her directly to JFK Airport in New York, where she was able to get a better flight than Boston. But she didn't go back to her father's apartment before she left. She knew it would make her too sad.

She was taking an evening flight to Paris, and arriving early the next morning, and had the day to settle in before she started with Yael. She called the convent from the airport before she took off, and Mother Elizabeth reminded her how much they loved her and would be praying for her. She was grateful to know that they would. She had no idea what to expect from Yael, but Mother Elizabeth still thought it was a good idea, and Ariana trusted her judgment in all things. It was the parental guidance she no longer had, and still needed, especially after her experiences of the past year. The anniversary of the date of her kidnapping had been difficult, and she hadn't wanted to leave for Paris until after that. Now she was on her way.

The flight took off over the lights of New York and headed over Long Island, then north toward Boston. As they flew over Massachusetts on the way to Europe, she thought of her beloved nuns. She hadn't completely given up the idea of joining them one day, but yet again, she trusted Mother Elizabeth's advice, insisting that she belonged in the world. And now she felt very bold moving to Paris on her own. But it was just for a short time. She'd be back in a couple of months, she told herself, as she laid her head against the seat . . . she'd be home by April or May at the latest, in time for spring in the Berkshires, at St. Gertrude's. She couldn't imagine living anywhere else anymore, except with them. But now she was going to Paris, to drink café au lait and eat croissants, and meet a mysterious deprogrammer called Yael.

Chapter 9

The flight landed at Charles de Gaulle Airport just after eight A.M. Ariana collected her two large suitcases. She'd had Sheila send her a few things from New York, but she didn't think she'd need much. She had brought a lot of warm sweaters and jeans, and a warm coat, but no summer clothes. She was planning to be finished with Paris then, and back in the Berkshires, or New York, where she had been thinking about getting a job. She wanted to work with kids, orphans maybe, or in a homeless shelter, something to do with the poor. Jorge's influence on her life was still strong.

She got a cab from the airport and gave the driver the address on Avenue Foch. She had been given the outer door code, and when she got there, the guardian looked annoyed as she handed Ariana the keys. The guardian had a cigarette hanging out of her mouth and looked very French. Ariana introduced herself as the new tenant, and she didn't seem to care. **Welcome to France,** Ariana thought to herself, with a grin. But it felt like an adventure. She had taken French in college and spoke enough to get around. After almost a year in Argentina, her Spanish was better now, but she could manage in French and had had no trouble with the cab.

The neighborhood looked very respectable, and Avenue Foch more luxurious than she had expected, and it was as close to the Arc de Triomphe and the Champs-Élyseés as they'd said. It was a pleasant, central location in a good, residential neighbor-hood, which was what she had wanted. And the building was impeccable. It had a small elevator, which she took to the fourth floor, let herself into the apartment, and was pleased with how sunny it was, even on a cold, wintry day. And the apartment was warm.

Looking around, she remembered that she had promised to send the nuns photographs of every-thing, and postcards all the time. And she planned to do it soon, starting with the apartment. The bedroom was pretty, all done in pink chintzes with a narrow canopied bed. The living room looked a little tattered, as if most of the furniture came from the flea market, but it had charm. And the kitchen was tiny but adequate for what she needed, and the fridge was ridiculously small.

She set her bags down in the bedroom, and there was an antique armoire instead of a closet, but it was big enough for what she'd brought. And the bathroom had an enormous turn-of-the-century tub. She sank into it an hour later with a sigh of relief. It was hard to believe. She was in Paris. It was her first time living in a foreign country alone, and she felt very grown up. She was alone everywhere now, except with her beloved nuns. It frightened her sometimes to realize that with her father gone, she was on her own in the world. If anything happened to her, no one would know or care. Sheila might eventually realize she had disappeared, if she stopped writing checks and using her credit cards, but there was no one else. She hadn't seen any of her friends in New York since she got back. She felt too different from them now, and disconnected after everything that had happened in Buenos Aires. And her friends in Buenos Aires hadn't been in her life long enough for her to stay connected to them once she left. She was totally solitary, and it was daunting to the point of terrifying at times. She tried not to think about it, got out of the bath, and got dressed. She put on jeans and running shoes and a warm jacket, and went out for a walk. She walked down the Champs Élyseés all the way to the Place de la Concorde, and then managed to find the Place Vendôme, and then walked down Rue Royale to the Louvre and into the Tuileries Gardens, until she got back to the Place de la Concorde. She had brought a map, but she remembered enough of Paris from trips there with her parents to find her way around, at least in the best part of town. She had thought of going to the Hotel Ritz for a cup of tea. But she had last stayed there with her father, and it would make her miss him too much.

It was fun looking at the people and glancing into the shops as she walked along. And by the time she got back to her apartment three hours later, she was tired but happy. She went out again a little while later, to get something to eat, and found a shop that sold cooked chickens, French bread and cheese, and some fruit. She took it home and ate a very pleasant meal.

She thought of reading Jorge's letters that night, because she felt lonely in the apartment, but decided not to. Instead she put the box away, on the top shelf of the armoire. She went to bed with a book instead, and was sound asleep by ten o'clock. She woke up at seven the next morning, toasted a piece of the French bread she'd bought and ate some fruit, and by eight-thirty she was dressed. She thought of taking the metro but was afraid to get lost, so she took a cab to Yael's address instead. He was on Rue de Naples, in the Eighth Arrondissement. She had the outer door code, and found her way to a little house at the back of a courtyard. The door was painted red. She pressed the bell, and heard a dog bark.

And a moment later, a man was standing in the doorway with a rugged face and long hair. He was somewhere in his forties, stood ramrod straight, and smiled as he waved her in. But everything about his stature and demeanor told her he was tough, and suddenly she was scared. What if he was horrible to her or what he wanted her to do was too painful? For an instant, she wanted to turn and run, and then the old German shepherd he had next to him looked at her and wagged his tail. Even the dog looked scary to her at first.

"Hello, I'm Ariana Gregory," she said politely, acting as if she'd come to visit a friend.

"Yael Le Floch," he said, and waved her into a small living room with comfortable old furniture. It was the kind of room where you could spend late nights, drinking, smoking, and talking to friends. There was an ashtray on the coffee table, and he told her she could smoke. He didn't offer her anything to drink, and pointed to a chair where she should sit.

He waited a few minutes until she'd taken off her jacket, and then settled into a big comfortable armchair across from her. He waited another minute and then fixed her with his dark brown, almost black eyes. His hair was jet black, and despite the winter season, he had a tan. He looked like a man who spent a lot of time outdoors, and there were photographs of sailboats on the walls. It was obvious that he liked to sail.

He got straight to the point. "Why did you go to Argentina?" he asked her. There was no judgment in his voice, only the question, and his eyes never let her go for a second. Her instant reaction was to say that her father had made her do it, but she knew that wasn't fair, although she had done everything to talk him out of it at first, and even refused to go. But she couldn't let him go alone. So she had given up her job, broken up with her new boyfriend, and gone with him.

"My father was appointed ambassador, and he wanted me to go with him, so I went." She left out the pertinent details.

"Did you want to go?" The relentless eyes kept their grip on hers. She had the feeling that he could see everything, straight into her soul, and you had to tell him the truth.

"No, I didn't. I'd just graduated from college a few months before. That was almost two years ago," she said, situating it in time for him. "I had just gotten a job I liked. I was dating someone I was having fun with. I wanted to stay in New York."

"Did you tell him that?" he asked, lighting a cigarette and watching her.

"Yes, I did."

"And he made you go anyway?" He was trying to get a picture of their relationship. But she didn't want to malign her father, especially now. She had never blamed him for what had happened, and she didn't now.

"My mother had died a year before, and he didn't want to go alone. He wanted me to go with him, so I went. He'd been sick, and with my mother gone, he needed my help, and he said it would be fun for both of us. And it was, for a while. We were out at parties every night, and I met a lot of great people I wouldn't have met otherwise. And it was only going to be for three years."

"That's a lot of time to give up at your age," he commented. He had a heavy French accent, but his English was excellent, and he understood everything she said. "It must have felt like forever to you."

"It did when we went, but I loved it after a few months. And he was right—it was an opportunity that would never come again."

"An opportunity to be kidnapped and held hostage for three months? That would have been hard to give up for a job and a boyfriend in New York." He said it drily, and she was shocked. "Have you gone back to work?" She shook her head. "Why not?"

"I think I want to do something different after everything that happened, like work for the poor. I'd been working for a fashion magazine, which seems kind of frivolous and pointless to me now."

"Why? You don't like fashion anymore?" he asked innocently. He wanted to get inside her head and was doing a good job of it so far. He looked at the way she was dressed. She was wearing designer jeans, a simple but expensive sweater, and Balenciaga flats and bag. He wasn't fooled that fashion didn't matter to her anymore.

"I just think it's more important to do things for the poor," she said with a look of determination.

"Who told you that?" He wanted to know who else was in her head, and before she could stop herself, she answered.

"Jorge."

"And who is that?" he asked her gently, leaning slightly forward to put out his cigarette.

She hesitated before she answered. She knew that he must know the answer to the question, but he wanted to see what she said. "The leader of the group that kidnapped me."

"Ah, yes. Rebels, I believe. Yes?" She nodded. "The champion of the poor, yet he asked for twenty million dollars ransom. Did you know he had accounts in Switzerland? Did he ever tell you that?" It was information they'd had from one of their informants since Jorge died. It was unsubstantiated but more than likely true.

"No, he didn't." Her eyes looked sad as she said it. He had been so pure about his ideas, so emphatic about them, and so hostile to the rich.

"Do you really think he gave the money to the poor?" Yael asked her.

"I don't know. He said he did, and I believed him."

"What else did he tell you?" He kept the questions coming at her at a rapid speed.

"That he loved me." She was being honest with

Yael. "I think he really did, whatever his politics were. We had an amazing connection. I've never known anyone like him."

"And now? Do you miss him?" He had eyes and a voice that made her tell him everything, even when she didn't want to. He was mesmerizing, and she felt hypnotized. A little bit like Jorge in a strange way. But all Yael wanted from her was the truth.

"Every day," she said, honest with him again. "I think about him all the time. Less than I used to, but I still do." Yael didn't look surprised.

"Did he give you anything to take with you, some article of his clothing, some symbol that was important to him, anything he'd written?" She nodded.

"I have love letters from him, in a box he kept on his desk. He gave it to me . . . right before"—she could hardly force out the words and felt breathless as she did—"the night they raided the camp and rescued me . . . he gave me the box right before he died. . . . There are some journals of his in it too. He wrote in them every night. I keep the love letters in that box. I put them in there when the camp caught fire in the raid."

"Do you read the letters every day?" She shook her head.

"I used to. Now I just read them sometimes at night, when I miss him and I'm sad. I don't think I'll ever meet anyone like him again."

"I hope not," Yael said softly. He didn't say it, but

he hated men like him who twisted other people's minds until they no longer knew who they were. "Do you read the journals too?"

"No. They're very ideological, and too esoteric for me. I looked at them a couple of times in the beginning. They're too political. I read the love letters, but not the journals, but I keep them too."

"And where is the box now? Did you bring it to Paris?" She had taken it everywhere with her since the day he'd given it to her.

"It's in the armoire in my bedroom, on a high shelf."

"And if someone took it from you, or you lost it, would you be upset?" She looked panicked as he said it, as though she were afraid he would demand that she give it to him, but he didn't. She couldn't have. But he knew better than that—it was the whole point of their work together, which had only just begun. He wanted to get the lay of the land first.

"Yes," she said in a small voice in answer to his question. "I would."

"Then that will be one of our goals. That one day, you no longer read his letters. You don't have to make up for his sins, by working with the poor, and doing what he told you to do. You owe him nothing. And if your father hadn't paid the ransom, he would have killed you." Yael said it matter-of-factly, but Ariana didn't believe him.

"He protected me from the other men," she said in his defense.

"Who do you think gave them their orders?" Yael said simply. "He was the leader of the group. He wanted you to believe he was rescuing you from them. It made you more dependent on him, as your only protector in his camp. That's part of what confused you about who he really was." And then he asked her another question he already knew the answer to. "You were lovers?" She nodded, and then she went one better.

"I was pregnant with his child. I lost it the night of the raid." She called it a raid and not a rescue, because that was still what it was to her, and it had been just as terrifying as the day she was kidnapped by Jorge's men. Even more so, because it was so efficiently carried out, among the flames and in the dark, and she had seen Jorge die as a result. And she didn't know who her rescuers were.

"All of those were devices to confuse you and turn you around. His protecting you in the camp. I assume he was the only one who fed you and gave you water, and released you from whatever bonds you wore or wherever they confined you." She nodded, that was true. "Making love to you, telling you he loved you. And he got lucky if you got pregnant by him so quickly—that created an even greater bond to him. I know you don't believe me, but he didn't love you, Ariana. He used you. It was part of his plan, just like the ransom. He wanted your father's money and your mind, and he got both. He was a clever man. And one day, if you had stayed with him, he would have used you as part of his revolution against the establishment. He's still using you, if you want to work for the poor to please him, instead of following the career you enjoyed before. You owe him nothing. He would have killed you in an instant, if it served him better. You were more useful to him alive. And he's still controlling you with his letters now. I want you to promise me that you'll tell me each time you read them. I won't punish you or scold you, but knowing how often you read them, and when, will be part of our work together."

"I think he really loved me," she said sadly.

"Trust me," Yael said quietly, "he wasn't capable of it. He was a dangerous man. And he played a dangerous game with your mind." And then he looked at her even more intently. "Do you want to be free of him now?" She hesitated and then nodded. "Even if that means knowing he didn't love you?" She nodded again, with tears in her eyes. "Have you ever been in love with any other man?" Even if she had, she was an innocent, naïve, decent girl, and she was young. She shook her head.

"Not really. I've gone out with guys I liked, and I was starting to really like the boy I was going out with in New York when we left. I had a boyfriend in high school for a few months, and another one in college sophomore year. But they were boys. Jorge was a man with a fascinating mind."

"A dangerous, sick, fascinating mind," he corrected her. "A mind that destroys people. He would have used you and thrown you away the moment you weren't useful to him. He probably would have killed you after he got the ransom, and never sent you back. You already knew too much by then. You would have been dangerous for him. He was just playing with you, Ariana. You can't give him the rest of your life. You need to get free of him and his manipulations if you want to have a good life. One day there will be a man you love in your life. You don't want Jorge keeping that man away forever. One day you will need to put this behind you as a very bad thing that happened, like a terrible accident. But you survived. I don't want you walking with a limp forever, because of him."

"Neither do I," she said softly. "That's why I'm here."

"Good," he said, then he smiled at her and stood up. "Then we know what we have to do. We got a good start today. I'll see you tomorrow," he said, and as she stood up and followed him to the door, she realized that she was dripping with sweat and felt as though she had been hit by a bus. She had been there for three hours, and it had flown by.

She went for a long walk in the Bois de Boulogne that afternoon, thinking of everything Yael had said to her. She still had a hard time believing it was true. Part of her still believed that Jorge had loved her. It had been too real not to be true. She could accept what Yael said intellectually, but not in her heart.

She went to the Louvre after that, then walked home, and Sam Adams called her on her cell phone to see how it had gone.

"It was hard, but he was nice."

"That sounds about right," Sam said, sounding relieved. Over the years, Sam learned that Yael wasn't always "nice," but he was usually tougher on men than on women. Maybe because he was French. But he was glad that Yael hadn't scared Ariana off. She needed everything he had to give.

And when she opened the armoire in her bedroom that night, she saw the box on the top shelf and glanced at it. She had a powerful desire to take it down and read his letters again, but she didn't. She wanted to be able to tell Yael the next day that she hadn't. She suddenly wanted to please him, which was a first step in her recovery too.

She lay down on her bed without even having dinner, and slept straight through until the next day. She woke up just in time to take a bath, dress, and go to meet Yael again, and this time when she saw him, it all seemed less scary to her. She knew what to expect. He showed her an EMDR technique he was going to use, tapping her knees rhythmically, as he asked her to close her eyes and relive the day she was kidnapped. It was a technique sometimes used for people who had suffered extreme trauma. She didn't want to do it, but she trusted him, so she agreed. She told him all of it, with her eyes closed. Then he asked her to open her eyes, and relive it again, and when she did, she felt as though she were flying backward and the men who had kidnapped her were getting smaller as she flew away. They didn't talk about Jorge at all that day, only about the men who had taken her from the car on the way to the **finca,** and she was astounded to discover that she remembered each of them in minute detail, like a strip of film that remained in her head. It was all still in there. It took four hours to relate it all to Yael, and she felt sick when they were through. But the feeling of flying backward at a great height had impressed her, and the men looked less menacing to her now from far away. But she threw up when she went home that afternoon, and told Yael about it the next day. They used the same process to go over each day of her captivity that she remembered, and then Jorge was in the film, in their early days together.

It was a long, laborious, slow process, and by the end of the first two weeks, she realized that they had a lot of work to do. Six months maybe, or three, but the dream of going home in six weeks had disappeared. She had read Jorge's letters twice in the last two weeks, always on the nights that she felt frightened by what she remembered and wanted to remind herself that he loved her. His love was so much less frightening than anything that had happened to her, when they lowered her into the box each day and left her there in the blazing sun until he rescued her. She began to see what Yael had meant in the beginning. It was always Jorge who gave her food and drink and took her to the outhouse, ordered her taken out of the stifling coffin she was in, had the ropes taken off her legs and wrists, took her to the stream to get clean and swim in the cool water. He was the only source of good in her life, and relief. It was easy to see why she had thought he loved her, and it saddened her to realize that it was just a clever manipulation to make her trust him. But she still believed, at the end of two weeks with her sessions with Yael, that he had genuinely fallen in love with her. That had seemed too real to doubt now, and she still didn't. Yael didn't argue with her about it. They had work to do, and things were proceeding at a pace that he was satisfied with. She was a good subject, earnest and unfailingly honest with him and a bright girl. He knew that one day they'd get there. He just didn't know when. But eventually, she would be free of Jorge. He was certain of it, and when she was, she would look back wondering how she had fallen for him and believed what he said. And when she finally was free of him, their work would be done. Until then, they had much to do.

Chapter 10

For the first three months until the first of May, Ariana saw Yael every day, five times a week. They ground through each day of her kidnapping, her impressions, the things that were said, the things they did to her, the men who had taken her, her driver's murder and why she felt responsible for it when she hadn't set herself up to be kidnapped, and her father's death. It was he who had insisted on going to Argentina, and she had begged him not to, but now she felt, like everything else, that his death was due to her. She was beginning to see how Jorge had manipulated her, and controlled and distorted her thinking, but she still had a long way to go on that. And after the May 1 holiday, which was French Labor Day, when everyone exchanged sprigs of lily of the valley in France, Yael told her to come in three times a week, so they could proceed more slowly and give her time to do other things.

She often felt sick after they met, particularly after he used the EMDR technique on her, which was intense.

At first she objected to his only seeing her three times a week.

"I'll be here for the next ten years if we start slowing down now," she complained. She had been there for exactly three months.

"Is that so terrible? Why are you in a rush to go back?" He knew how little she had there waiting for her. There was nothing but the cloistered nuns at St. Gertrude's, and her father's empty apartment. No man and no job, and she still hadn't figured out what she wanted to do as work. She didn't need the money to live on, particularly after her father's death, but she wanted an activity that was meaningful to her. And she had mentioned to him in passing that she hadn't collected any of her inheritance from her father's estate and felt guilty about it, another holdover from Jorge's disapproval of the rich, "Los Ricos." She didn't want to be one of them. And the ransom her father had paid, although not in full, hadn't even made a dent in his estate. He had been a very, very rich man, and left it all to her. But Jorge had made her feel wrong about who she was, and she wasn't over it yet. Yael pointed out that her new concern for the poor was admirable, if it was for the right reasons, but if rejecting her father's money was to maintain Jorge's approval and standards for her, then it was for the wrong ones. And he was still a man who had demanded a twenty-million-dollar ransom. And who knew how he would have used it? To help the poor, as he claimed, or feather his own nest? The CIA had indicated to Yael that they believed Jorge had sent money to Switzerland, and was amassing a personal fortune there. He reminded Ariana of it frequently, to debunk Jorge's claims of his holy mission.

"I think you need time to do some other things, enjoy Paris, make friends, meet people, do things you enjoy here, not just work with me," he told her in answer to her desire to work with the poor in a sincerely selfless gesture. She was willing to sacrifice anything to atone for her sins, and live the life of a martyr. "Let's not make erasing Jorge your whole life," Yael said sensibly, "nor giving up your life to serve the poor just yet. You need to have fun, and do some of the things you did before. Go to the theater, the movies, go shopping." She listened, but she was still unconvinced when she left his office. She didn't feel ready to go out in the world yet. It frightened her. There was still no end in sight, but she was feeling better, and hadn't touched the aviator's box, nor read Jorge's letters, in three weeks, which was the longest she had gone so far. But she always kept the box close at hand, just in case. Yael didn't argue about it. He knew that ultimately, when their work was finished, the box would be gone. And until then they jokingly referred to it as the bottle hidden under the bed. She could read Jorge's letters anytime.

She was enjoying a stroll along the quais one day, after looking in the bookstalls, and at the Bateaux Mouches sliding by on the Seine, when she noticed a string of pet shops, and decided to go in. It was the funniest assortment of pets, with lizards, iguanas, rats, mice, a ferret, and even chickens in cages, and a wall of woebegone-looking puppies waiting for homes. There were various terriers, a poodle, several Yorkies, and a particularly sorrowful-looking French bulldog who the pet store operator said was the runt of the litter and was unusually small. She had a black patch over one eye, and a pink nose, and the rest of her was white, and she looked at Ariana intently and barked, a ridiculous tiny bark. She was eight weeks old. Ariana asked if she could hold her, and the moment the attendant took her out, and Ariana set her down, she ran around Ariana's feet barking and playing, and when Ariana picked her up, she licked her cheek. She was intolerably cute, but Ariana told herself she didn't want a dog. What would she do with a dog? She had serious work to do here, with Yael, about the trauma she'd been through, but there was nothing traumatic about the puppy, she was just an adorable little creature to love.

"Thank you very much," she said, giving him

back the dog, and walked out of the store, looking resolute and proud of herself for not succumbing. She could still hear the puppy barking when she left, and told Yael about it the next day.

"Why didn't you buy her?" he asked, curious about it. "Were you depriving yourself, or do you really not want a dog?"

"I don't know," she said, thinking about it.

"It might be good company for you." He glanced over at his old shepherd as he said it, asleep at his feet. She came to every session, and seemed to follow him everywhere. It reminded Ariana of how much French people liked dogs.

"I'd have to walk it, and then what if something happened to me?" And then she said what she was really thinking, "What if someone attacked me, or kidnapped me, when I was walking the dog?" It had taken a lot to say it, and he was pleased.

"Are you afraid you'll be kidnapped again?" he asked her, and she nodded, with tears in her eyes. "That's not likely to happen, particularly not in France. There are no bandits on the road here. It's not a common occurrence. I can't remember the last time there was a kidnapping in France." She knew that was true, but she was scared anyway. "Would you feel better with a bodyguard?" he asked her seriously. He assumed she could afford it, if it would make a difference to her. He was flexible about things like that, and she had every right to be scared after her experience in Buenos Aires.

"No, I'd feel stupid," she admitted. "I should be able to go out alone like everyone else."

"But you're not like everybody else. You were kidnapped and held hostage by rebels for three months. Other people haven't been through that. It's okay if you're scared."

"I guess I am." She felt better now that she'd said it, as she thought about the little dog. She was thinking about her again when she left Yael's house, and she went back to the shop on the quais that afternoon. The white bulldog puppy was still there, and she jumped and started barking when she saw Ariana. This time she couldn't resist her, and didn't try to. Talking to Yael about it suddenly made it all right. She bought all the supplies she needed, a pink leash and collar with rhinestones on it, and took her home. The puppy was ecstatic as soon as she got there, and Ariana was laughing as she chased her around the apartment and played with her, and the puppy played with the toys Ariana had bought her. She had a great time with her, and the next morning, with a day off from Yael, she took her for a long walk at Bagatelle. She was too young to play with other dogs, but Ariana set her down on the grass, and they ran until the puppy was exhausted and rolled over on her back with her paws in the air. She was incredibly cute. People were smiling as they watched her. Ariana had decided to call her Lili, and she took her to meet Yael the next day. The old shepherd looked annoyed by their guest, sniffed her, and sauntered away. Lili slept at Ariana's feet for the entire session. She took her for a walk in the Tuileries after that. She was turning out to be great company. Ariana felt like she had a new friend.

For the next three months, they met three times a week, and she was feeling better, and then Yael surprised her by saying he was going away for a month. He had a sailboat in the south of France, and he was planning to sail to Italy with his wife, his children, and another couple.

"Are we done?" They had been working together for six months.

"Do you think we are?" he asked her pointedly, and she shook her head. The aviator's box was still in the armoire, and she had read his letters again only a few days before. She was wondering if she'd ever get past it. But she was in no hurry now to leave France. She was happy here, she loved her apartment, and she had rented a car and driven into the countryside several times, which was a big step for her. At first she kept expecting to be waylaid and kidnapped, but now she no longer thought of it as she drove. And she took Lili with her everywhere. She felt safer in a car than on foot, but took Lili to the park too, even if walking around alone still made her nervous, but she was getting braver, and forcing herself out of her comfort zone more now.

"When will you be back?" She had no idea what to do with herself while Yael was gone. He was the focal point of her life in Paris, although she went to museums, exhibitions, auctions, and shopping, and walked all over Paris with the dog. Having the dog with her made her feel bolder too, although Lili was too small to protect her. But the dog gave her an illusion of protection.

"I'll be back in a month, at the end of August. We'll resume our work then," Yael answered. It seemed to Ariana that all of France would be closed for a month, even some restaurants and stores.

"When do you think we'll be finished, Yael?" she asked him, sounding discouraged.

"When that box isn't in your closet or under your bed, and you don't need the letters anymore." That was their goal, and she wondered now how long it would take. Yael said that one day it would just happen, but neither of them could guess when. Ariana thought of Jorge far less often, but in subtle ways, his influence was still there. She was still trying to please him and be the woman he had loved, or claimed to.

Yael's leaving the city for a month made Ariana think of doing that herself. She rented a car, and drove down to the south of France, stopping at various places she had wanted to visit. And of course, Lili came with her, and slept on the front seat next to her. She went to Aix en Provence and St. Paul de Vence, got as far as St. Tropez, spent ten days there, and then drove slowly home to Paris. In all, she was gone for three weeks, and sent postcards to the nuns at St. Gertrude all along the way. She'd been sending them photos of Lili by e-mail for the past three months.

And while she was away, she had time to read a book Yael had given her on Stockholm Syndrome, and a biography of Patty Hearst that she'd bought herself—she had also become enamored with her captors when she was kidnapped. Both books gave her further insight into what had happened to her, and her feelings for Jorge, the deep love she had felt for him, and the dependency on him he had fostered, as her only means of survival.

In September, she and Yael resumed their work. He pushed her harder now, because she said she was anxious to finish. But it was Christmas before they had a real breakthrough, when she realized that Jorge getting her pregnant had been yet another way of manipulating her. He had been trying to possess her and turn her mind inside out, and she had been so desperate and frightened that she had clung to him for dear life, wanting to believe his love for her. She had lost everyone else she trusted and relied on, her mother when she died a year before, and her father when she was taken from him.

"Are you ready to give up the box now?" Yael asked her, as the final challenge. "It might be a nice Christmas present to yourself. You could gift-wrap it and bury it and throw it away." But the thought of relinquishing the last vestige of him terrified her. She still wasn't ready to give up the illusion of Jorge's love, nor the symbol of it through his letters in the aviator's box.

"What if no man ever loves me again?"

"At twenty-five, with your looks, brains, and charm, that's not likely to happen," he said, smiling at her.

"Maybe after the new year," she said cautiously, and he didn't push her. She had to be ready to give up the box herself.

It was January, after Yael had gone skiing for a week over Christmas, before the subject came up again. She had been working with him for almost a year. The anniversary of their first meeting was coming up in a few weeks, and suddenly it dawned on her.

"I'm ready," she said, sounding breathless. "I think I'm done." She didn't want Jorge in her life anymore, his journals or letters, and the box she was tired of seeing at the top of the armoire, as a reminder of the worst days of her life. "Our first meeting was on February second. I'm going to get rid of it that day." Suddenly she was absolutely sure.

"How are you going to do that?" he asked with interest. The scenario had to be hers, just as the victory would be, and the freedom once she did.

"I think I want to bury it somewhere. Maybe when I walk Lili. We can bury it together."

"Are you going to leave the contents of the box intact?" She thought about it then and shook her head.

"I think I want to burn the letters and journals, and put the ashes back in the box. Kind of like a cremation." She could visualize it as she said it, and Yael nodded approval. Each person had to find their freedom in their own way.

"On February second then. Do you want me to come with you?"

"No," she said quietly, "I want to do it alone." In a way, it was like burying Jorge and everything she had thought they shared.

And on the night of February 1, she put the aviator's box in the metal sink in her kitchen, carefully took out the letters, and held up a lit match, as Lili sat next to her and watched with interest, as though she knew something important was going on. Ariana's hands were shaking, as the edges of a page turned brown and the letter began to curl, and without thinking, she blew the flames out. Suddenly all she could see was his body burning under the fallen tree the night they rescued her. She felt as though she were setting fire to him again and knew she couldn't do it. The fire was still too symbolic to her and reminiscent of that night. She tried again on another letter, and blew the flames out just as fast. She contemplated the journals then, but they were too thick to burn. There were seven of them, all filled with Jorge's handwriting, just like the stack of letters. She thought about calling Yael to ask for his advice, but knew she had to figure this out on her own.

"So what do you think?" she asked Lili, who cocked her head to one side. In the end, she decided not to burn the letters. She would leave them and the journals intact in the aviator's box and bury the whole thing in the park the next morning when she took Lili on her walk.

She found a small scoop in one of the kitchen drawers, for lack of a shovel, and hoped that the earth would be soft enough for her to dig a hole large enough for the box. And then it would be over at last. She was burying Jorge in Paris, and expunging him from her heart and mind. It was time. She was ready to move on.

She lay in bed, thinking about him that night, and she was anxious for morning to come. She was awake before first light, and it was snowing when she woke up, making it too hard to go to Bagatelle and bury the box. She hoped the weather would change—she wanted to do it on that day. It was symbolic. It was just slightly more than two years since she had been rescued by the Israelis, a year since she'd been working with Yael to get her mind back. She didn't want to wait another day. It was time.

The snow turned to rain in the afternoon and finally stopped at four-thirty, and it was still light out. The ground was wet, but she put Lili's leash on, and took the battered metal box under her arm. She hadn't let it out of her possession since Jorge had entrusted her with it. She had done him honor and justice, far more than he had ever deserved. He hadn't been worthy of her love, dedication, and confusion after she was released. He had deserved nothing except the fate he had gotten in the end. She knew that now. She had no doubt. And she couldn't wait to get rid of the box with his letters and journals in it. She felt as though it were on fire under her arm.

She walked Lili to Bagatelle, carrying the box and the metal scoop. She walked for a while, and found a clearing with some hedges around it, and saw that there was soft earth under the bushes. She dropped Lili's leash and knew that she would stand nearby, as Ariana began digging with the scoop. After the rain, it was easier than she had thought it would be, and the hole in the ground grew large enough very quickly. She set the box down in it and said a little prayer, for her own peace of mind and the life she had nearly lost and finally regained. And then she covered the box with the damp earth until it vanished completely. It was gone forever from her life. The rest of her life could begin now, forever changed, but maybe stronger and better after all she'd been through. She stood looking at the earth that was the shallow grave for the aviator's box and what was in it.

"Goodbye," Ariana said softly, and walked away, as she picked up Lili's leash, and they ran back to her apartment. She had never felt as free in her life.

Ariana and Marshall

Chapter 11

The day Marshall arrived in Paris, it was snowing, and he stood on the terrace of his apartment watching the giant snowflakes fall from the sky. It looked like a winter wonderland, and he thought he had never seen anything as beautiful. He unpacked his suitcases, and went to buy groceries so he'd have something to eat for dinner and bought himself a great bottle of red wine. He was giving himself a treat that night to celebrate his arrival in Paris. The snow had turned to rain by the time he got back to the apartment, and Stanley was looking at him mournfully. He wanted to go out, but it was still raining hard.

"I'll make you a deal," he said to Stanley. "Hold it for a while, and I'll take you to the park as soon as it stops." The huge dog whined and lay down, as though he had grudgingly accepted the deal but didn't like it. And an hour later the rain stopped.

Marshall wasn't looking forward to it, but he lived up to his end of the bargain. He put his coat back on, and a wool scarf. It was colder than it had been in Washington, but the air was clean and crisp, despite the bitter cold. Stanley didn't like the weather either, but they loped along at a good pace. Marshall had already seen where the park was and headed there, as he noticed a pretty blond woman ahead of them with a small white dog. He saw her pay her entrance fee to the park at the gate, and then she started walking with her dog, holding a box under her arm. There was something graceful and mysterious about her that intrigued him, as he entered the park far behind her.

But even at that distance, Stanley picked his head up and became interested in the small white dog. He wanted to run after it. Marshall held him back on the leash, and walked along at a leisurely pace. The blond woman disappeared up ahead, and then he saw her again, as he and Stanley rounded a bend. She was leaning over something next to a hedge. He thought at first that she was cleaning up a mess her dog had made, with a scoop. The box she had been carrying was sitting on the ground. Her back was turned, and the dog was watching her dig a hole. And then Marshall saw her reach for the box. It was an old tin box of some kind, and it shone in the light, as the sun came out of the clouds. He was embarrassed to be watching her so intently, but he was fascinated by her. She was beautiful, but there was something deeply sad about her face as she turned and put the box in the hole. He could see her close her eyes, and say a few silent words as he and Stanley continued on the path and walked past her at a distance. And then her face looked peaceful as she picked up the dog's leash, and they walked away. She looked as though she had just been relieved of a great burden, and he couldn't help wondering what was in the box.

He had been trained to observe people and un-usual occurrences, and something about the young blond woman put him on alert. And then he saw her run out of the park with the dog. She looked as though she were flying, and she had a big smile on her face. Whatever she had come to do had ob-viously been accomplished, and suddenly his old instincts made him wonder if she had been doing something illicit or wrong. She didn't look the type, but you never knew. Stranger things had happened. The box was too small for a body—he laughed to himself at his suspicions. Maybe a pet, but then she wouldn't have been smiling. And she had looked happier when she left the park than when she had arrived. Everything that he'd seen her do seemed strange and suspicious to him, and when he and Stanley walked back the way they had come, Stan-ley pulled him toward the bush where he had seen her bury the box, as though he sensed something too. He was a bloodhound after all.

"Easy, boy," Marshall cautioned him. The ground

was slippery under his feet, from all the rain, and his balance wasn't as good as it used to be, with his dead arm. Marshall used a long leash when he took him to the park, and Stanley was already pawing at the hole when Marshall reached him. He was digging frantically, and Marshall couldn't help wondering what he had picked up on the scent of the box. Stanley was looking at him as though he expected him to help. "Don't look at me, you're doing fine. I only have one good arm." The dog had uncovered the box by then, and was barking at it. He wondered if the bloodhound had picked up the woman's scent, or the dog's, or what was in it, and although he felt foolish digging up whatever she had buried in the park, his old instincts made him too curious to resist. He bent down and pulled the box free of the soft earth.

Marshall could see that it was an old aviator's box. He opened it cautiously, afraid of what he would find. You never knew what people buried, but as he pulled the box open with one hand, he saw a stack of letters, one of which looked as though it had been burned around the edges. And when he dug deeper, under many letters, he found a group of small notebooks. There was nothing frightening in the box, no drugs, no small animal remains, just letters and notebooks, and he was about to put the box back in the hole, when curiosity got the best of him again, and he wondered why the woman had buried them instead of just throwing them away.

Something was drawing him to the contents of the box that he couldn't explain. He brushed the dirt off the box with his one good hand and stamped the dirt down again with his shoe so she wouldn't know the box was gone if she came back. He glanced at Stanley with a sheepish look.

"I know this is ridiculous, but I'm retired DEA. What can I tell you? I was born to be suspicious. They're probably letters from her mother-in-law whom she hates, or the diaries of her fourteen-year-old kid." But the pretty blonde didn't look old enough to have a fourteen-year-old—more likely it was a boyfriend she was pissed at. Still, the old aviator's box seemed strange to him. There were a lot of things she could have put in it, other than notebooks and old letters. He sensed a mystery afoot, or maybe he was just wishing for one. By then he had stood up, with the box under his good arm, holding Stanley's leash, and headed back in the direction of the gate. Stanley was looking at him as though he disapproved, and Marshall spoke to him like a friend.

"Don't look at me like that. You dug it up. What did you expect me to do?" The dog sniffed and looked away, and then tried to chase after a bird, despite his leash.

They left the park a few minutes later, and Marshall felt as though he were bringing a treasure chest home with him. He could hardly wait to see if he could figure out why she had thrown the letters away. It was probably a banal answer, but maybe it would turn out to be more interesting. And after he finished reading them, he was going to just dispose of the contents and the box. He didn't want to risk burying them, and getting caught while he did, if she happened to come back to the park while he was there. He would have to dispose of the evidence some other way.

He dropped the box onto his kitchen table, got out a damp rag, and cleaned it off. The soft dirt came away easily. He opened the bottle of wine masterfully with one hand, using his knees to hold it, as he had learned to do, and poured a glass of Château Margaux. It was his gift to himself to celebrate his arrival in Paris. And he grinned, thinking that now he had a mystery to solve too. He felt like Sherlock Holmes as he carried the metal box to the leather couch, and went back to the kitchen for his glass of wine. He sat down with it, opened the box, and took the letters out. He read the one with burned edges and was startled to realize the letters were in Spanish. He wondered if the blond woman was Spanish. It was a torrid love letter addressed to someone called "Ariana" and signed "Jorge." And it was clear that they had had a passionate romance. There was no sign of trouble in it, no argument. It was pure passion as he described the wonders of her lips, her eyes, her body as he made love to her. It was faintly embarrassing reading such an intimate letter to a lover, particularly since he'd seen the woman who had buried it. And he noticed that there was no date. He was intrigued by the charred edges, and wondered if she had started to burn it, changed her mind, and buried what was in the box instead.

He took a sip of the Château Margaux, and sat back to read the letters and journals he had found in the aviator's box in Bagatelle. Night had fallen by then, and he sat in the warm cozy apartment, fascinated by what a man called Jorge had written to her. All he knew was that Ariana, whoever she was, whether she was the blonde he'd seen or someone else, had to be quite a woman to inspire letters like that.

Chapter 12

Marshall had intended to read only a few of the letters—there were at least thirty of them in the box, neatly stacked on top of each other. But they were so loving, passionate, and intense that he couldn't stop himself. By midnight he had read them all, and started one of the journals, which he found more interesting. The letters were a little too Romeo and Juliet for him. The man who had written them, who signed himself Jorge, talked about their being fused into one being, and sounded as though he were trying to convince her that she could no longer exist without him, and should want to abandon all that remained of her "old life" now to be with him. He said it frequently. And if Marshall had to guess, it sounded as though all thirty-two letters had been written in a short span of time, and among them, he had been talking about the child that was now within her. So clearly she had been pregnant, but

whatever had happened between them, and whatever line he had tried to sell her about following
him forever into a new life, hadn't worked, since she
had buried the letters in Paris, and was alone when
she did. Maybe she had a husband or other man
in her life now, and didn't want him to find them.
There were dozens of romantic possibilities as to
why she wanted to get rid of the letters. And maybe
Jorge was a bad guy, despite his adoring words. He
sounded a little unhealthy to him, with his notions
about "fusion," and abandoning every memory
of her "old life." It sounded excessive to him, and
maybe had to the blond woman too.

The journal he had begun reading was also written in educated Spanish, with elegant penmanship,
the kind that Jesuit schools often produced, particularly in Europe. His ideologies sounded as extreme
as his romantic ideals. He talked about starting a
new order and a new world, where everything that
had existed until now had to be destroyed, and the
poor would rise to conquer the world, and all the
rich had to be punished and removed from power.
It was classic revolutionary philosophy and went
on and on and on—he sounded like a man who
liked to hear himself talk. He appeared to have a
God complex and wanted to rule the world, and
apparently had a profound hatred for the upper
classes and anyone with money. Marshall looked at
Stanley when he took a break.

"He sounds like a Communist to me," Marshall

said with a grin, and took another sip of the fabulous wine. The dog rolled over and played dead.

He went back to reading the journals, and couldn't
tell what order they were supposed to be in, so he
just started with the nearest one at hand. And as he
read further, the writer referred to the woman they
had taken, and said that her father was going to fund
their movement for years, which Jorge apparently
thought was ironic. And whoever the woman was,
he clearly considered her a meal ticket. He talked
about keeping her in a box, and he had freed her
from it that afternoon, and he bragged that soon
she would be his. The way he said it made Marshall
read it again. Her being "taken" and "kept in a box"
sounded ominous to him.

He mentioned her again later on, and this time
he referred to her as Ariana. He talked about how
beautiful she was and about watching her bathe in
the stream. So the journal mentioned her as well.
And something about the way it was written, and
what he said about her, made Marshall uncomfortable. He felt like a peeping tom, but other than
that, there was an undercurrent of violence, power,
and possession about what he wrote about her, and
total control. It gave him the creeps. He already
didn't like the guy, when he came to a passage later
on that mentioned his men killing her driver. Something about what he was reading suddenly brought
Marshall wide awake, and what he'd read was starting to ring a bell. He didn't know what it was, but

pieces of what was in the journal sounded vaguely familiar to him.

He tried to finish the first journal he'd started, but with the time difference and jet lag from the trip, he fell asleep with it in his hand. He woke up the next morning, with the sun streaming into the room, and Stanley nudging his good arm. He wanted to go out. It was after ten A.M.

"Okay, guy, give me a minute," he said, and stood up. He washed his face, looked at himself in the clothes he'd slept in, put a knitted cap over his unbrushed hair, and rapidly got into his coat. Stanley was waiting at the door.

Marshall put his leash on him, and together they bounded down the stairs, walked outside, and headed to the park. He bought a multiple-entry ticket at the gate, and jogged down the path with the dog. And as soon as he came around the same bend in the path, he saw Ariana, standing near where she had buried the box with her dog. She was wearing a peacoat and red scarf, and he just hoped that she hadn't decided to retrieve the box, and discovered it was gone. She didn't see him, but he had guilt all over his face, as Stanley strained at the leash to get to the little white dog.

"Come on." Marshall tugged at the leash, and Stanley grudgingly followed as they walked past her. She didn't look upset, and walked by the place where she had buried the box, so he assumed she didn't know the box was gone. He slowed his pace then, and watched her. Her long blond hair was in a braid, and as though sensing him watching her, she turned and their eyes met, and then she walked away. There was no expression in her eyes. She seemed distracted and uninterested in him, and a few minutes later she and the dog left the park. He exercised Stanley for a while, and then he went home.

Marshall flopped down on the couch and started reading the journal again. He finished the first one before lunch, took a shower and changed his clothes, had something to eat, and read the second journal. He found nothing interesting in it, other than the rambling political dogma he found tiresome. But the third one woke him up again. In that one, Jorge referred to his brother, Luis. He said he would be president one day, and when he was, he would help Jorge to change the world. According to Jorge, Luis was very cleverly hiding his true allegiances, and had fooled everyone, and they were biding their time. Jorge wrote that he had promised him a portion of the ransom money, which Luis intended to use to buy arms for them in Bolivia and Ecuador, and would put the rest in a secret account.

Marshall started to pace when he read it. He had no idea which South American country Jorge and Luis were from. It was impossible to tell. He referred to mountains and forests, which could have been anywhere, and for a moment, he wondered if it was Colombia. And more than ever now, he wanted to know what he could discover about the girl. She obviously wasn't Spanish, as he had guessed from the love letters. He assumed she was from somewhere in South America, and he was dying to know who she was. He had a sixth sense that she was more important than she appeared when he saw her in the park with her dog.

He read all afternoon, and had finished three of the journals by then. It was crazy, he was in Paris, and had stayed in his apartment all day, thinking about a woman he didn't know, and reading the journals of her lover, who was clearly a revolutionary of some kind. He wondered if she was in Europe to buy arms, but then why would she have buried the box with his love letters in it? Maybe so they wouldn't be found if she got caught. The girl in the park looked wholesome and innocent, but after years in undercover work, he knew that didn't mean anything. He wondered where she lived, obviously somewhere close by. What he had gleaned in his reading that day troubled him for the rest of the night. He made himself an omelet for dinner, and finished the rest of the wine.

Ariana had had a much better day than Marshall. She had gone to see Yael after taking Lili to the park, and she looked victorious the moment he opened the door.

"I did it!" she said happily, as she took off her

coat and laid it down. She had brought Lili with her, who sniffed at the shepherd, and then hopped onto the couch and lay down. She was used to their sessions, and most of the time she slept on Ariana's lap. "I buried the box yesterday just before dark. That's it. It's done. I don't need any of it anymore." She had never thoroughly read the journals—they were full of the dogma he had explained to her. It was the love letters that had kept her hooked, not the rest.

"How do you feel?"

"Like a free woman for the first time in two years. I'm finally, finally free!" She had worked hard for this. Yael smiled at her and looked pleased. It had been a difficult case. She was such a decent person, had such strong integrity, and was so passionately loyal that she had hung on to the memory of him and her belief that underneath it all Jorge was a good person, that it had been hard for him to convince her of the truth. Nearly impossible, in fact, but she had gotten there at last. She looked like a different person, and the agony of the past two years had finally melted from her face. She was free at last, and Yael was happy for her.

"What are you going to do now?" he asked her. She still hadn't made up her mind. But the future was open to her. She hadn't been able to move forward until she exorcised Jorge from her life.

"Enjoy Paris for a while." She had just extended her lease again. "Maybe travel a little." She wanted to go to Italy, although she was still nervous about traveling alone, but she felt that Italy was safe. She would never have gone back to South America again. But here in Europe, she knew she was all right. "I might try to work for the online fashion magazine again or get a job at one of the big fashion magazines like **Vogue** or **L'Officiel.**" She didn't want to go back to New York. There was nothing for her there. But now she was twenty-five years old, with her whole life ahead of her. Jorge had finally lost his grip on her. Burying the box hadn't liberated her—she had freed herself, with Yael's help, which had allowed her to finally get rid of the box that had been like a ball and chain around her leg. Now it was gone.

"It sounds like you have a lot of plans." He was very proud of her. She had come far, worked diligently to get there, and taken all his advice.

"Are we done?" she asked him cautiously, afraid of what he'd say. She knew she'd miss him when they were.

"Yes, we are," he said quietly as he lit a cigarette and watched her from his chair. She was a beautiful girl, and a wonderful woman in many ways. And he knew that one day she would make someone a lucky man. He hoped for her that it would be soon. He hated to think of her alone. And he had grown fond of her, in a wholesome way, through their work. He wanted only the best for her.

"I'm going to miss you," she suddenly said sadly.

He had been the mainstay of her life for a year, and her salvation. She could never have freed herself of Jorge without his help. He had saved her life, and she was deeply grateful to him.

"Keep in touch, Ariana. I want to know what you're doing."

"I promise I will. I'm going to stay in Paris for a while. Maybe until next summer. Or longer if I find a job."

Yael hugged her when she left, and it was a strange feeling for her, knowing she wouldn't come back again. She had seen him almost every day for a year, and he knew everything about her life.

When she went home that afternoon, she called Sam Adams in Washington. He was just getting to the office, and he was surprised to hear from her. He hadn't spoken to her in a year.

"Is everything all right?" he asked, sounding concerned.

"Very much so. I called to thank you. I just finished a year of work with Yael Le Floch."

"Oh my God. I thought you'd finished with him months ago. You're still in Paris?"

"Yes. I just graduated today. That's why I called. It took longer than we thought."

"How do you feel?" She sounded great, and he was happy for her. She was a nice girl and didn't deserve what had happened to her.

"I feel terrific." She didn't tell him about burying the box and the letters. He didn't need to know.

That was between her and Yael. All that mattered was the end result. She was free now. The ghost of Jorge was no more. He had no power over her. He was gone at last. And she finally understood now how evil he had been. All she needed now was to pick up the threads of her life and move on. She didn't even feel guilty for her father's death anymore, just sad that he was gone.

"When are you coming back to the States?"

"I don't know. Not for a while. I like my apartment. I have a dog. I might try to find a job here. I want to travel around Europe before I leave." A whole world had opened up to her, with the freedom she had won. And Sam respected her a lot for the courage she'd had to deal with it. He knew Yael could be tough, but he was the best in his field.

He didn't ask her if she was seeing anyone. The question was too personal, and he suspected that she wasn't. She had to get Jorge out of her head first. But it sounded like Yael had helped her exorcise his ghost at last. Sam was happy for her, and she was young enough to start a whole new life. He could only imagine how tough the last two years had been for her.

"Well, stay in touch. Let me know if you come back to the States." But he wondered if seeing him, even for a friendly cup of coffee, would bring back painful memories for her.

She took Lili back to Bagatelle for a walk at the end of the day. By then Marshall was deep into

Jorge's fourth journal, and he talked about his brother again. It was obvious from everything that Jorge said that he was high up in the government, playing a double game and secretly sympathetic to his brother's small army of revolutionaries. He was apparently doing all he could to help them establish a sound financial base. Jorge even intimated that committing a series of random kidnappings had been his brother's idea as a sure moneymaker for their cause. Jorge also said that his brother would help overthrow the government one day, and that day was near at hand.

As Marshall read the journal, he tried to guess who it could be, but he didn't even know what country they were in. And Jorge never used last names. It was driving him crazy, and he read all through the night and into the next day. It wasn't what he had planned to do in Paris, but he was hooked on what he was reading. He had a nagging suspicion that he had stumbled on something important, but he had no idea what to do about it, or even who to call. He would sound like a lunatic if he explained that he had unearthed a box full of love letters and journals in a park in Paris, and a South American government was at risk for being overthrown, but he didn't know which one. So many of them were in the delicate balance that existed there.

It bothered him so much that two days later, when he'd finished the last journal and was more convinced than ever that he was right, he called

Bill Carter at the DEA. One of the things that was worrying him was that Jorge had said in several of the journals that he had told the woman Ariana everything. And if his brother in government was aware of it, she would be at risk from him as well. Jorge sounded like a dangerous piece of work. He was one of those strange luminaries with a brilliant mind that had gone awry and turned to the dark side. And his brother clearly was no better, and was playing an extremely dangerous double game. And throughout the journals, Jorge said their time was drawing near.

Bill Carter was surprised and pleased to hear from Marshall. Bill was still sorry about what had happened to him. He had been an outstanding agent. Bill had no idea what Marshall would do now, other than collect his pension, and he had a long life ahead of him. A brilliant career had ended with the bullet in his left arm. There were lots of other things he could do, but he knew that Marshall's passion had been undercover work. And he had nothing to replace it that he cared as much about.

"So where are you now?" Bill asked.

"In Paris."

"Lucky guy." But they both knew that wasn't entirely the case.

"I got here four days ago, and it sounds crazy, but I think I'm on to something."

"Please God, don't tell me you're chasing drug dealers around Paris."

"No, but maybe revolutionaries. I happened on some journals here, and I'm not sure what I've got. They're in Spanish and all I have are first names. Some of it sounds vaguely familiar, but I don't know why. The man who wrote the journals is named Jorge. He has a brother in government named Luis. And there's a woman in the thick of it. Jorge is in love with her, and I think I've seen her here. Blond, blue eyes, name of Ariana. I've got a lot of little pieces of the puzzle, but not enough to figure it out. Jorge keeps talking about overthrowing the government in his journals, which may just be wishful thinking, but maybe not, and damn if I can figure out which country they're from."

"How the hell did you get involved in that?" Bill asked, startled by what Marshall had to say.

"Don't ask. My dog dug up the journals. The woman I think is Ariana had just buried them. I'm not even sure it's her, but it makes sense. Does it ring any bells for you?"

"No," Bill said honestly. "Have you been drinking a lot since you got there?" He was teasing him, but none of what Marshall had said sounded familiar to him. "Are you sure your dog didn't dig up this woman's first novel? It sounds a little far-fetched to me." But they both knew that leads like that happened sometimes and that fact was always much stranger than fiction. Most leads turned out to be nothing, but others turned out to be hot and blew wide open when you started digging.

"Can you run any of that for me? I know it sounds crazy, but it sounds like Jorge may have abducted this woman called Ariana, then fallen in love with her. I don't know, it all sounds a little nuts to me too. Can you try checking around with the South American desk and see if anything surfaces? Maybe it's old history, and never went anywhere. I don't know how old the journals are."

"Are they dealing drugs?"

"Not that I read about in the journals. It's all revolutionary dogma. The usual crap about changing the world and raising the poor to power. Nothing we haven't heard before, but sometimes these guys actually manage to pull it off, or cause a hell of a lot of destruction trying." Revolutionaries weren't usually Marshall's specialty, drug dealers were, but occasionally the two were combined. And they both knew that sometimes drugs provided the money for revolutionaries.

"Yeah, but if they're not dealing drugs, we may not have much on them. This sounds more like CIA. Let me think about it. There's a guy I call over there when I'm stumped. Sometimes he gives me good stuff. I'll run this by him, and see if it rings any bells for him." They hung up, and Bill had to deal with a minor crisis in Chile after that— they had an agent going haywire who had gone out of contact on his way to Bolivia—and Bill forgot about Marshall's inquiry until the next day. He called Sam Adams at the CIA, who was out, but he called Bill back just as he was about to leave the office. It had been a bad day for Bill. The agent in Bolivia had been killed, and the whole operation blown. Two years of careful groundwork had gone down the drain, and an agent was dead.

"Sorry to call so late," Sam apologized. "Bad day here."

"Yeah, me too," Bill said. "We lost an agent in Bolivia and blew two years of work."

"What's up?" He knew Bill never called unless he was looking for information he couldn't track down at the DEA.

"I have a retired agent in Paris, a young guy, name's Marshall Everett, he was one of our best agents, and he thinks he might be on to something. It might just be a witch hunt or something you guys already know about, but he's all worked up about it. Smart guy. One of our top men, six years undercover in Ecuador and Colombia. We put him on sabbatical for a year to cool off before we sent him back to the field somewhere else. And we lent him to the Secret Service. He practically got his arm shot off protecting the president and his family. He took a bullet for the president's daughter, and that was the end of a glorious career. Now he's in Paris and thinks he fell into some information. All I've got are first names. Jorge, Luis, and a woman called Ariana. Marshall thinks Jorge may have kidnapped the woman, and is in love with her. He thinks he may have seen her in Paris, a girl somewhere in her twenties, blue eyes, blond hair, about five feet eight."

Sam sighed when he heard the story. "It's old news," he told Bill, "if it's the same Ariana. Argentina, two years ago. The U.S. ambassador in Argentina, Robert Gregory—his daughter was kidnapped by rebels on her way to their country home. The driver was killed. They held her for three months for twenty million dollars ransom. The Brits and the Israelis helped us raid the camp and killed Jorge, and they got her out. Her father had a heart attack and died the next day. Funnily enough, I just talked to her a couple of days ago. She just finished with a deprogrammer in Paris we sent her to. So your guy probably has seen her there. She's in Paris, but the trail is cold on this one. Nothing much has happened with Jorge's rabble since he died. Other than kidnapping her for ransom, Jorge never amounted to much, and I think his followers are pretty ineffective without him. We haven't heard anything about them in a couple of years," Sam reassured him. "We killed a number of his guys with him when we raided the camp."

"Apparently Jorge has a brother in government, Luis, who plans to overthrow the government, or was planning to two years ago, I guess," Bill told him.

"We know about the brother," Sam said, unimpressed. "I think he was a left-wing activist in his youth, but he's calmed down since and become part of the establishment. Our reports told us the two brothers didn't even speak and were estranged. I can check it out again, but I think the brother is okay." Sam sounded calm about it, and unimpressed.

"Maybe not as okay as you think," Bill suggested. "My guy thinks she may be at risk if the brother thinks she knows something, and Jorge claimed in his journals that he told her everything," Bill informed him.

"I hope he's wrong on that one," Sam said, sounding tired. "She had a hell of a time after we got her out. It's taken her two years to get her head back on straight. Jorge did a real number on her. She had a heavy case of Stockholm Syndrome. She was in a convent for a year, and then went to the deprogrammer in Paris. This is the last thing she needs, to have someone bring it all up, or wonder if Jorge's brother is after her. She disappeared from the press and public eye for the last two years, which was a good thing. Only I knew where she was."

"Can you shoot me a photo of her," Bill asked, "so we can see if it's the same girl? It might not even be her. Maybe she found these journals in the trash somewhere," Bill said hopefully.

"Sure," Sam said, also hoping that Ariana wasn't the girl the ex–DEA guy had seen in Paris. If Jorge's brother had had men looking for her, they would have had no way of knowing she was in Paris, with her living in seclusion for the past two years, and he didn't want them finding her now. He didn't even want to tell her she was at risk. And they had no confirmation of that yet, only Marshall's suspicions.

"I'll send you a picture of her right away. I really hope it's not her. And if it is, I hope Jorge's brother doesn't find her. There's no reason why they should be in Paris." But they both knew that drug runners and rebels had a way of finding the people they wanted even halfway around the world. They never forgot a debt or a face. And Sam was sure that they still blamed her for Jorge's death, just as she had blamed herself.

After Sam hung up, he suddenly remembered the box of love letters Ariana had brought back with her and defended fiercely. It was an old tin box. He had rifled through it himself, and had only seen the letters and thought they were of no interest. He had never seen the journals beneath them, which concerned him now. And if the agent in Paris ID'ed her from the photograph, he'd want to see the journals immediately to read them himself.

Sam sent a photograph of Ariana to Bill by e-mail, who forwarded it to Marshall in Paris. It was after midnight in Paris by then, and Marshall heard the e-mail come in. He opened it, and sat staring at it for a minute. She was a beautiful young woman, and the rough details of the case were there. And it was her, without any question—it was the same woman he had seen burying the box with the letters and journals in it, and whom he had seen again the next day, Ariana Gregory. Marshall read about what had happened, and then called Bill on his cell.

"That's her. Sounds like she had a rough go."

"Very rough, according to my contact at the CIA," Bill said. "She just finished with a deprogrammer in Paris." That was why, Marshall assumed, she had buried the box, maybe as some kind of ritual to get rid of the last physical evidence of what had happened. The report he'd just read even said that she'd been pregnant by her kidnapper and had a miscarriage after the rescue. "Apparently her father had a heart attack and died the day after they got her out. She has no family. It sounds like it's taken her two years to get over it, no surprise. And they're concerned about the journals. Somehow they missed them in Buenos Aires. They knew about the brother but thought he was respectable. You're on to something, Marshall. And if the brother is looking for her, this girl could be in big trouble."

Bill called Sam as soon as he hung up with Marshall. "She's your girl," Bill confirmed as soon as Sam answered.

"Shit, I was hoping it wasn't, and just some kind of crazy coincidence that a stranger found her letters. And I don't know how I missed the journals in Buenos Aires. She said they were just love letters, and Jorge was dead by then, and so were all his men at the camp. Maybe she didn't even know she had the journals in the box. I didn't see them. And I was so worried about her and her dying father, her box of love letters seemed like the least of our problems. We left the box with her at the embassy. She must not have known she had the journals. She was out of her head then, furious with us for killing what she referred to as a 'holy man.'" Bill nodded as he listened. It sounded like a bad situation to him as well, for everyone involved.

"Who's the brother?" Bill asked him.

"A guy called Muñoz. He's the number three or four in the government. A very smooth operator. He could do a lot of damage if he's playing a double game and preparing a coup of some kind, although it's been two years since Jorge died and nothing has happened, so maybe it's all talk and no action, and petered out. He disavowed his brother years ago, and claimed he was relieved when we killed him and said he was a madman. Maybe they both are," Sam said, sounding worried. "We'll get on it right away and see what he's been up to. I don't want to scare Ariana until we know more. Can your guy keep an eye on her in Paris until we figure this out?" No one had bothered her for the past two years, and no one in Argentina had any way of knowing she was in Paris, nor reason to suspect it, so she was still safe for now. But if she surfaced and became visible, she could be in serious danger, and Sam didn't want to alarm her until he knew what Muñoz was up to now and he got some recent reports.

"Everett in Paris is retired," Bill reminded Sam.

"He seems to have trouble remembering that himself, if he's gotten this far. I'll tell him to keep an eye on her for now, but she'll need more than that if they've been looking for her. And if they are, sooner or later, they'll find her." Sam knew that too, and didn't deny it. He felt sick thinking about it. He liked her.

"Just tell him to stay on it. I'll get back to you after I check Muñoz out and find out what he's doing. And I'm going to want to see those journals, but I've heard enough for now. I'll call you when I know something." Sam hung up after that, and Bill called Marshall and asked him to watch Ariana from a safe distance. Sam had promised to e-mail him her address, which he did within the hour. Marshall was lying in bed thinking about her when Bill sent it to him. She lived barely more than a block away. Marshall felt sorry for her. If Jorge's brother was looking for her, there was a good chance he'd find her, and the nightmare would begin again.

Chapter 13

Finishing her work with Yael felt like graduating from college again to Ariana. Suddenly it was as though the world had opened up to her. She went out more freely, went to museums, out to lunch on her own, and went to Deauville for the weekend, winning five hundred euros in the casino. She had no sense that Marshall was following her and had no reason to suspect it.

Sam had been checking out Muñoz through their contacts in Buenos Aires, but there were no reports of revolutionary activity. He appeared to be even more respectable and firmly entrenched in the government than two years before. And Sam relaxed a little when he heard it and told Bill he was less worried, despite what Jorge had said in the journals. Maybe Luis had only been humoring him, pretending to sympathize with his cause. Sam still wanted to see the journals just for good measure, but it sounded now like Jorge had been delusional about his brother. Marshall had promised to copy the journals and send them, but he was busy watching Ariana and hadn't had time.

And after her weekend in Deauville to celebrate her "graduation" from Yael, Ariana put out feelers for a job at French **Vogue.** They said they didn't have anything for the moment, but they invited her to a spectacular event to celebrate a new designer at Dior. She hadn't been to a party in two years, but she bought a new dress and decided to go. She was nervous about going alone, but she went anyway. She wore a fabulous red dress, and her picture was in the **Herald Tribune** the next day, with a short article that upset her. It said she was the daughter of the late U.S. ambassador to Argentina, and mentioned that she had been kidnapped by rebels in Argentina two years before, and her father had died shortly after she'd been rescued. It was a piece of her history she didn't want mentioned anymore, but it was in all the press archives so it was bound to come up. And she looked beautiful in the photograph. After she read the piece, she called Yael and complained about their digging up the old story again.

"You can't help that kind of thing, Ariana. It's bound to come up. The press don't forget anything, particularly if it's shocking, tragic, or sensational." Her kidnapping had been all three.

"I guess so." She sounded sad about it, but it

brought back bad memories and put them into her daily life again, even here.

"You look beautiful in the photograph, so to hell with them. Give them something else to write about," he teased her. "Start kicking up your heels here." It was why she had gone to the party and bought the new dress. But the article brought up everything she wanted to forget.

"The box is buried, Ariana," Yael said. It was code to remind her that the past was dead and buried, and to put it behind her. She thought she had, but now it was in her face again. She didn't want everyone she met in Paris to bring up the kidnapping. It was still painful for her, even if she wasn't in love with Jorge anymore. "Just try to forget about it and go have fun. They won't write about it every time. It will get old."

"I hope so," she said, but she was hesitant about going out socially again.

Sam hadn't contacted Yael to tell him his concerns about Jorge's brother. They had checked on Muñoz thoroughly, and there seemed to be nothing to worry about. And having Marshall watch her temporarily seemed like enough.

The weather was getting a little warmer. It was March and felt like spring was just around the corner, which boosted her spirits after the article in the press that day. And as she and Lili walked through the park, Ariana noticed a man she had seen there before. He had a bloodhound who was trying to

chase the peacocks in Bagatelle, and he looked distracted with his dog as she walked by.

Marshall had felt sick when he saw the photograph of her in the newspaper that morning. It was
the kind of thing that could wind up on the Internet or anywhere in the world. Her father had been
an important man in business, and she had inher-
ited his entire fortune, which the article didn't say,
and which Marshall only assumed since the CIA
report said she was an only child. But the article
mentioned the kidnapping in Argentina, and the
photograph of her could be seen anywhere in the
world, as a follow-up to what had happened two
years before. It was exactly what Marshall didn't
want for her, if Jorge's brother was interested in
her. Without realizing it or trying to, she had successfully disappeared for two years, because she had
avoided the press and been in seclusion. But now,
thanks to Yael's successful efforts, she was emerg-
ing into the world again. And that worried Marshall. The article in the paper said she had been
living in Paris for a year, information that had been
supplied to them by **Vogue.** Marshall just hoped it
wasn't picked up by any of the wire services. And
although Sam said he was less worried about Luis
Muñoz after unexciting reports about him, he still
wanted Marshall to continue watching her until all
their reports were confirmed.

Marshall followed Ariana to the park every day
when they walked their dogs, and she never seemed

to notice him or be concerned. And with all he had been told about her now, Marshall felt as though he knew her. He still had the aviator's box with the letters and journals in it at his apartment. He didn't want to get caught burying it again, and he wanted to hang on to the information for Sam, until he had time to copy the journals, but Sam said there was no rush. Marshall also followed Ariana at a discreet distance, whenever she went out all day, which was usually a walk along the Seine, or to a museum, or to the grocery store. Although she felt freer now, she was still leading a quiet life, and didn't go out at night again after the party at Dior. The article in the press had slowed her down a little. Marshall would sit in his apartment, thinking about her, once he was sure she wasn't going out again. She never went to dinner alone, and she seemed to have no friends in Paris, and saw no one.

Several days went by when she didn't emerge, and he wondered if she was sick, particularly when he saw the guardian walk her dog. He was totally absorbed by thoughts of her and worried about her, which seemed strange even to him since she didn't even know he existed.

He had planned to go to Florence and Venice for a long weekend but canceled his trip. He wasn't going to leave her until Sam Adams in Washington told him it was safe. It felt good helping her, even if she knew nothing about it. It made him feel useful again. He had rented a car at his own expense, just so he'd have it if he needed it to follow her, but so far she went out on foot or on the Metro in the daytime, and walked her dog.

He was thinking about the strange mission he'd been on for the past two weeks, when he was walking Stanley one day, at the same time he knew she always walked Lili, which gave him the cover he needed. And he noticed that a man was watching her from a park bench, and then followed her at a discreet distance when she left. Marshall thought it was strange, and he followed both of them with Stanley, and saw her go into her building on Avenue Foch. She was oblivious to anyone following her, just as she had been to Marshall for the past weeks. The man who had followed her stood outside for a while, got into a car, and left. Marshall felt a ripple of fear run down his spine. He told himself that it was probably nothing, but he made a point of watching her even more closely, sometimes hanging around outside her building as though waiting for someone, or sitting in his car. He then observed a different man following her a few days later, and then he saw both men in a car outside her house. Each time Marshall saw her, she seemed to be completely unaware that she was being watched. He called Bill Carter after the fourth time.

"I know I sound like an old agent," he apologized, "but something's up, no matter what Adams says. I've seen two different guys following her in the park, and they were sitting in a car together outside her house. You should have Sam warn her of what's going on. I think she needs to know. If one of these guys gets in her building, she could open the door." Marshall knew that if someone made a move on her, or tried to kidnap her, there was nothing he could do. He was only one man, and he wasn't armed.

"She's a pretty girl. Maybe they're just horny French guys who think she's cute." Bill was hoping that was true, but the fact that Marshall was worried, worried him. Marshall had almost infallible instincts, as he'd proven before.

"They're not that kind of guy. They look like tough customers to me. And they were definitely following her. Tell your guy to call her." Out of respect for Marshall, Bill called Sam at the CIA that afternoon, and told him what Marshall had said. Bill was still hoping it was nothing, and that only Marshall's overdeveloped instincts were making him zealous, but he respected him enough to call.

But Sam didn't agree with Marshall's assessment. After the benign reports on Jorge's brother Luis, Sam was skeptical that he was after her. Maybe it was someone else.

"If I call her, it'll scare the shit out of her, and it may have nothing to do with Jorge or his brother, or the kidnapping. There are plenty of bad guys in the world, and she's a rich girl. She should be careful anyway. And if this is nothing and I terrify her, it'll set her back two years." And he also knew that if he didn't tell her and something happened, he'd never forgive himself. "Just tell your guy to stay with her a little longer until this shakes out," Sam told Bill, over Marshall's report. "I want to hold off a few more days before I call her. Can he get me pictures of the two guys? I'll run a check on them."

Bill called Marshall back and told him what Sam had said, and asked him to take photographs of the two men.

"I don't have any high-tech equipment here," Marshall said, sounding distracted. "I'm out of the business. I can do it with my cell phone, I guess." He walked by her house that afternoon and got a picture of one of the men sleeping in a car. And he got the other one the next morning, sitting on a bench in the park, pretending to read a newspaper and watching her. He sent the photographs to Bill immediately, who passed them on, and Sam called him the next day.

"Your guy is on to something, and I don't know what it is. I doubt this has anything to do with Jorge or his brother. One guy watching her is from Chile, the other one is Panamanian. They're both small-time operators for hire who've been in and out of jail for a dozen things, mostly drug dealing, forged checks, prostitution. They don't have ties to government or anyone in Argentina. Someone must have hired them, but damn if I know who. And I still don't want to scare her. Tell your guy to keep watching her. He seems to be pretty sharp if he picked up on this just walking his dog."

"He is," Bill confirmed. "He was one of our best agents." And then he called Marshall back and told him what Sam had said.

"Is he crazy?" Marshall exploded at him. "What is he waiting for? For someone to grab her again? I don't even know her. I can't follow her around like a bodyguard. She'll think I'm after her and have me arrested. He has to tell her what's going on."

"He doesn't know what's going on, and neither do you," Bill cautioned him. "They could be trying to steal her purse, for all you know."

"That's bullshit and you know it. She was kidnapped by rebel forces two years ago, and their leader has a brother high up in government in Argentina. If he thinks she knows something that could expose him in some way, he'll go after her. And she's only just become visible again. She's an accident waiting to happen. If I say something to her about two men watching her, she'll think I'm insane." He was beginning to feel it, but he knew something was going on.

He was panicked when he saw two more men in a car, different ones, watching her the following day. There were four of them now, and every instinct Marshall had told him they were getting ready to make a move. They had doubled their forces, and two of them followed her home from the park, and the other two were parked outside her house with the motor running.

He saw Ariana heading straight for them on her way home from the park. She was wearing shorts and sandals and a T-shirt, on a particularly warm May day. And as he watched her, and then glanced at all four men, he saw two of them nod to each other. Marshall took four long strides to reach her and blocked her path with a broad smile, pretending to greet her like an old friend. He took her arm and propelled her down the street as he spoke softly to her.

"Ariana, please trust me. I'm with the DEA. There are four South American men moving in on you right this minute. I think they may have something to do with Jorge's brother, if he's looking for you. I want you to get in my car and drive away with me." She looked at him in total panic with wide eyes, not knowing what to believe, while he continued smiling and walking down the street with her as the men waited for her outside her house, sure she would come back that way in a minute. Marshall's car was parked just down the street. And by sheer luck he had his car keys in his pocket. Marshall and Ariana reached his car, and he opened the doors with a clicker he held in one hand. "Get in now," he said quickly, praying she wouldn't hesitate. He didn't think the four men would grab her while someone was with her, but if they shot him, they could take her immediately, and they had started moving toward them at a slow but steady pace and would reach them in a minute. "Don't look back, get in, and smile at me."

She didn't know why she believed Marshall, but despite her terror at what was happening, she did. What he was saying to her sounded too true not to believe, and she knew she couldn't take the chance. She grabbed Lili and jumped into the car, as Stanley climbed into the back, and Marshall got behind the wheel with one swift movement, locked the doors, and drove off, just as two of the South Americans approached his car. He had driven away before they could react or stop them. But they knew she'd be back eventually. As far as they knew this was just a casual unplanned outing with a friend.

Marshall turned to look at her as they drove away, and he turned the corner as quickly as he could. She was deathly pale and shaking as she held her dog on her lap and stared at him. "I'm sorry if I frightened you. My name is Marshall Everett, I'm a retired DEA agent. Drug Enforcement Administration. Those men have been watching you for weeks. Two of them, then they added two more yesterday, and they were moving in on you. I reported it to the CIA via my agency. They know who the men are, two of them at least, but they don't know who hired them. If you know anything about Jorge's brother, he could be after you. If so, it's taken him two years to find you." He could see that she was shaking in her seat, and she glanced nervously at Stanley and clutched Lili to her. "My dog won't hurt her," he reassured her.

"Where are you taking me?" she said in a choked voice. "I don't know anything about Luis except that he's high up in government, and was going to overthrow the government with Jorge. But I don't even know their last name. Jorge never told me. He said that his brother was a double agent, operating for the people's good."

"Meanwhile they kidnap you," he said through clenched teeth. He had taken several sharp turns, and got on the Périphérique at Porte Maillot, and from there to the freeway heading toward the airport, although he had no idea why he was heading there. He just wanted to get her away from the four men on Avenue Foch.

It occurred to her that Marshall might be kidnapping her, and not the South Americans he claimed were after her. But something about his story rang true. She didn't know who to believe, and every bad memory of two years earlier was rushing through her head. But there was something credible and trustworthy about him. He was **not** like Jorge in any way.

"I don't know where I'm taking you," he said honestly. "Somewhere safe." It was a promise he hoped he could keep as he called Bill Carter on his car phone then, to reassure her and contact him to tell him what had happened. It went straight to voice mail, but the message on speaker in his car said that it was Senior Special Agent Bill Carter of the DEA, which gave him some credibility at least, although the message could have been a fake for all she knew.

She had been afraid to resist him when he told her she was in danger and insisted she go with him. She was terrified of Marshall, although she recognized him from the park, where she'd seen him with his dog, and never paid much attention to him, or anyone, and now she was in his car and didn't know where they were going, and neither did he. He left a message for Bill to call him, and told him he had Ariana Gregory in the car with him, that four men had been moving in on her outside her house. And he requested that Bill call him immediately. The situation was serious. And he must call Sam Adams and tell him what was happening.

At the mention of Sam's name, Ariana relaxed considerably. It told her that Marshall was for real. But so were the men who were after her, in that case, and she turned to Marshall with terror in her eyes. "Why are they after me?"

"I don't know, but they've been following you for weeks. I reported it as soon as I saw them. I called my old boss at the DEA, and he called Sam Adams." He didn't tell her that he'd first called about the journals he'd read. He didn't want her to know he had them and had dug them up after he saw her bury them.

"Why didn't he call me?" She looked frightened and confused. This was a terrible déjà vu for her.

"Because they don't know what's going on or who's behind it. And he told my old supervisor at the DEA that he didn't want to scare you for nothing. I hate to say this to you, but I don't think this is nothing." It had just grown exponentially more serious with what Marshall had seen and sensed was about to happen, and she knew it too. There were tears running down her cheeks, as she continued shaking and looked sick. She felt as though she'd been catapulted two years back, into the past. She had thought the nightmare was over, dead and buried, and now she was in it again.

"I thought this was all over," she said miserably through tears, and he felt sorry for her as he drove.

"Everyone else did too. I think the photo of you in the **Tribune** must have hit the wire services and the Internet, and now they know where to find you. We'll figure out what it is and who's behind it," he reassured her. And he suddenly had an idea and punched in another number on his phone, and she noticed he was driving with one hand. The phone rang, and a man with a heavy Scottish accent answered immediately.

"MacDonald. New Scotland Yard." He sounded alarmingly official.

"Mac? Marshall Everett. I need a favor."

"Not you again," he said with a groan. "The last time I saw you, you damn near got me arrested in Panama. How the hell are you, lad? Keeping out of trouble? Where are you, by the way? You're a hard man to keep up with." It had been nearly four years since they'd seen each other and a lot had changed, which Mac didn't know.

"I'm in Paris, with a lady friend. Do you have room for two houseguests?"

"Don't they pay you guys a decent wage? Can't you take your woman to a hotel?"

"I'm too cheap to pay for one. I'll take the couch, if you've got one."

"And leave your woman to me? Good man," he said, as Ariana smiled in spite of herself. He sounded like a nice guy, and he was further credibility for Marshall. "Scotland Yard" had done it for her, unless he was part of a plot too, which seemed unlikely. As terrified as she was, she believed Marshall now, although she was still shocked that she had gotten into the car with him, but he was very convincing, and the look in his eyes had told her she had to, or something terrible was about to happen. He had saved her. "When are you coming?" Geoff MacDonald asked him. He was a commander of the Specialist Crime Directorate of the London Metropolitan Police Service, in the unit to investigate organized international crime. They had first met when Geoff MacDonald took a special train-

ing class at the FBI Academy in Quantico while
Marshall got his DEA training there. And they had
worked on a few cases together over the years, and
become friends.

"We'll be there in about five hours. We wanted
to surprise you. We're on the road from Paris now,"
Marshall said, trying to sound more casual than he
felt.

"Are you still undercover?"

"At the moment, yes. In real life, no. You'll see
why when I get there."

"That must be a blessing to those blokes in South
America, with you screwing up their business. I'm
surprised they haven't killed you by now."

"They tried," Marshall said, laughing. "And listen, Mac, don't tell anyone I'm coming. Nor the
lady."

"Ah, cheating on your wife, are you? I hope I'm
not on speakerphone," he said with a broad guffaw,
and even Ariana laughed.

"You are, and I still don't have one. No one will
have me."

"Sounds right. What's your poison these days?
Tequila or scotch? I'll go round the shop and get
some before you get here."

"I'm working, Mac," Marshall said, trying to
sound respectable to Ariana. He and Geoff had
shared some rowdy times after hours, and at the
end of a case.

"A likely story, with a woman with you. Is she an agent?"

"No. I'll tell you when I get there. I'll call you when we get to London. You can give me the address then."

"Have a nice drive. Keep both hands on the wheel, lad. Eyes straight ahead," he said, and laughed at his own joke, and then they signed off, as Marshall looked apologetically at Ariana.

"Sorry, he's a little rough around the edges, but he's a great guy. We've done some DEA work together. I'd trust him with my life. In fact I have." He grinned. And as he drove, he realized how much he missed his job. The adrenaline was pumping, and all he could think of were the four men on Avenue Foch who had come within a hair of grabbing Ariana for the second time. "We can't go back now, until we know who those men are and what this is about. I think we should stay out of Paris till Sam tells us," he said seriously, and she nodded. She didn't want to be anywhere near them, and was grateful Marshall had been there. "We can stay with Mac while the CIA boys figure it out. Those men are going to expect you to come back in a few hours. They won't realize you're really gone for a while. They'll probably think you're shacked up with me. But by tomorrow they'll know something went wrong. Do you have anything sensitive in your apartment?" She shook her head as Stanley put his enormous head over the backseat and sniffed at Lili, and she licked his nose. They were doing fine so far. "Is there anything they shouldn't find? Anything that links you to Jorge or his brother?"

"No. I got rid of all that a while ago." Marshall had to stop himself from saying "Yes, I know. Now I have it," but he just nodded. "How did you know what was happening?" she asked him. If all he said was true, and she was beginning to think it was, she was in danger all over again.

"I saw one of them watching you. There were only two of them at first. They took turns follow-ing you to the park. I called my boss at the DEA, and he got the rest from Sam Adams at the CIA. I ID'ed a photo of you." The explanation was too thin, but she was too upset to realize it just yet. Her mind was in a jumble from what had almost hap-pened, again. She shuddered at what would have occurred if he hadn't noticed. She'd be gone by now, with a hood over her head, in the trunk of their car. Or maybe even dead. She wondered if they'd been looking for her for all this time, and if the photo in the **Herald Tribune** was really how they found her.

They drove on in silence for several hours, and reached the tunnel at Coquelles near Calais. Mar-shall had called ahead for a reservation. And they arrived in time to board half an hour before de-parture time of the shuttle. Marshall drove the car onto the platform, and they opted to stay in it. He didn't want Ariana wandering around, in case there

were more of them than he knew and they'd been
followed. He didn't think so, and had been watching the road closely, but he wanted to be cautious.
He wanted to get her to London safely. He was
grateful that he always carried his passport in his
pocket, and Ariana said she had hers in her purse.
She always carried it on her abroad as ID, and Marshall was planning to say that both dogs were service dogs if they were questioned, and he still had
one of his old cards on him that identified him as a
senior special agent of the DEA.

It took thirty-five minutes to cross the English
Channel, and they left the shuttle at Folkestone,
where they both showed their passports. And then
they drove on. And just as they reached the outskirts of London, Bill called him from his office,
and Marshall told him what had happened. He
kept him on speakerphone so he could drive and
Ariana could hear him too. She was still quiet and
deathly pale.

"Where are you taking her?" Bill asked with deep
concern.

"To a friend of mine from Scotland Yard."

"Not that maniac they sent to Panama with you?"
Bill laughed as he said it.

"The very same. I figured she'd be safe there.
We're going to his house in London." He told Bill
about the four men then.

"I hope she drinks a lot." Marshall glanced at
Ariana, and she smiled. At least it lightened the

moment. "I'll call Sam right away." And then he addressed Ariana. "Miss Gregory, are you all right?"

"Yes, yes, I am," she said hesitantly. It had been a stressful few hours, and she was fighting the memory of her terror of two years before, but this was far more civilized, and she was reassured now that Marshall was what he said he was. By sheer luck, she had made the right decision to go with him.

"You're in good hands—the best," Bill reassured her. "We'll get to the bottom of this quickly. Agent Everett did the right thing getting you out of Paris."

"I'm glad he did," she said in a small voice, and looked gratefully at Marshall as she said it. "Why do you think they're after me again?"

"We don't know yet. But I think Special Agent Everett may be right. It may be Jorge's brother, worried about what you know and trying to silence you before you expose him. It's taken him a while to find you."

"I don't know anything about him, except that he's in the government. That's all I know."

"It sounds like he's playing a double game, and your knowing that puts him at great risk. That's enough to make him want to get you out of the picture. Sam Adams can figure out the rest," he said calmly. He wanted to talk to Sam too about arresting the four men in Paris and holding them for questioning. Some or all of them were probably on a terrorist list, which would give them grounds to deport them. But they had to get to the root of the problem and find out who had hired them to grab her. More than likely it was Jorge's brother, if that could be traced.

Marshall called Geoff MacDonald after that, and he gave them his home address and said he'd meet them there in twenty minutes. It took them that long to get to his house. Mac was waiting for them when Marshall rang the doorbell. It wasn't as warm as it had been in Paris, and Ariana was cold in her shorts and T-shirt, as they walked into the house. Mac clapped Marshall on the shoulder.

"Good to see you, lad." And then he saw Ariana and smiled broadly. He was in his early fifties, a tall, burly man who had played rugby in his youth. He looked admiringly at Ariana and waved vaguely at the house. "Sorry, my wife left me thirty years ago, and I haven't had time to clean the place since." They had brought both dogs in with them, and Mac didn't seem to mind. Ariana went to the kitchen to give them each a bowl of water, and the two dogs acted as if they had grown up together. Stanley got Lili soaking wet as he lapped up the water, and Marshall left them both out in the back-yard for a few minutes. Mac offered Ariana and Marshall a drink, which they declined. He said he had a guest room upstairs for Ariana if she wanted, and he waved grandly at the couch for Marshall. It looked like it had no springs left, but he didn't care. Then Mac noticed his arm and frowned.

"What happened there?" He looked sympathetic

as he said it. He didn't see how he could do the work he did with only one good arm.

"Instant retirement. Six years undercover in South America, and I got loaned to the Secret Service for a year, and took a bullet for the president's daughter. Go figure. So I'm hanging out in Paris. I miss the work, though. There's nothing in the world like getting shot at by bad guys." He tried to be lighthearted about it, as Ariana listened and felt sorry for him. She hadn't realized until then that he had almost no use of his left arm, and minimal use of his left hand.

"So what's going on here?" Mac asked as they sat down in the living room. Marshall filled him in on what had happened that morning, and two years before that.

"They sound like a bad lot. Seems like it might be his brother." Mac agreed with Marshall's assessment of the situation, and who was most likely behind it, and why.

"They're working on it now," Marshall said quietly.

"Maybe we can give you some help with it too." Mac smiled at Ariana appreciatively. "We can't have a girl like you dragged off by those bastards. We'll get them."

Sam Adams called them at Mac's that night, while he was cooking dinner for them. It was some sort of stew with vegetables. Sam said they were canvassing their informants for new information and expected some responses within hours. He said something would turn up soon, and he thanked Marshall for getting her to London. "Good work." He praised him for getting to Mac's safely. He knew Mac by reputation. Everyone did. He had been horrified to hear from Bill Carter how close Ariana had come to being kidnapped again. It had been sheer good luck and good instincts that Marshall had seen the men and acted quickly, and that his car was near at hand. Everything had conspired in their favor, and he was glad too that Ariana had cooperated with Marshall even though she didn't know him. A sixth sense had told her she had no choice.

They had a relaxing dinner with Mac that night, and ate the stew that he prepared for them, which was surprisingly delicious, and Ariana even ate a generous portion too and got some of her color back. And afterward, the two men shared a brandy. Ariana was exhausted from the shock and emotional strain of the day, but she felt safe with the two special agents, and she thanked Marshall again for saving her and bringing her to London.

"There's no better man in the business," Mac vouched for him. "Can't hold his liquor worth a damn, but best agent I've ever worked with," he said as Ariana laughed, said goodnight, and went upstairs to the guest room.

"If I were you," Mac advised him as he poured the brandy into two snifters with a heavy hand, "I'd get confused tonight, and wind up in her bed in the guest room. Might do it myself if you're too cowardly to try it." Marshall laughed at him, but he knew that Mac was brilliant at undercover work, and one of the most respected agents at the Yard. All the talk about drinking and carousing was just an act he put on to entertain them. He had literally saved Marshall's life in Panama in a drug deal that went sour.

The two men talked long into the night, and Mac was genuinely sad about Marshall's retirement. He knew that the loss of the use of his arm must have been a terrible blow, and he was being very brave and gracious about it. Losing his career at thirty was a tragedy in Mac's eyes, especially for an agent as good as Marshall. It just wasn't fair. They discussed Ariana's situation then, and Mac said he didn't like it. If Luis Muñoz was after her and they didn't stop him, she could be hunted down for years and be constantly in danger. "She can't lead a decent life like that, and she seems like a nice girl." They both acknowledged that she'd been through a lot, though she seemed to have recovered fairly well. And she looked shaken by her sudden escape from Paris.

Sam Adams called them the next morning, and said that the four men on Avenue Foch had been arrested. The two original men who'd been following her were the low-level thugs they'd identified earlier. But the two more recent additions were more alarming. One appeared on a list of wanted international terrorists and was being detained in

France. And the other had a forged passport and no visa, and was suspected of terrorist activities as well. He was a known hit man in Peru, and had been convicted of murder. And all four claimed that they just happened to be in Paris, hanging out at that address. None of them gave the police a clue about who hired them and why they were there. And after Ariana got up, Marshall told her about the four men being arrested. But they had to get to the man in charge, and they hadn't found the link to Muñoz yet.

Eight hours later Sam called Marshall. "Bingo," he said, the minute Marshall answered his cell phone. "One of our best informants says that Muñoz has been quietly organizing a group of rebels in Bolivia, and he's cut of the same cloth as his brother. He's just smarter about it. And he's waiting for the right time to step up. He's been very careful till now. No one mentioned Ariana, but if Muñoz thinks she knows too much, he'll want her out of the picture so she doesn't blow it for him.

"One of our connections in Buenos Aires is going to expose him to the government, as a subversive. I don't think he'll be able to keep his seat after that. The Bolivian terrorist group he's working with isn't going to sit well with the current government. It makes them look bad. And they can't hold it against him officially, but the connection to Jorge, if he subscribes to the same theories, will hurt him, and the journals will condemn him as a traitor. He may even be arrested. We don't know yet. The problem is that even if we get him kicked out of government, he's still going to be out there somewhere, angrier than ever. Unless we have him eliminated, which is a little heavy-handed by today's standards, Ariana won't be safe anywhere in the world. And you won't be either, if they find out you brought this to us, or they see you with her. It's a serious problem."

"What are we going to do about it?" Marshall said calmly. He wasn't worried about himself. Drug dealers had been after him for years, after he had burned them or destroyed their operations. But that was the life he had signed on for. Ariana hadn't, and she couldn't live in fear, or hidden, for the rest of her life. There would be no hiding from Muñoz, wherever she chose to live. "What do you want me to tell her?" Marshall asked him.

"Give us a few days to see how things shake out with Muñoz, and then we want you to come in. We can discuss it here. Don't either of you go back to Paris. Both your apartments are too dangerous for now. Do you have everything you need there? Passports?" Marshall told him they did. They had already used them on arrival in Britain.

"Where are the journals now?" Marshall still had had no time to copy them, while he was following Ariana.

"They're at my apartment in Paris. I can send someone to get them." It was going to be an embarrassing situation when Ariana saw that he had them. She had no idea that they were no longer buried at Bagatelle. But his reading them had saved her life, so he hoped she would forgive him.

"Why don't you have someone pick up the journals, and let us work on the rest here? I want more details about Muñoz and his activities, all we can get. And then we want you both to come in." It meant flying to Washington, which didn't appeal to either of them. But Marshall knew it would only be for a few days for debriefing, so he could explain how he had deduced what he had, when he had noticed the men following her, and she could explain any information she had from the past. Those meetings were better held in person.

When Ariana woke up, they had coffee together. Marshall filled her in and mentioned they might have to go to Washington, and she wasn't happy about it. But he reassured her that the debriefing would be routine. And he didn't say it, but they were both aware that she would have to find a safe way to live, with bodyguards around her all the time, from now on, if Muñoz was after her. For now, she had Marshall to protect her. He was legally entitled to carry a gun, as a retired DEA agent, and he had asked Mac to get him one the night before, which he had, so he was armed.

Marshall and Ariana went for a walk that afternoon with Stanley and Lili, and talked about everything that was going on. And after they left the dogs back at Mac's house, they took a cab to Harrods, so Ariana could buy something to wear. All she had with her were the T-shirt and shorts she had worn to the park the day before, and a pair of sandals. It took them two hours, but they came back with some decent clothes, and Marshall bought a jacket and a pair of slacks. If they had to fly to Washington, he wanted to be properly dressed for the meeting.

And on the way back from Harrods, Ariana thanked him again for everything he'd done.

"I've been worried about you for weeks," he admitted.

"How did you know who I was?"

"After I saw the first guy following you, I called Bill. He called Sam to ask him if anything sounded familiar, and he sent Bill a picture, and he forwarded it to me, with the summary report. Everything was there." Even the baby she had lost, which he didn't say to her. "It alerted me to the fact that you really were being followed. And I saw the photo in the **Herald Tribune** and recognized you from the park." But as he explained it, she realized there was a piece missing, and Marshall looked at her with embarrassment. He knew he had to confess—she would find out anyway. "I read the journals," he said in a small voice, and she looked shocked.

"How did you do that?" There were no copies.

"I saw you bury the box the day I got to Paris. And

Stanley dug it up. He's a bloodhound . . . and I'm an ex-agent. I wanted to see what was in the box. I took it home and read the journals. Something about the story sounded familiar. So I called Bill, and he looked it up. I'm sorry, Ariana. I shouldn't have done it." He looked morbidly ashamed and apologetic.

"Thank God you did," she said softly. There was nothing to forgive. His curiosity and good instincts had saved her.

And when Mac came home that night with an excellent Indian dinner, Marshall asked him if he had a junior operative who had time to go to Paris. Washington wanted the box of journals, and he needed some more clothes, as long as someone was going to his apartment.

"No problem, lad. I'll send someone over tomorrow. Give me your keys." Marshall handed them to him, and gave him the code, and told him where the box was, and the following night, one of Mac's agents walked in with the aviator's box. Ariana gasped when he did.

"I never thought I'd see that again," she said unhappily. And she didn't want to see it now. She asked Marshall to put it away. She was finished with it forever. And even if Marshall had unearthed it, it was no longer a part of her life. The wound had healed. She refused to allow it to reopen now, even if she was at risk of being kidnapped again. Jorge was out of her life forever.

They sat around talking to Mac that night, and spent the next week waiting for news, while Marshall stayed in constant contact with Bill and Sam on the iPad Ariana had in her purse when they left Paris, and Mac's agent brought his own laptop back from his apartment. And finally Sam called them on Friday night.

"I have good news and bad news," he told Marshall. The good news was that they had exposed Luis Muñoz as the double agent and revolutionary he was, and he had been removed from the government. The bad news was that he had vanished and no one knew where he'd gone, not even their best informants. "He could be anywhere," Sam said, sounding discouraged. "South America, North Africa, even Europe. He's a slippery sonofabitch, and a smart one. He has literally disappeared into thin air." Marshall dreaded breaking the news to Ariana. It meant that she would never be safe again. And then Sam added, "How soon can you both be here?"

"Whenever you want. We've just been sitting here waiting for news. And I'm sure Mac is tired of us by now."

"How about Monday?" Sam suggested. "We'd like to see you here. And bring the journals."

"That will work for us," Marshall confirmed. He told Ariana the next day, and he hated the look on her face when he told her that Jorge's brother had escaped. She knew exactly what that meant. It was very, very bad news for her.

"What happens now?" she asked Marshall sadly.

"I don't know," he said honestly. "I guess they'll tell us on Monday." But for certain their lives were about to change.

Chapter 14

Marshall and Ariana spent Saturday quietly with Mac at his house. Neither of them went out, and Ariana seemed unusually subdued. She didn't say anything to the two men, but her current circumstances were beginning to make her feel kidnapped again. There were no rebels and no box to confine her in this time, but she was trapped. Danger could have been lurking anywhere. As soon as she was recognized, she'd be at risk. Possibly for the rest of her life. And being under one roof with the two men for many days was bringing back memories of Jorge and his men, even if this was different. Mac and Marshall couldn't have been nicer to her, but Jorge had been kind to her too. She didn't want to fall into Stockholm Syndrome again.

Feeling claustrophobic and anxious, she called Yael that night, and told him that Jorge's brother had sent men after her, maybe after seeing the press

photograph in Paris at the Dior party. The photograph had gone everywhere on the Internet along
with her story. She wondered if he'd been waiting
for her to surface, so he could pounce. Because of
her, he had lost his position in the government, and
now he had vanished, which made the situation
even more dangerous for her. She told Yael that
she felt trapped and frightened. He listened quietly while she explained the situation, and it didn't
sound good to him either, particularly for Ariana
after all she'd been through and her hard work to
overcome it. She had just regained her freedom
and now she had lost it again, maybe forever. The
weight of it on her seemed crushing. He could hear
it in her voice.

"Are you feeling guilty?" Yael asked her after listening to her. "About Jorge's brother, or anything
else? This isn't your fault. It never was." He wanted
to be sure she understood that. And hearing his
calm voice centered her again.

"No," she said slowly, thinking about it, and
always honest with him. "I think I'm just scared,
and sad that I can never lead a normal life. I was
starting to enjoy my life again. I felt so free, and I
wanted to find a job and start working. And now
everything's gone wrong again." Just like when she
was kidnapped. "And they've been nice to me here.
But I can't do anything. I think I'll go back to the
convent when I go back to the States. Maybe I'll

become a nun," she said, sounding despondent. At least Muñoz and his men wouldn't find her there, and she'd have peace. She was twenty-five years old and felt like her life was over. And in many ways it was. It had ended, as she knew it, the day they left for Argentina. It had been the worst thing that had ever happened to her, other than her mother's death. It had ended her father's life ultimately, and now hers.

"Things will probably calm down eventually. He's not going to hunt you down forever," Yael told her. "He doesn't have the manpower or the funds." But they both knew that if he became allied with the drug lords, or already was, he would have the money, and maybe enough men, and he would try to find her for revenge if nothing else. "He has other fish to fry than to avenge his brother," he tried to reassure her. "And if he was worried about exposure, that's already happened. Now he'll go into hiding somewhere, Bolivia, Chile, Ecuador, Colombia, who knows where. Sooner or later he'll give up on you. But there's no question, you'll have to be careful for a while. Maybe even a long while." And it wouldn't be easy for her.

It was different for Marshall, if they were after him now too, if they had associated him with her, or recognized him. If one of them had taken a picture of him, even with a cell phone, they could identify him and find out he was an agent, from their sources. But Marshall had volunteered to give his life up many times, and his identity. Ariana hadn't. He was a willing recruit, even as a retired agent. Ariana had been dragged into it against her will, every time.

"We're going back to the States tomorrow night. To meet with the CIA in Washington on Monday." That brought up old memories as well. When the CIA were part of her daily life, it had been a terrible time for her. Now they were back in her life, as her saviors, once again. "I hope they let me come back to Paris soon," she said sadly, but she didn't sound as if she thought they would.

"You'll have to change some things if they do," Yael said candidly. "You're not set up for any kind of protection here. Maybe you can hire this retired DEA agent as a bodyguard," he said, and meant it. And she'd need more than just one. She'd need many, but fortunately she could afford it.

"He can only use one arm," she said, sounding matter-of-fact, and Yael laughed.

"Believe me, those guys are lethal even with no arms. They're trained to survive. Maybe he can help you. Seriously. What you need is a strong protective system around you, and to lie low for a while, until Muñoz surfaces again, disappears for good, or gets killed. All three are possible. And in the meantime, you just have to keep your chin up and be smart. You know you can survive this. You'll be okay. This is different from last time. You're well protected, you're not being held captive, and you're not at the mercy of the men you're with," he reminded her.

"They feed me and keep me safe from the bad guys," she said. "Just like Jorge."

"No," he insisted, trying to give her perspective. "This is very different. The lines are clear, and the players. The good guys are the agents from all those alphabet agencies, and the one from Scotland Yard. The bad guys are the others. Last time the bad guys were pretending to be good guys. That's what screwed up your head. This time the teams are clear, and everyone is doing what they're supposed to. The bad guys are out to get you, and hurt you if they can. And the good guys really do want to protect you. And you're not dependent on anyone for food." He reminded her of that too. Even a simple detail like that made a difference. She would have died of starvation and thirst in the forest without Jorge. "You can order your own pizza. And champagne if you want to. This really is different, Ariana. I know it's awful and unfair and very stressful, but you're not totally out of control. You can make choices. They may not be great ones and you may not like them, but you can make some decisions here about how you want to be protected. With Jorge, you had no choice. He had total control." She sighed, thinking of what he said, and knew he was right, but she didn't like it anyway. He told her no one would.

While Ariana talked to Yael, Marshall and Mac

were drinking coffee in the kitchen. It was like
old times when they'd worked on an assignment
together.

"How do you think she's doing?" Mac asked
him, and Marshall wasn't sure. He could see how
stressed she was, but she was keeping to herself and
not confiding in him.

"This is bound to be hard on her, and give her
flashbacks of when she was kidnapped," Marshall
responded. He had seen it in her eyes, from the
moment he approached her in Paris. He was grateful she had gone with him willingly. For some reason that neither he nor Ariana could fathom, she
had trusted him, just long enough to get her out of
immediate danger. She'd probably have been dead
by then if she hadn't. "She only just got over this
with the deprogrammer. Now she's up to her ears
in it again." She seemed depressed about it, and he
didn't blame her. And he had noticed that she was
eating very little. She didn't look like she ate much
anyway, and was very thin.

"What do you think the boys in Washington will
tell you?"

"To get our asses out of Dodge, for a while at least.
They may want to hide her somewhere. I can't see
them letting her come back to Paris, to live by herself. That would be insane." Mac agreed with his
assessment, and she couldn't live in his guest room
forever, although he would have liked it. There
hadn't been a woman in his life in years. He'd been

involved with another agent, in a different section, for several years, but eventually even she couldn't put up with him, and had moved on to someone else. He was a confirmed bachelor, and made jokes about it. His work didn't leave him much time for fun, or women, and he liked it that way. His assignments had always been more important to him than anything else. Marshall had been no different while he was working, until Paloma. Until then, women hadn't been a priority in his life. Fighting the forces of evil was. It was all that had mattered to both Mac and Marshall for years.

"What about you? You need to be careful for a while too," Mac said with a fatherly look. He had always been fond of Marshall, he was a great agent and a good man, and they had worked well together and had good times.

"I can take care of myself," Marshall said, and glanced at his useless left arm, "even with this," and they both knew he had a gun in his pocket and would use it if he had to.

"Shit luck that," Mac commented about his arm.

"Maybe not. I would never have forgiven myself if Amelia Armstrong had been killed because I didn't move fast enough. Or her mother. She was eight months pregnant."

"So you're a hero," Mac said cynically. "And the bad guys win now, without you to fight them."

"Nah, you and I are replaceable, Mac. We're good at what we do, but so are a lot of other people.

We'll outnumber them in the end. We just keep on trucking."

"And so do they. They've taken out a lot of good men, just in the years I've been working," Mac said with a sober look.

"It's kind of ironic that what got me in the end was a random shooter. He got out of a mental hospital six months before. At least it should have been someone clever who had reason to shoot me. This seems so stupid, like killing yourself falling in the bathtub."

"Not exactly." Mac grinned at him. "You were defending the president of the United States. That's a little different." Marshall smiled, and Ariana walked into the kitchen after talking to Yael, and made herself a cup of tea. She looked calmer than before.

"Can I do anything to help?" she offered as she sat down at the kitchen table. She was growing comfortable with both of them, in her forced seclusion with Marshall, and she felt better after talking to Yael. He always got her head back on straight. He had called it a tune-up when they talked, and it had helped. He always did.

"Yes," Mac answered her emphatically. "Clean my house, woman, and don't forget the windows and floors. You don't expect me to live in this pigsty forever, do you?" Ariana laughed when he said it. Her apartment in Paris had come with a cleaning woman who came twice a week. Ariana hated housework, and had never done it in her life, and had always had others to do it.

"I'm not so great at that kind of thing myself," she admitted, and Mac made a face.

"None of you young girls are. Argh, modern women, they're useless. All they know how to do is shop and get their nails done. What are we supposed to do with that? Cooking, cleaning, laundry, scrubbing floors—now that's a **real** woman for you!" Ariana chuckled. She loved him. It was hard not to. She thought it was sad he was alone, with no wife and no kids, but Marshall had told her a lot of old agents were like that. And young ones too. There wasn't much room in their life for marriage, relationships, and romance. And it was a bad deal for their women. It made Marshall think of Paloma then while they were talking. She had gotten the worst deal of all, because of him.

They chatted for a while, and then she went upstairs to pack her few things. Mac cooked stew for them again that night, and threw everything in it he had in the fridge except a couple of limes and some packaged chocolate pudding. He had the contents of a bachelor's fridge, usually with the leftovers of some fish and chips he bought on the way home and never finished.

And he produced a bottle of decent wine for the three of them. Ariana only took a sip. She was anxious about their trip to Washington the next day and what the CIA would say on Monday.

"You'll be fine," Mac reassured her, but she wasn't convinced. And the next morning when Mac said goodbye to them at the airport, he had to choke back a lump in his throat as he hugged Marshall. He had the terrible feeling he wasn't going to see him again, and had never had that feeling about him before.

"Take care of yourself, lad," he said in a voice thick with emotion after they had checked their bags, and put Stanley with the luggage in a crate. Lili was traveling in the cabin with them, in a travel bag Mac had picked up for them. Ariana was dealing with the woman at the desk and getting her board-ing pass while the two men talked. "You two make a nice couple," Mac said to Marshall in a low voice. "You could do worse, and probably have." He was only half teasing. He had come to admire Ariana a lot in the past week of living closely with her, and he had great admiration and affection for Marshall, and always had. He thought Ariana a very intelli-gent, discreet young woman, who had none of the airs and graces she could have exhibited given who she was and how she had lived. He had grown very fond of her.

"Very funny." Marshall made a face at him, at what he said about them as a couple. He was acting as an active agent, even though he no longer was. His mission was to get her to Washington in one piece, and leave her to the CIA after that. He had no designs on her as a woman. She was a potential victim who needed protection, which was his job, whether officially or not.

"You've got to teach the woman to cook, though. She'll be useless to you otherwise." Both men were laughing when Ariana joined them with her boarding pass and luggage stub, carrying Lili in the bag. She was only bringing one small suitcase, with what she'd bought at Harrods. Everything else was in Paris, although she didn't have much there either. Her life in Paris had been simple until recently, just working with Yael.

Ariana hugged Mac when they left, and thanked him for his hospitality, and she was sad to leave him too.

"Next time you'll sleep in my room," he told her with a wink, and she laughed. She knew he was harmless, and had only pretended to flirt with her. Both men had been totally circumspect and nothing but kind and respectful to her. Yael was right. This wasn't like when she'd been kidnapped at all. And she was grateful to both men.

"Take care, you two. Play nice" were his last words to them, and he never left them with his eyes as they went through security. It was old habit, and he could have used his Scotland Yard badge to take them through, but he didn't. He knew that Marshall had it covered, and he was sad to see them leave, particularly Marshall. He had that terrible feeling again that this would be the last time they'd meet, and he didn't know why. Marshall had returned the gun to him right before they left.

Mac's eyes were damp as he drove home, and he felt his heart ache as he walked into the empty house, saw their breakfast dishes in the sink, and poured himself a stiff drink, thinking about his friend. He hoped he'd be all right, and nothing untoward would happen to either of them.

Ariana stopped and bought magazines on the way to the plane. She bought Spanish, French, and American **Vogue, Time** magazine, and the **International Herald Tribune,** and they settled onto the plane in first class on British Air. Normally Marshall traveled coach or occasionally business, but the CIA was bringing them home in first class for security reasons. And they wanted Marshall as close as possible to her, never out of her sight or reach.

"You're lucky they didn't put you in steerage with me," he teased her, as she looked up from her magazines and smiled. Everything had gone smoothly so far, and he was thinking about Mac as the plane took off. He had enjoyed seeing him again and missed the old days when they'd had occasional assignments together. He had been fantastic to work with, and one of the smartest, bravest men he'd ever known. You couldn't judge from his disheveled, tweedy appearance and casual style. He looked like a befuddled college professor, and was the fastest man with a gun he'd ever seen. Mac had killed three men in seconds one night, and taken the fourth out with a knife with lightning speed. Marshall had been forever impressed by him after that, and they had become fast friends. He promised himself to make time to see him when he returned to Paris and went on his travels around Europe in the coming months.

Ariana didn't say much, and they ate a light meal. She started to read her magazines and was asleep in a few minutes. He covered her gently with a blanket, and the flight attendant smiled. She wondered if they were honeymooners. It would never have occurred to her that they were an ex–DEA agent, and a woman being hunted down, on their way to a meeting with the CIA.

Ariana woke up after two hours, noticed the blanket, and thanked him with a sleepy smile. He'd been watching a movie and stopped it, and took the headphones off when she awakened.

"Are you doing okay?" He looked concerned. He was worried about what might be happening in her head, and how stressed she was. She relaxed back into her seat and sighed as she glanced at him.

"I'm nervous about tomorrow," she said quietly. "What are they going to do with me? I don't want them to lock me up to keep me safe." He didn't want that for her either. It wasn't fair, and she was young. She needed to have a life. It never occurred to him that he did too—he hadn't had one in so long. There had been no woman he cared about since Paloma, three years ago. Sometimes it still felt like days. He hadn't looked at a woman since, and knew he never would again. It was too painful to lose someone you loved. And in his case, she had died because of him. He knew he would feel guilty about it forever and had her blood, and their baby's, on his hands.

"They'll probably just assign you a detail of guys for a while. And you might have to hire bodyguards on your own. I can help you find them, if you like. There are a lot of good men around, with minor injuries who can't work for the DEA anymore, or CIA, but are still capable of working in the private sector. A lot of guys do that when they retire, or go out on disability."

"Is that what you do?" she asked, curious about him. He was very discreet, and never talked about his injury or personal life. She knew he had come to Paris for several months, but didn't know why. She had heard him tell Mac that he'd lost the use of his arm, taking a bullet for the president's family while working for the Secret Service, but Marshall had never told her himself.

"No, I'm done," he said simply. He didn't sound bitter about it, just matter-of-fact. "Shit happens, as they say. I wouldn't feel right hiring myself out with only one good arm. Maybe at half price." He grinned, and she winced at the awful joke. She had seen that he could use his hand enough to help himself, but the arm was limp at his side. But he had just saved her in Paris nonetheless. "I was lucky for long enough. The bad guys would have gotten me sooner or later. I pissed a lot of people off when I was working undercover. You can't do that forever, though I would have tried. Sometimes destiny intervenes." It was one way to look at it, and she had the feeling he was philosophical and at peace about it, which couldn't have been easy, since he was young. He had said he had just turned thirty-one—six years older than she was.

"What do you think you'll do now?" she asked him.

"Travel for a while. Do all the things I never had time to do when I was working. I hadn't taken time off in years." With his enhanced pension he could do whatever he wanted, except work as an agent. "Sometimes I think I'd like to teach. I know a lot about South America. Maybe foreign policy or something. I'll figure it out eventually. What about you?" He knew she didn't need a job, but he wondered what she did with her time, or would when she was free again.

"I wanted to go into fashion. I was working for an online fashion magazine when we left for Argentina. It was just an entry-level job, but I loved it. I'd kind of like to go back to work in fashion, but I wasn't ready until now. I was going to start seriously looking in Paris, with one of the magazines.

Now I don't know what they'll let me do." She told him then about living at St. Gertrude's for almost a year, with the nuns.

"That always seems like a sad life to me, and such a waste," he said cautiously, not wanting to offend her, and she instantly shook her head.

"It isn't, honestly. They have so much fun, they're wonderful, and they have such a good life. I loved living with them. They taught me how to grow vegetables." She was smiling as she said it, thinking of Mother Elizabeth, Sister Paul, Sister Marianne, and the others.

"You can be a gardener then," he teased her.

"I was terrible at peeling potatoes," she confessed. "For a while I thought maybe I had been led there for a reason, but the mother superior talked me out of it. I was just scared to go back into the world, and she knew it. I came to Paris to work with Yael Le Floch after that. I'm glad I did, and now here I am again. On the run from kidnappers and rebels. It seems to be my destiny, for now."

They both watched movies then after that, and landed in Washington on time. They were cleared through customs and immigration instantly, were met by two CIA agents as they came off the plane, picked up Marshall's dog from the cargo, and were taken to the Four Seasons in Georgetown, where they had a two-bedroom suite, and shared a living room. And there was an agent posted outside their door.

"Traveling with you is certainly an experience," he teased her again. "Last time they brought me in from somewhere, they put me up at a hotel at the airport." They had put them in the double suite so he could keep an eye on her, and they had the agent outside for insurance. There was no way for anyone to know she was there, but they were playing it safe. There would be no excuse if she got kidnapped or killed right under their noses on U.S. turf. Last time she was kidnapped hadn't been their fault, since she hadn't been in their care. This one would be.

They had been told to stay in for dinner that night, and Marshall ordered a cheeseburger and Ariana a salad from room service. And the hotel was allowing them to have both dogs in the room. Ariana ordered hamburger meat for Stanley too, after she checked with Marshall, and sliced chicken for Lili. Stanley was still looking insulted after the trip. He had hated the crate and traveling with the baggage. And Lili had slept all the way in her bag. The agent outside their room had thought Stanley was great, and played with him whenever he came out when Marshall walked him. He had offered to take Lili out for Ariana, so he took both dogs. The CIA wanted her to stay in the room and out of sight.

Marshall had brought the journals with him in a briefcase, with the letters to Ariana, and had left the battered tin box with Mac. They didn't need it, and he knew that seeing it was traumatic for Ariana. He had offered to make copies of the letters for her, if she wanted them, before he turned them over at the meeting, and she shook her head. All that was over for her. She didn't want to see them again and undo her work with Yael.

They watched a movie together in the living room of the suite, and they both went to bed early. Lili slept on her bed with her, and Stanley was stretched out on the couch in the living room of the suite, nearly the size of a man. Marshall laughed when they left him there, snoring. "He likes traveling with you too."

Ariana lay awake in her bed for a long time, wondering what would happen the next day, and if there was any news. Maybe by some miracle, Jorge's brother would be found, and she'd be free. It was almost too much to hope for. Sam Adams had called them when they got in, and said he'd see them the next day. They were scheduled to be at the CIA offices in McLean, Virginia, a few miles outside Washington, at nine-thirty. Ariana was up at six.

She ordered coffee and sat reading **The Washington Post** peacefully in the living room with both dogs, until Marshall emerged from his room in jeans, to take them out.

Ariana thanked him, and they had breakfast when he came back half an hour later, and they both got dressed. They left the dogs at the hotel, with a Do

Not Disturb sign on the door of the suite, so they
wouldn't escape if a hotel maid opened the door,
and were in the CIA car waiting for them downstairs at nine-fifteen. Ariana was wearing a black
skirt and sweater she had bought at Harrods for
the meeting, and Marshall was wearing a suit he'd
had Mac's agent bring him from Paris. They looked
serious and respectable, and Ariana was nervous as
they walked in.

Sam Adams was there to greet them, and he and
Marshall shook hands. Sam gave Ariana a hug to
reassure her, and a few minutes later, half a dozen
men assigned to their case walked in. The situation
was the same. They explained that Muñoz had not
been found. He was loose somewhere, presumably
in South America, but he could have been anywhere. And they felt it was more than likely that
he blamed Ariana and the information he thought
she'd had, for his fall from grace, and certainly for
his brother's death. And they knew now that he
was a vengeful man, just as Jorge was. Sam Adams
suspected that Luis was smarter than his brother,
infinitely better connected, and had successfully
played his double game for a long time, which suggested he was more clever.

"We have good reason to be concerned," one of
Sam's men explained to her as they sat around a con-
ference room table. They had met the day before to
formulate a plan, and Sam approved. Marshall listened without saying a word. He had a feeling he

knew what was coming, but hoped he was wrong. "You're in serious danger, Miss Gregory. And until something changes—we locate Luis Muñoz, put him behind bars, or kill him—we can't give you the kind of protection you need. You saw what almost happened in Paris. It will happen again. The minute they locate you, they'll try again, and they won't kidnap you for ransom this time, but for revenge. Or they'll keep you alive for long enough to have you turn money over to them to fund their cause, and then they'll kill you. Your risks are much higher than they were before. Kidnap for ransom is child's play compared to this. And we don't know yet who else is on Muñoz's team, what other government officials we don't know about, who would carry out his orders or do his dirty work." The foursome in Paris had been a motley crew, recruited from all over South America, among mercenaries, rebels, and paid killers. "You're up against some really bad people here," he said as Ariana's face grew pale.

"So what am I supposed to do? Hide for the rest of my life? How can I do that?" And she didn't want to—she'd almost rather be dead, she thought as she listened to them. And Marshall was worried by the look of despair on her face, but he could understand how she felt, particularly at her age. Her life was just beginning again, and they wanted to turn it into a prison.

"You don't have to hide for the rest of your life," Sam explained gently to her, "but maybe for a while.

A few years. We want to make that as livable as we can for you, Ariana. I know it's hard. We brought you here to offer to put you in the Witness Protection Program, at a very elite level, with maximum security, in a way that's comfortable for you, while still keeping you safe. We'll work with you to set it up."

"Like moving to Montana and pretending to be someone else?" she said with a look of horror, as the men around the table nodded. Tears came to her eyes. "What would I do there? I'd be all alone." It sounded like a fate worse than death to her, not because of the location but because of the way she had to live. Hidden, under an alias, with strangers who'd never know the truth, or who she was. She would have to live a lie, and for how long?

"We can help you hire staff, and we could place some agents with you for a while until you acclimate, but our hope is that you wouldn't need them there. We'd like you in a safe environment until something changes here, or in Argentina with Muñoz. Of course we'd continue looking for Muñoz during the entire time. It might not take long," he tried to encourage her as tears spilled down her cheeks and Marshall wished he could comfort her, but there was nothing he could say in the meeting, and he knew they were right. It would have been his plan of preference for her too. It was just too dangerous for her out in the world right now, and could be for a long time.

"And what if I won't go?" she said stubbornly, suddenly looking and acting her age.

"You'd be taking an enormous chance, and living with that risk every day. Like you just experienced in Paris. We can help you pick a location—there are several we prefer. In rural communities, states with low crime activity, and where you wouldn't attract attention. Obviously not in a city like Washington or New York." She hadn't been far off with Montana. Wyoming was one of their favorite states for Witness Protection. "We really think this is the wisest course for you right now. Normally the Witness Protection Program is for people who are going to testify in a trial, and we need to protect them until then. Your case is somewhat different, because you are a potential victim of people who kidnapped you once before, and we want to protect you from them. But a trial could arise from this at some point, and you would be subpoenaed to testify. But what we're really focusing on right now is your safety."

He explained to her then that before making her the offer of protection, they had already gone through the appropriate channels to put it into effect immediately. While she was still in London, they had gotten approval from the U.S. Department of Justice, through the Office of Enforcement Operations, who had agreed to her admission into the program, and Marshall's. And their admission into the Witness Protection Program had been confirmed by the U.S. Attorney General's Office, according to their normal procedures. Sam had asked all the agencies involved to speed their applications through, so they could move quickly. Ariana had been shocked to hear that her application to the Witness Protection Program had already been made and approved. It made it feel like a done deal, which upset her even more.

There was no one to advise her or tell her what to do. She was entirely on her own, which was a disadvantage too. She was young to make such a major decision, which might impact the rest of her life, or even her survival. "Why don't you take a day or two to think about it? We know it's a big decision and a lot to absorb. We can give you a list of the places we're considering. And we'll do everything to make it work for you. We can help you both find jobs, we have housing for you, and we can provide you a stipend of up to $60,000 a year. We'd handle all the documents, and counseling if you felt you need it." Her head was spinning as she listened. She was also in a very particular situation, because she had inherited a great deal of money from her father, and could set up an extremely comfortable life somewhere, more so than most people. She nodded, and looked like she was in shock when they left the office. She felt totally overwhelmed.

Marshall had turned over the journals and letters to Sam in a manila envelope before they began the meeting. Now Sam turned to Marshall as they left.

"We feel the same way about you, Everett. You're at high risk right now too. If the four operatives who saw you in Paris took photographs of you, they'll be after you in no time. We want you in the WPP too. With Miss Gregory, once she decides on a location, or on your own. That's up to both of you." Sam handed both of them a list of preferred places and states where they felt the Witness Protection Program would function best for them.

"You want me put away too?" Marshall asked him, surprised, and Sam Adams nodded.

"You have just as much reason to be in the WPP as she does. Maybe more, given your history and now that you've been seen with her," Sam said seriously. He escorted Marshall and Ariana from the room, and took them to his office, where they discussed it for a few more minutes. Ariana was fighting back tears, and Marshall looked subdued.

"It's like sending me to prison, or Siberia," she said to Sam as they left the meeting.

"It's about saving your life," Sam said somberly. "We worked hard to get you out of Jorge's camp. We don't want to lose you now." And he knew they could. Marshall knew it too.

They went downstairs to the waiting car then, and Ariana burst into tears the moment they left the building, and cried all the way back to the hotel. Marshall hated to see her so distraught—it had been an overload of information for her. And when they got back to the suite, he put his arms around her, and she cried against his chest.

"I know it sounds awful. But it won't be so bad. And it won't be forever. Guys like me find guys like Muñoz all the time. You just have to give them some time to do their job. And now I'm in the same boat as you are. They want to lock me up too. Or send me to Siberia, as you put it." But he didn't look as distressed as she did, just startled. He was used to going to far worse places under bad conditions, for extended periods of time.

"I'm sorry," she said miserably, as she blew her nose when he handed her a tissue. "It's all my fault."

"No, it's not. This is what I've always done as my job. I've been having people try to kill me for years. When I left Colombia, there was a leak." It was the first time he had told her about himself. "I had to get out in a hurry, like within minutes. I had a woman and a baby, her brother was the drug dealer whose camp I had infiltrated for three years. He killed her and the baby the day I left. These people don't play for small stakes. Sam is right. Muñoz will kill you if he can. Let's not let him do that. You have a long life ahead of you, and this will only be for a while." He tried to make it sound as benign as he could, and just an intermission in her life.

"It could be years," she said, and blew her nose again. She couldn't stop crying, thinking of what was ahead, and then she looked at him. "Will you go to the same place?" He was becoming her only friend, and the thought of "disappearing" alone scared her. At least if he came, she'd know someone, and she felt safe with him. And she was touched to hear about the woman and the child. "I'm sorry about what happened to you. Why are these people so awful?"

"They just are. No morality, no conscience, twisted ideals, and motivated by money, or power, or both. That corrupts people. And I guess some people are just made that way." He had seen a lot in his years in the DEA, and it showed in his eyes.

He handed her a glass of water then, and they sat down to look at the list of options. Wyoming was at the top of the list. Washington State, Alaska, North and South Dakota, Montana, Oklahoma, Arkansas, and New Mexico. There were a lot of rural, less populated, and farming states, none of which appealed to her, and she burst into tears again. And then she thought about Wyoming.

"I used to want to live on a ranch when I was a kid. For about ten minutes." She smiled through her tears. "I rode a lot when I was young. Maybe we could start a horse farm." She didn't really want to, but it made it sound not quite so bad. At least she'd have something to do if they bought horses and she could ride.

"If we pick something near a university town, I could come with you, and teach, if they let me," Marshall suggested with a thoughtful look. "I don't think I'd be much help as a ranch hand." He smiled ruefully and pointed at his left arm.

"I had a riding master with one arm once," Ariana said, smiling at him. "He was the best teacher I ever had." She looked sincere.

"I'll leave the horses to you," he said again, but he was willing to go with her. That reassured her somewhat, but she needed to think about it. They went for a walk in Rock Creek Park with four agents, and talked about the plan again. Wyoming was definitely the state they both preferred on the list. And the idea of a horse farm was growing on her, as long as it was only for a year or two, or hopefully even less, if they caught Luis. Marshall had almost convinced her that that would most likely be the case. He hoped he was telling the truth. It was also possible that Muñoz would disappear for many years, or forever—and she'd be stuck in Wyoming indefinitely.

"What would you teach?"

"Political science, with a specialty in South American countries. I could teach Spanish, if they have nothing else. But I'd rather do poli sci. Or both." He was ready to get busy again, and he liked the idea of going into seclusion with her. He didn't want to be in the Witness Protection Program on his own either. He was a solitary, independent person, but going to an unfamiliar place, knowing no one at all, with a new identity, sounded lonely to him this time. He had done something similar in undercover work, taking on different identities, but there it had been far more exciting. He had been active and living by his wits all the time. This would be a lot tamer, less interesting, and a lot more comfortable than some of the places he had lived. But it was less liable to keep him busy, which he missed. He told her about Raul's jungle camp then, and she asked about Paloma. He talked about her for a few minutes, and then changed the subject. She could see that it was still painful for him, just as Jorge was for her.

They called Sam the next morning and asked him to come to the hotel. Marshall spoke for both of them and said that they would agree to go into the Witness Protection Program, and they were considering Wyoming, but they wanted to know more precisely the locations the CIA had in mind. He said they'd like to be near a college town, and Ariana wanted to start a horse farm, which she intended to fund herself, and was well able to do so. She had even come up with the idea of having underprivileged kids come to ride, and giving them lessons, although Marshall had told her he didn't know how many underprivileged kids there were in Wyoming, away from urban areas. But they liked the idea. And Sam surprised them.

"We actually own a fairly large ranch in Wyoming, which we've used for these purposes before. It's unoccupied for the moment. And it probably needs some work. It has a good-sized main house,

large enough for a family. Our last witness who
stayed there had four kids. And there's a house for a
foreman, and several other smaller buildings on the
property. You'd have to do some work on it when
you got there, at our expense of course. And there
is a college town nearby. It's not Harvard, but it's
a respectable school. It sounds like that might fit
the bill for both of you." Sam looked enormously
relieved, and Ariana was still cautious.

"How would I access money?" It was a problem
most members of the WPP didn't have. But in her
case, it was an issue, which they had foreseen.

"You can have funds wired into one of our trust
accounts. We can handle it for you, so nothing is directly traceable to you. And we would disburse the
funds you want into your account under your alias
in the program. Retrieving your funds shouldn't
be a problem. And you'll both have to pick new
names, by the way," he reminded them.

"Can I do whatever I want to the house?" Ariana
asked as Sam smiled.

"Yes, within reason," Sam answered. "If you
paint everything shocking pink with purple stripes,
the next witness who lives there might not be too
pleased. But I guess we could work that out later."
He wanted her to be happy, as much as she could
be in the circumstances. She liked what Sam had
said, because it made it sound like they weren't
going to be there forever. And maybe it would be
okay for a year or two. And at least Marshall had

agreed to go with her. Facing it alone, in isolation, would have been infinitely harder. She didn't know Marshall well, but she had come to trust him in the short time since they'd met. He had already proven himself to her.

"When do we have to go?" she asked Sam with a look of dread.

"Soon," Sam said seriously.

"Like tomorrow?" Ariana looked panicked. It was Tuesday.

"Let's say by Friday. We want you two to disappear as soon as possible. For all we know, they're looking for you here, or someone might happen to see you. The world is a small place, and we don't know where Muñoz is. That makes us very uneasy. He could be here, using an alias and a false passport. Let's get you out as soon as we can." Marshall nodded agreement.

"Can we take our dogs?" she asked, looking worried.

"Of course. And we want to work on your identities and your stories. Where you came from, why you're moving there, what you did before. Where you went to school. You can make friends in the community, but there can't be any slip-ups. Marshall here can show you how it's done." Sam smiled at him, knowing he was an expert in taking on a new identity and sticking to the story. His life had depended on it for six years. He had literally learned to become the person he pretended to be.

Members of the WPP came to show them photographs of their new home that afternoon. It looked like a large, slightly battered farmhouse, and Ariana made an immediate decision to repaint it out of her own funds, and put up new fences. And the furniture looked battered—she wanted to improve that too. The house Marshall would be using looked spacious and had been decorated for the foreman when it was a ranch, before the government bought it. And Marshall said it was fine for him, he didn't need anything fancy, and didn't care about how it looked. He had lived in a hut for three years in Colombia, and a tent in Ecuador before that. Living in a house would be a vast improvement for him.

"You'll be going as . . . friends?" the agent from the WPP inquired politely. "Husband and wife? Brother and sister? Employer and employee?" They hadn't thought of that, and Ariana spoke for both of them.

"Friends. He came out to help me start the horse farm, after he lost his wife. And I just lost my father." In a way, it was true. Masquerading as brother and sister seemed too weird, and he wasn't her employee. Going on equal footing, as friends, was more comfortable for both of them. And staying closer to the truth was less confusing.

Marshall was planning to apply to the college for a job, once they arrived. And the WPP offered to help him locate a job opportunity, and provide him the necessary credentials, which they always did.

They were told to select new names and said it usually worked best if they kept their own first names,
or the same initials, which was standard procedure
too. Marshall was going to use his mother's maiden
name of Johnson. And Ariana was going to use
"Robert," after her father. They had to get credit
cards, ATM cards, passports, drivers' licenses, bank
accounts, and a host of other ID in place in their
new names by the end of the week. The WPP would
handle it all for them.

Ariana fell into bed that night utterly drained
and totally exhausted. And Marshall made a phone
call to the White House after she fell asleep. He
wanted to see the Armstrongs before he and Ariana
left for Wyoming. It had been too long since he'd
seen Brad and Amelia. Melissa was happy to hear
from him when he called—she owed him a debt
for life. And he said he wanted to see his namesake
too. The president was in Tel Aviv on a state visit,
but Melissa and the children were at home and invited him to come over after school on Thursday,
and he agreed.

And taking four female agents with her, Ariana
went shopping the next day, for everything she
thought she'd need in Wyoming. Marshall did the
same with one agent, on a smaller scale. He bought
suitcases for both of them, and had to order more
when he got back to the hotel. He hadn't expected

the quantity of clothes Ariana had bought "just in case." She looked faintly sheepish about it and he laughed. He had never lived with a woman other than Paloma, and life on Ariana's scale was entirely new to him.

The next day he invited her to visit the Armstrongs with him, and Ariana was touched and surprised by the invitation. She had met Phillip Armstrong and his wife before, and gone to the Inaugural Ball with her father, as his staunch supporter, and the president had come to her father's funeral, but she was surprised by the warm, affectionate relationship Marshall had with the first lady and the children. Amelia talked to Ariana about how he had saved her life, and told him everything she was doing, while Brad flew a new remote-controlled helicopter around the room and narrowly missed their heads. And they got to hold the baby, which touched them both. Marshall and Ariana spent a happy two hours with them, which was a blissful relief from the tension they'd been living under since her near kidnapping in Paris.

"I'm going away for a while," Marshall said to the kids before he left them, and their mother raised an eyebrow, worried about him. The children had already asked if Ariana was his new girlfriend, and he said she wasn't and they were just friends. Amelia looked relieved, but she looked sad when he said he was going away.

"Under the covers again?" she asked with her big

blue eyes that had won his heart the first time he saw her.

"Sort of."

"I thought you couldn't do that anymore."

"They're making an exception, but I won't get hurt. I'm going someplace very safe, right here in the United States. And as soon as I can, I'll come back to visit." He didn't see why he couldn't visit the president with his new alias. And maybe it would all be over soon.

Melissa told him in an undervoice to take care of himself when he left, after he hugged the children, and she thanked Ariana warmly for the visit. Her secretary had reminded her who Ariana was and what had happened to her, and she wondered if Marshall was acting as security for her. Melissa thought she was a very nice young woman, and remembered meeting her before.

In the car, on the way back to the hotel, Ariana raved about the children. It touched her to see how sweet with them he was, and how much they obviously loved him. They were lodged deep in his heart forever, and she could see it. He seemed like he would have been a good father, if his life had worked out differently. It occurred to her that they had both lost babies with the people they had loved, in shocking circumstances that had traumatized them. Destiny had intervened.

And when they got back to the hotel, they found Stanley and Lili sound asleep together. She was tucked between his paws, burrowed against the bloodhound's huge chest, and Stanley had rested his huge nose on her, while she snored softly. It was nice having the dogs with them, and that they got along. Stanley looked as though he could have devoured Lili with one bite, but fortunately he had no desire to, and sometimes she hung off his long floppy ears, playing with him, and he put up with it, and then finally swatted her away and walked off to lie down somewhere.

The next day, after their visit to the White House, was the day of reckoning. Ariana emerged from her bedroom in the suite in blue jeans, a pink checkered shirt, and a pink sweater, with flat shoes and no makeup. Her long blond hair was pulled back in a ponytail, and she looked about sixteen as she put Lili in her travel bag. Everything else was ready. They had been given all their identity cards the night before, and even cell phones and computers in their new names, and everything associated with their old names had been replaced. A federal judge had approved their new last names and all record of the changes had been sealed. It was all handled by the Justice Department through the OEO. And both their Paris landlords had been notified that they were giving up their apartments, with sixty days' notice.

Marshall had done it all before, but this time was a little different, and it was all new to Ariana. She was silent and subdued as they rode to the airport.

They were being flown by private jet to Wyoming, and they had four CIA agents with them. Paperwork had been drawn up to make it look as though they'd bought the house for a modest amount of money, in case anyone checked. And Ariana sat staring out the window mutely on the flight. She had called Yael in Paris that morning to bring him up to date, and he told her to call if she needed him. It felt strange now going to a new place with Marshall, whom she barely knew.

The flight to Casper, Wyoming, took four hours, and Ariana didn't sleep, speak, or eat. She just sat there looking out the window and staring into space, and Marshall was worried. She had been traumatized before, and he didn't want this to bring back old memories for her. She looked haunted by the past. The OEO had reiterated its offer of counseling to help make the adjustment, and she had refused. She preferred to speak to Yael.

Having a new identity was familiar to Marshall, and in places a lot worse than this, so he wasn't upset, just slightly apprehensive about settling in, and adjusting to life with a woman he didn't really know. Ariana was giving up everything familiar to her yet again, and he wasn't sure what to say, so he left her to her own thoughts, and chatted with the agents. He had called Mac to say goodbye the night before, and hinted in veiled terms what was going to happen, but didn't tell him where.

"I figured they'd do something like that with her,

and put her on ice for a while. It's the only thing they can do. Well, take care of yourself, lad. I hope it's a decent place. It can't be worse than the ones you've been before. Hell of a way to get a woman, though," he teased him. "Make sure you have her clean the house. She's got a lot to learn on that score."

"She'll probably have me cleaning it for her." Both men laughed.

As the plane descended at the airport, Ariana noticed a few houses and some ranches, but mostly it looked like unpopulated land, and she felt as though they were landing on the moon.

"Are you okay?" Marshall asked her softly, and she looked at him and nodded. But she didn't seem convinced. It was suddenly all too real. She missed Paris, Buenos Aires, New York, and even Geoff MacDonald's cozy, disheveled kitchen in London. She wanted to be anywhere but where she was. And with tears silently rolling down her cheeks, she followed Marshall and the four agents off the plane.

Chapter 15

It was a half-hour drive from the small airport to the ranch owned by the Witness Protection Program outside Casper—a van had been waiting to drive them with their dogs and luggage. The gate to the property was battered and needed painting. There was a rural mailbox, and they'd been told they had a P.O. box too, and they both knew that Casper College, where Marshall hoped to teach, was forty minutes away, a reasonable commute for him.

Once through the gate, they drove down the long driveway, past the foreman's house, and several small buildings and equipment sheds, and saw a large barn on the left, where Ariana wanted to house the horses she was planning to buy. And they saw the main house with a porch and a picket fence, surrounded by old trees. Casper Mountain was visible in the distance—it was warm, and there

was a gentle breeze. One of the agents walked up
the front steps with a set of keys and unlocked the
door. And a pickup truck and a small sedan had
been delivered and were parked outside. Marshall
and Ariana exchanged a glance, and she looked apprehensive and followed the senior agent inside.
There were no other houses around for miles. It
was beautiful there, but it felt deserted to her. She
had never lived in such a quiet, rural place. Everything was unfamiliar to her, and she missed the big
cities that she knew. Even the convent hadn't been
as quiet and isolated as this.

The agent turned the lights on, and the rest of the
group walked inside and looked around. There was
a living room, a dining room, a den with a fireplace,
a big airy kitchen, and a wide staircase leading to
four bedrooms upstairs. It was simply furnished in
a sparse, impersonal way, like a motel, and there
was nothing on the walls. There was nothing warm
or cozy about it, and it instantly made her miss the
charm of her apartment in Paris. Her father's old
secretary Sheila was going to Paris to send all of
Ariana's belongings back to her father's apartment
in New York. Sheila essentially knew what Ariana
was doing, but had no idea where they were sending her or under what name, and Ariana had been
told she couldn't call her, in case her cell phone was
traced. Any messages for Sheila would have to go
through the WPP or the CIA. Sheila was desperately sorry for what was happening to her, and wor-

ried she'd never see her again. And as Ariana looked around the simple farmhouse, she gazed at Marshall with sad eyes.

"Welcome home," he said softly, wishing the house were prettier than it was. It was very plain and would take some real effort to make it look inviting and warm.

The WPP advance team had left food in the refrigerator for them, just basics, milk, eggs, butter, bread, lettuce, yogurt, packaged ham and turkey, bananas, breakfast cereal, instant coffee, and sugar. Just enough to have something to eat when they first arrived and the next morning. There was a list of the local stores on the counter, which were all ten miles away. Ariana looked around the house with an expression of desolation, and half an hour later, the agents left, and she and Marshall were alone.

"We can warm it up with a little paint and some new things," he said, trying to sound encouraging. He could see how unhappy she was. Luis Muñoz had stolen all semblance of a life from her, just as his brother had two years before.

She sat down at the kitchen table, and Marshall made them both coffee. He had hoped for her sake that the house would be nicer than this. The grounds were beautiful, and the area majestic, but it was a brutal change from Paris or New York. She was suffering from culture shock as she sipped the coffee from an ugly chipped cup. And then she looked up at him and smiled.

"I'd never survive this if you weren't here," she said honestly. She didn't mind the lack of luxuries, but the isolation was terrifying and depressing. And the more she looked at the house, the uglier it seemed. It was hard to imagine living there for several years or indefinitely. It was so impersonal, and she felt like she was living someone else's life, not her own.

"Yes, you would survive," he reminded her, "you've been through a lot worse."

"Thank God, I bought decent clothes before I came here," she said ironically, and he laughed while Stanley and Lili chased each other around outside, barking furiously. "The dogs like it." It was the only hopeful sign so far, but Marshall knew it could have been worse. And she could have been kidnapped in Paris or dead by then.

"We'll get used to it," he encouraged her, but the house seemed depressing to him too. Somehow a hut in the jungle didn't seem as dreary as the slightly forlorn house with nothing to warm it up, pretending to be a home. It didn't feel like one to either of them.

"How the hell did it come to this?" Ariana said softly. She stood up to examine what was in the cupboards. There were a lot of very ugly plates and a few mismatched glasses. There was cutlery for six, which looked like it had been in the garbage disposal in the sink many times. The forks and spoons were bent. "Okay, that's it," she said, facing him. "That does it. I hate ugly china. We're going to town to buy new stuff." She felt better as she said it, and he smiled. Living with a woman and the things women thought about was entirely new to him.

She ran upstairs to examine the sheets and towels and pronounced them ugly too. "Let's go shopping. There has to be a Target or IKEA here somewhere. Maybe we can find some furniture and even things for the walls." It was what she had done at the embassy in Buenos Aires, although with beautiful antiques and Aubusson rugs, and on a much grander scale, with spectacular results. But she was determined to meet the challenge of the ugly house, which Marshall thought was a good sign.

They left the dogs in the house and got in the truck. They stopped at the foreman's house, and looked around, and it was just as uninviting as hers, although she liked his kitchen better, and there was a wonderful old carved wooden bed in the master bedroom that appeared to be handmade.

"You need some decorating here too," she said as they got back in the truck, and headed to town. She put on some music and stared out the window with a sigh. Marshall felt sorry for her. She was trying hard to make the best of it, but it all seemed so unfair that they had to be there at all.

They drove through a small town on the way, where the grocery store was. There was also a Laundromat, a dry cleaner, a bookstore, a gas station, and a few other stores, but they didn't stop to check them out. And half an hour later they were in Casper, which was full of young people and life, with restaurants and bars and coffee shops, some art galleries, and an antique shop on Main Street, and Ariana cheered up. They stopped for something to eat and a cappuccino, and then Ariana went to work, trying to find things she could use for the house. She found two pretty tables and a desk at the antique store, a large painting at one gallery, and half a dozen good-looking framed photographs at the next one. Then they drove to Target, where she found sheets and towels for both of them in decent patterns and colors. She bought tables, chairs, knickknacks, and bright-colored implements and accessories for the kitchen. And a set of blue and white Italian ceramic plates, simple wine and water glasses in blue Murano glass, and simple stainless flatware with bone handles. None of it was fancy, but all of it was bright, pretty, and in good taste. Marshall was impressed, and even more so by the efficiency with which she gathered it all up. They loaded up the truck, and she asked to have the furniture delivered the next day. She had even bought some things for his house. It had all happened with lightning speed, and he was floored. She said that her mother had loved to decorate, and had taught her how. And Ariana put her new credit cards to good use.

"You're good at that," he said admiringly. "It would have taken me a year to figure all that out, and what to buy for the house."

"It's fun," she said, and was happy for the first time since they'd arrived. "You should have seen what I did with the embassy in Buenos Aires. It was practically empty when we got there. It was beautiful when I finished setting it up. I left it all there, as my father's contribution to the embassy. I just hope we get out of here in less than a hundred years. I don't want to spend the rest of my life in Casper," she said with a tone of desperation, but she looked better than she had a few hours before.

"You won't be here for a long time," he said, and sounded convinced.

"How do you know?" She wanted to believe him but didn't.

"Because the boys in the CIA are good at what they do. They'll find him. They're not as good as the DEA, of course," he said, teasing, and she laughed. He had a knack for cheering her up and making the best of difficult situations. He had done it all his life. And he liked her, and wanted her to be happy, even if the situation wasn't ideal. And he admired that she was trying to be positive about it.

They stopped at the grocery store to buy food for dinner, and he bought a barbecue and put it in the back of the truck. He swore he was good at it, although he hadn't done it in years.

"That's lucky," she said, grinning, "because if you're depending on me to feed us, we'll starve. I live on salads and takeout, and cheese in Paris."

This was definitely not Paris, and she had never really learned to cook.

"I'll make you a deal. I'll cook, you decorate." She smiled as he said it. It was strange getting to know him here, like survivors on a desert island. And as night fell, she realized she was worried about being alone in the house. Over dinner, Marshall sensed she was nervous and said something about it. "I'll keep my cell phone on tonight. Call me if you have any problems."

"Like what? If a wolf comes in and eats me and Lili alive?" She was kidding, but not completely. She had never lived anywhere this isolated before. She felt safer in the city, even with paid gunmen hunting her down.

"Would you feel better if I slept in one of the guest rooms?" he offered, and she looked sheepish, but nodded.

"I know it sounds stupid, but I'm scared here. It's hard to believe this is safer than a city with people around."

"No one is going to kidnap or shoot you here, Ariana. They have no idea where you are." Which was the whole point. She nodded but didn't like it anyway. Casper was beautiful but didn't look like fun to her. And he could tell she was a city girl. He was looking forward to fishing, and some hikes, neither of which appealed to her, although they'd been told there was good skiing in winter, which they both liked. And there was a theater, a symphony, and a museum, which Ariana had said she wanted to check out, and so did he.

He went back to the foreman's house after dinner, got his suitcase, and moved it to the main house. He took the bedroom farthest from her larger one so he didn't disturb her if he watched television at night, which he usually did. There was one in every bedroom, and a large flatscreen in the den. And a decent stereo system, and Marshall had promised to download some music for her.

Ariana went to her bedroom to unpack, while he sent e-mails from his computer in the kitchen after he came back. She heard him come upstairs later, and opened her door and thanked him for staying at the main house with her. She looked relaxed and was wearing a frilly white cotton nightgown with blue ribbons on it that she'd bought at Harrods and had worn at Mac's. And her long blond hair was loose, falling over her shoulders. She looked so young and pretty that it startled him for a moment. He was living in this house with her, and they had already come a long way together. It felt strange being there as friends, like being roommates, which was a far cry from his life in the jungle, or his solitary time since.

"Sleep tight," she called out to him and closed her door.

He lay in bed for a long time that night, thinking about her, and when he fell asleep, he dreamed of Paloma. He could still feel her in his arms, as though she had never left them.

They explored the barn together the next morning, after he made breakfast. And she thought the barn was better looking than the houses. They went back to town and found a Best Buy to buy DVDs of movies, and CDs, and found they liked a lot of the same artists, although he liked Latin music too, after being in South America for so long. She said she had learned to tango in Argentina, and he smiled. They bought a few more things for the house, and the furniture was delivered, and she pushed it around, and he helped her. He was amazed at how much better it all looked with a few cushions, some candles, the new furniture, a large mirror for the hall, and the paintings and photographs she'd bought, which he helped her hang. She knew exactly where she wanted to put it all, and the house was instantly improved.

"Wow! Magic," he said, impressed by the result. "Never mind raising horses, you should be a decorator. You're good at this stuff." The place looked infinitely better after she was finished, and he made barbecued ribs and chicken and put some music on. It almost felt like home to both of them, though not quite. It was all still very new. She was easy company and grateful for his help.

They watched a movie on the flatscreen together, and she fell asleep, watching it, leaning on his good shoulder. He raised his arm and put it around her as he enjoyed the movie, and Stanley gave him a quizzical look, as though asking him what he thought he was doing.

"Mind your own business," Marshall whispered, and kept his arm around Ariana while she slept. She woke up at the end of the movie, and he teased her about falling asleep. She was tired from everything they'd done that day, and it was still new and a little unnerving.

They spent the next few days cleaning all the houses together. Aside from the foreman's house, there was a tackhouse, and several buildings for equipment. And Marshall promised to hire a crew to help her clean out the barn. She wanted to go to some local horse auctions once she got the barn set up, and she was looking forward to the local rodeos, which Marshall thought sounded like fun too. It was something to do.

The following week, he went to the college and filled out an application for a teaching position in political science, Spanish, or some criminal justice classes they had that were right up his alley. On the application he filled out his new "credentials," which said he had been in military intelligence for two years. He had the documentation to prove it. Ariana went with him and checked out the bulletin board to find someone to clean the house for them, and a crew for the barn, and jotted down several names and e-mail addresses. Eventually they'd need someone to help take care of the horses when she bought them, so she glanced at those listings too.

Sam Adams called to see how they were doing after the first few days, and Marshall said they were fine. And Ariana sounded better to him too. By the end of two weeks, she was comfortable in the new house, although Marshall was still sleeping in the guest room, and she was nervous about being alone at night. She didn't want him to move out. They could hear coyotes in the distance, and she was always careful with Lili when she took her out. But Stanley was enjoying the space to move around.

At her request, they went to church on Sunday, and they met a few of their neighbors who were very friendly. And after a few weeks, they started dropping by to bring them cakes and pies and homemade jams and other offerings, partially out of curiosity to see what they were doing with the ranch. Their neighbors appeared to be nice people and were welcoming to them. And they worked at a variety of jobs in town. They met the head of the symphony at church, the curator of the museum, and several of the professors from Casper College.

They'd been there for six weeks when one of the women from church stopped by to bring them homemade blackberry preserves. "How long have you two been married?" she asked Ariana, who looked startled by the question. Marshall was mowing the front lawn and waved when she arrived, and then Ariana led her into the kitchen, where she asked the question, while she admired Ariana's decorating.

"I . . . uh . . . actually, we're not married. We're just friends. Marshall lost his wife, and my father died, and I decided to buy the ranch, so he offered to come out and help me. It was good timing for both of us. We've been friends for years, and we needed a change from Chicago." That was where they were claiming to be from. The story sounded lame even to Ariana, and the woman looked like she didn't believe it for a minute. She just nodded and smiled, while Ariana stammered. She told Marshall about it when he came inside for something to drink. He looked over at her in surprise as he took some Gatorade out of the fridge.

"Maybe we should just tell them we're living in sin, and get it over with," he suggested with a grin. "It's probably what they think anyway." He was laughing about it, and her shirt was soaking wet and plastered to her from washing the dogs after the woman left. And then, without thinking about it, he walked over to her, put his right arm around her, pulled her close to him, and kissed her. He didn't know how or why it happened, but it felt totally normal to him, and she put her arms around his neck and kissed him as he held her, and they were both breathless when they stopped.

"Is this a good idea?" Marshall asked her in a

hoarse voice between kisses. It had been so long since he had allowed feelings and passion to enter his life that they overwhelmed him now, and Ariana was swept away on a tidal wave of the same passion. He picked her up with one arm and carried her up to her bedroom. They pulled their clothes off and made love to each other like starving people discovering food for the first time. They had both been so lonely for so long that their feelings engulfed them. And Ariana lay there afterward looking at him in wonder. She kissed him tenderly again then, and laughed softly.

"Wow! What would have happened if that woman from church hadn't asked me that question?" He laughed in answer and propped himself up on his elbow to look at her. She had a gorgeous body and was a beautiful, sensual woman. And he hadn't realized it, but he had wanted her from the first moment he saw her in the park. He hadn't allowed himself to have feelings for a woman in years, and was concerned about it now.

"It probably would have taken a little longer, but not much," he answered her, feeling this was inevitable even if scary, as he touched her nipple with gentle fingers, filled with desire for her again. He was an extraordinary lover, as she had discovered. "It's been driving me crazy, thinking about you in the other room at night." But he also didn't want her to think that he only wanted her because it was convenient and they happened to be there together. He had begun to care for her deeply when he read Jorge's journals and understood what had happened to her. She had snagged his heart then.

"I kind of thought about it too," she confessed. "Is this a crazy idea? What if we decide we hate each other?" He didn't think that was likely to happen. They had gotten along remarkably well as house-mates for several weeks, and she was an easygoing, gentle, considerate person, and so was he.

"We can always have the WPP relocate us separately if you want. Or I could move to the foreman's house," he said seriously. "I want you to know I've never done anything like this," Marshall said to her. "When I was working undercover, I had no time to get involved with anyone at home, the rare times I was on leave. I didn't really have a home after my parents died when I was in college. And I didn't want some girl waiting around for me for years while I broke her heart or got killed. I didn't think I had the right to do that to anyone, just so I could have the comfort of knowing someone loved me while I didn't go home for three years. It wouldn't have been fair to them. I was always very careful about it.

"And then Paloma happened. I never expected to get involved with someone while I was work-ing, but I fell in love with her, and she was killed because of me. I feel like everyone I love winds up

dying, my parents, Paloma, our baby. It's kept me
from getting involved with anyone since she died.
I don't want to love someone and lose them again,
or worse, have them get hurt, or die, because of me.
I'll never forgive myself for what happened to her."

There were tears in his eyes when he said it, and
he had never been as honest in his life as he was
being now with Ariana. He had never been honest
with Paloma, since she didn't know his real identity. He couldn't tell her. But their life together had
been a lie because of it. And if he shared a life and
his heart with Ariana, he wanted it to be honest
right from the beginning, and he was being truth-
ful with her. "I'm not sure how much is left of me,"
he said sadly. "Part of me died in Colombia, when
she did." Ariana nodded as she listened and gently
kissed him. She was touched by everything he'd
said.

"I'm not sure I'll ever fully understand what happened to me with Jorge. I thought we loved each
other, and now I know he was a terrible person, and
I could never fall in love with him or respect him.
But what happened between us was magical, or it
seemed like it. I became someone different when I
was with him. Not all of it was bad, and it felt so
right when it was happening. I was so happy to be
having his baby. I lost my mind for a while, I guess.
But it seemed so real. And he was killed because of
me too. I can't forget that, or the baby I lost."

"He died because he kidnapped you, which was a

terrible thing to do to you," Marshall corrected her gently, as Yael would have. "He was killed because of his acts, not yours." Unlike Paloma, who had been an innocent victim, but Ariana and Marshall had both lost people they loved passionately, and a baby. And they had both been in impossible situations that could never have worked. They knew it now, but had loved them anyway, and had been deeply hurt, and had the scars to show for it.

"I'm afraid of something terrible happening again, if I love someone," Ariana admitted, echoing Marshall's fears. "I don't want anything bad to happen to you because of me."

"I don't want anything bad to happen to either of us. That's why we're here. And I'll do everything I can to protect you," he promised, and meant it, and she believed him. And the agents who had flown them to Wyoming had left several weapons with him, at his request.

"We just have to trust that all that bad stuff is behind us. It can't happen again," she said cautiously, "and that one day we'll get out of here."

Marshall couldn't help wondering if she'd ever want a life with him, when they left Wyoming. It was hard to imagine, given all the options she had. What did she need with a one-armed retired DEA agent, when she could have anyone? But it was already too late for him to retreat. He was in love with her, and he could see that she was in love with him too.

"I love you, Marshall," she said to confirm it as she kissed him.

"I love you too, Ariana," he said, and then he took her in his one strong arm and made love to her again.

Chapter 16

After they made love, Marshall moved into the main house officially, and into her bedroom. They lived together as a couple, slowly getting the ranch house and grounds in shape. She worked hard on the barn with a crew she hired, and one by one she began buying horses at local auctions, until she had six in freshly rebuilt stalls, and two men to help her care for them.

They continued meeting people at church, and went to a Fourth of July picnic at their neighbor's ranch, and invited them over for a barbecue. The two men went fishing together, and Ariana liked the wife and invited their kids over to ride her horses. She began training them herself. And she spoke to two charitable organizations to offer free riding lessons to underprivileged children. She taught them how to ride and care for the horses, and enjoyed riding with the children. And at the end of August,

Marshall got good news from Casper College. They had a fill-in position in the Spanish department, and Marshall was delighted to accept it. They were both busy and enjoyed the people they met, but never got too close to them, afraid to blow their cover. They were happy as they were, got along beautifully, and constantly got closer. They had met people, but were each other's best friends.

Marshall still had a bid in to the political science department at the college, and they said it might work out for the spring semester. He was thrilled. Ariana wanted to buy more horses. Everything was going smoothly, although it still felt strange at times to be cut off from everyone and everything they'd ever known, as though they had been born the day they got there, with no history before.

In November, it started snowing. They spent long lazy weekends in bed, making love, and sleeping in each other's arms as they listened to music or watched movies. Ariana said she had never been as happy in her life, and he could see it. And he felt fulfilled as he never had before. He had loved Paloma, but she was a child, and had never lived in a bigger world. She would never have been happy or understood his life in the States if he had taken her out of the jungle. He and Ariana were perfectly matched, equally capable. They talked for hours at night and shared a thousand similar opinions. They shared books and music, went to the theater and symphony. And they were both happy when Phillip Armstrong was voted into office again for a second term.

Marshall and Ariana felt like a match made in heaven. They had paid their dues and had earned the happiness they'd found. They spent Christmas alone at the ranch together, and went to parties in the area when they weren't snowed in. He was enjoying his Spanish class, and had just gotten confirmation that he could teach political science, with a specialty in South America, for the spring semester. It was hard to believe that they had been there for six months by the holidays. In some ways it felt like forever. Their relationship grew richer every day. They had lost everything familiar in their life and had found each other. And everyone who met them thought they were an adorable couple.

Ariana loved going to town with him when he taught his class. She would browse the art galleries and shops, and meet him afterward at their favorite café. And best of all, they felt safe here. They knew that nothing bad would happen to them here, and Muñoz's men would never find them. They rarely talked about it anymore, and Ariana stopped agonizing about when it would be over. She never wanted this to end.

Marshall started teaching political science in the spring, and Ariana bought two more horses, and a mare and a foal. She was giving regular lessons, and loved doing it, and rode every day herself. And she had gotten Marshall to relax around the horses and enjoy riding with her.

And just after Marshall had finished teaching the spring semester of political science, Ariana was out for a ride in the hills, and came back and saw a car sitting in front of the house. She didn't recognize it, dismounted, and led her horse to the barn and put him in his stall. She strode back to the house in her riding boots with her hair loose in the summer breeze. She walked quickly up the steps and into the house. She didn't know why, but she had a sense of dread when she walked in. And she saw Marshall and Sam Adams sitting on the couch in the living room. She had a feeling that something terrible had happened, that Muñoz had discovered where they were and was after them again. Marshall could see it in her eyes and was quick to reassure her.

"It's all right, Ariana. They found Muñoz and killed him. He was in Bolivia, recruiting a rebel army. It's all over," Marshall said as he stood up and put his arm around her. For them, it was the end of the war, and they could come out of hiding. It took her a minute to realize what Marshall was saying and what it meant to them.

"You can go home now," Sam said quietly as he stood to give her a hug. He had noticed the exchange between her and Marshall, and the obvious intimacy between them when he held her. And he wasn't surprised. They were both good people and had been through a lot, before they met. Their being a couple seemed right to him. They had been living together for the past year.

Ariana was looking at Sam with astonishment after he said it. They could go home. But where was that now? Her father's empty apartment in New York? Another rented apartment in Paris? And Marshall had no home—the CIA had packed up his belongings in Paris and put them in storage until he returned. Neither of them had family, they only had each other, and the home they knew now was the ranch in Wyoming, with their horses and their dogs, in a house that belonged to the Witness Protection Program and that they would use for someone else.

"Does this mean we're homeless?" she said to Marshall, looking confused.

"Not exactly," he said, smiling, as she sat down with them in the living room.

"It's all over?" she asked again, unable to believe it. Sam nodded. He had wanted to tell them in person. They had earned it.

"I came as soon as I could. It happened yesterday. They're still doing some cleanup in Bolivia and Chile, but our risk-assessment people feel comfortable with your coming home." Marshall was no longer at risk from Muñoz either, and his tracks had cooled after his work in Colombia. He had been gone for several years now, and they had no idea who he really was. There was nothing to tie him to Pablo Echeverría, the man he had been then.

"I think that means we're being evicted," Marshall added, smiling at her. There was a bittersweet feeling to it too. They had been happy here, and now they didn't know where to go, and he wondered if she would stay with him, once she had the choice not to. She had so many options that he didn't. He didn't want to assume anything. All he knew was that he loved her.

"How soon do we have to go?" Ariana asked Sam. "I have to sell my horses." She had ten now.

"We can take care of that for you," Sam offered generously. "You can leave as soon as you want to. Tomorrow if you like. You're free to go." They were words Ariana had been afraid she would never hear, and now she had and wasn't quite sure what to do about it. She looked at Marshall for guidance.

"Let us know when you want us to move you out," Sam said to both of them. He was sure it would be as soon as they caught their breath.

Sam left shortly after. He was flying back to Washington that night. He had come on official business.

As he drove away, Ariana sat down on the front steps, and looked at Marshall. They had a lot to talk about.

"Wow . . . I never expected that. I thought it would take years."

"I didn't think it would," he said, sitting down next to her on the top step. "What happens now?" He felt a ripple of fear as he asked her.

"We go home, I guess. Wherever that is," she answered. "What do you think? Where do you want to go?" They could go anywhere in the world now, but their lives had been so uprooted and turned topsy-turvy for so long that neither of them was sure where to go. Marshall had no reason to be in Washington, and Ariana didn't really want to go back to New York. Neither of them had a place in Paris anymore. And they no longer had a home in Wyoming as of that day. The whole world was open to them. "I told you. We're homeless," she said, and he smiled at her and leaned over to kiss her.

"What about the rest?" he asked her seriously.

"What rest?" She looked at him blankly. She didn't understand.

"Us."

"What do you mean 'us'?" She looked confused.

"You've kind of been stuck with me for the last year. A little bit like being kidnapped, or shipwrecked. Now the boat has come by to rescue us. You're not stuck with me anymore, Ariana. You can go anywhere you want, and be with anyone you want. You don't have to be with a one-armed bandit like me. You come from a much bigger world than I do." He wanted to give her every chance to walk away if that was what she wanted. He loved her enough to want what was best for her.

"Are you crazy? You're not a one-armed bandit, and I love you. And I wasn't 'stuck' with you. We could have picked separate locations. We didn't have to live together here in this house. We wanted to. Why would that be different somewhere else? I don't want to be with someone else. I want to be with you. I love you, wherever we are, or wherever we go from here." He was beaming as she said it, and she kissed him.

"I just wanted you to know you had the choice. I didn't want you to feel that you were obligated to be with me."

"I don't. But I hope you do, because I'm going to follow you forever if you leave me," she said looking at him seriously. They had both gotten over their fears of intimacy and loss in the past year. "I couldn't live without you, and I hope I never have to. I wouldn't know what to do if you weren't here." They sat on the front steps kissing for a few minutes, and then he turned to her with a serious expression.

"So where are we going to live?"

She closed her eyes pretending to spin an imaginary globe and then stopped it. "Paris!" she said with a broad grin. "What do you think? It's where we met, and I don't want to go back to New York. At least not yet." There were still too many memories there for her. Paris had been clean, except for the last day. "We could start all over again in Paris and do it right. I still want to get a job. Maybe you could teach there like you did here. We could have a real life like regular people." She was beaming, and he smiled at her.

"On one condition," he said, and stood up. He walked down the front steps as she looked at him in surprise. She had no idea what he was doing as he turned to face her, and then he dropped down on one knee and looked her in the eye. "Ariana Gregory . . . Ariana Robert . . . whoever you are . . . will you marry me, before we go to Paris? Or immediately after, if you insist. Will you be my wife?" She hopped off the front step and threw her arms around him and almost knocked him down. They had gotten their freedom, and he had proposed. She had been freed so many times now, from Jorge's camp after she was kidnapped, by Yael in Paris, and now they had been released by the Witness Protection Program. But the one person she didn't want to be free of was Marshall, ever, in her life.

"Yes," she said breathlessly, and he kissed her again. It occurred to them both that if Luis Muñoz hadn't tried to have her kidnapped, they might never have met, wouldn't have lived together for the past year, and might not be getting married. "We owe him a lot," Ariana said happily as they walked inside with his arm around her waist.

"Let's not go that far," Marshall said, smiling at his future wife. And then he stopped and looked at her closely. "Are there babies in our future?" he asked her, not sure what she would say. They had each lost an unborn child, which had traumatized both of them. He didn't know if Ariana wanted to try again. She looked up at him with wide eyes and nodded, and he kissed her again. At that moment in time, their life was perfect in every way.

Chapter 17

It took them three days to organize every-thing and pack what they were taking. Ariana sent the horses to be sold at auction. She was sorry to see them go, but it made no sense to try to keep them and have them sent somewhere else. She didn't want to send them to a stable outside Paris, or New York. It was simpler to sell them here.

They called a few people to say goodbye and that they were moving, but they had made no close friends here, in a life they believed was temporary and fraudulent. She was thinking of selling her father's apartment in New York, but hadn't decided yet. She had so many memories there of her parents, and she didn't need to sell it.

Marshall called the university and told them he wouldn't be signing the contract to teach poli sci in the fall, although he would have loved to. He said that he and his future wife were moving to Europe, and they told him how sorry they were that he was leaving. They thought he had done a fine job that spring, which was why they'd offered him the job.

Marshall and Ariana took very little with them, and left all the new linens and china and furniture for the new tenants. In the end, they took their clothes, their music, their dogs, and very little else. They were going to start fresh, all over again, together in Paris. She had already started sending e-mails to find a job. And Marshall had e-mailed the U.S. embassy in Paris for a civilian position there, and was researching teaching positions at the Sorbonne.

Ariana called Yael and told him all the news, and he was delighted, especially that she was free again, and coming back to Paris. He said he thought she might, she had been happy there. And it was a great city to start a new life. She sent Mother Elizabeth an e-mail and told her she was getting married. And she wrote back with congratulations from all the nuns.

And Marshall spoke to Mac the night before they left Wyoming. He told him about Muñoz, and that he had proposed to Ariana.

"I hope she said no," Mac teased him, but sounded very pleased. "Have you taught her to clean the house yet?"

"Not exactly." He had done more housework than she had, but didn't say it.

"Well, come to London, and we'll celebrate.

I hope she sticks around longer than mine did. I think she left with the postman or something. But you're a much nicer bloke. I'm sure she'll stay with you." He was happy for both of them, and told Marshall to give Ariana his love.

The plane came for them on Friday, and they were ready to go. A U.S. marshal picked them up at the house, more as a formality than a necessity, to escort them back to Washington. They had some papers to sign, and then they were free. They stayed at the Four Seasons in Washington that night and left for Paris the following afternoon. Ariana went shopping that morning and came back with a plain white silk dress for their wedding. They had decided not to spend any more time than they had to in the States. They were both anxious to get to Paris, and start fresh. They wanted to find an apartment, and had made a reservation at the Ritz until they did, which was Ariana's favorite hotel. She had already heard back from **Vogue** and **L'Officiel,** and a website she'd contacted, offering her interviews. And the U.S. embassy wanted to meet with Marshall when they got to Paris. They had been vastly impressed by his CV.

They talked about all of it on the plane to Paris. They wanted to get married when they arrived, even before they settled in. And once they were at the Ritz, while she was calling real estate brokers, he called the embassy, about their wedding. It seemed simplest to him to get married there, rather than cut through miles of French red tape for foreigners to get married in France. And he was startled to learn that diplomats were not authorized to perform weddings in France. It required a French government official to do it, and often there was a waiting period.

The secretary at the embassy told him what he had to do. He told her that he was a retired DEA agent in good standing, decorated by the president, and the bride was the daughter of an ambassador. She put him on hold then, and came back on the line rapidly. She assured him that everything would be done to move the process along quickly, they would find someone to perform the ceremony. And any time they came in to fill out the forms, they could be married the next day. It sounded fine to him. And he told Ariana when she was off the phone with the real estate broker. She looked excited and said they had three apartments to see that sounded perfect. One on Avenue Foch again, on the sunny side, one in a supposedly charming cul-de-sac, and the third in the Parc Monceau. She wanted to see them all that afternoon. And he mentioned stopping by at the embassy afterward, and she agreed. All they wanted was a simple ceremony. There was no one they wanted to invite, just the bride and groom. But she wanted to ask Yael to be her witness, since without him she would never have been able to do this, and would never have buried the box that had led Marshall to her. In a way, Yael seemed to be the father of it all, but when she called him, he was away for the week.

When they stopped at the embassy that afternoon, they discovered that there was a presidential visit, there were police cordons outside, and security was very tight. But they let them through anyway. And as they waited in the lobby to fill out their papers, Marshall had an idea, and approached the reception desk.

"Is the president in the building, sir?" he asked a marine at the desk.

"Why do you want to know?" The marine looked instantly tense, but Marshall looked respectable, so he relaxed a little.

"I'm a personal friend of the family. Ex–Secret Service, ex–DEA. My name is Marshall Everett, and I'd like to speak to him if possible," he explained discreetly. The Secret Service was a stretch since he had only been on loan, but the marine didn't need to know that.

The young marine dialed a number internally, spoke to two different people, and then handed the phone to Marshall, looking impressed while Ariana stood by. The president was on the line.

"What are you doing here, Marsh?" the president asked him in a jovial voice.

"Well, I'm moving back to Paris. And I'm getting married. And I'm sorry to ask you this. I know how busy you are. But if we make it fast, would you be my witness?"

Phillip Armstrong didn't hesitate, and instantly agreed. He spoke to someone standing next to him and asked about his schedule the next day. "If you do it at eleven-fifteen tomorrow, I'm all yours until noon. Melissa and the kids are here too. Can they come?"

"Of course! We'd love it."

"Who are you marrying, by the way?"

"A wonderful woman. Ariana Gregory. I think you knew her father." The president recognized the name instantly, and was amazed at how things turned out and how people found each other.

"I didn't know you knew her." He sounded surprised. He didn't know about their visit to his wife and children a year before.

"I didn't when I worked for you, sir. We met here a year ago. We just got off a year in the Witness Protection Program together."

"Tell me about it tomorrow," he said, and sounded rushed, and Marshall hung up and turned to Ariana.

"He said he'll be our witness. Melissa could be yours, if you want." Ariana smiled. Having the president and first lady as witnesses to their marriage was pretty impressive, and something to tell their children one day.

"Perfect." She beamed at Marshall.

They signed the papers then and were given an official eleven-fifteen A.M. time slot the next day.

The president's aide had already called down to arrange it. And everything went smoothly.

They went back to the Ritz and had a glass of champagne at the bar, and talked about the apartments they had seen that day. Ariana liked the one on Avenue Foch best, and had loved living there before, and it was fine with Marshall. It was a big sunny apartment with three bedrooms, and was unfurnished. So she would be decorating again. And it was big enough if they started a family while living in Paris.

And then they went upstairs to their room at the Ritz and made love. It had been a perfect first day back in Paris.

They arrived at the embassy promptly at eleven the next morning. Their papers were in order. The ambassador's aide was waiting for them, and took them upstairs herself. And Marshall was surprised to see the ambassador waiting when they got there—he recognized Ariana and was very pleasant to them both. And they had arranged for the assistant mayor of Paris to perform the ceremony. The waiting period had been waived at the request of the ambassador himself. And five minutes later the president walked in with Melissa, surrounded by Secret Service men, and Brad and Amelia were right behind them with their own.

Ariana wore the white silk dress she'd bought in Washington, and they'd stopped at a florist to buy a small bouquet of white lily of the valley. She looked simple and young and elegant, with her shining blond hair down her back. Amelia smiled the minute she saw her and then looked disappointed.

"You don't look like a bride. You should have worn a big pouffy white dress."

"I couldn't find one," Ariana explained, and then Marshall introduced her to the president, whom she had met before with her father. He told her she looked beautiful, and she kissed Melissa and the children, and then handed her bouquet to Amelia and asked if she'd be her flower girl. The child beamed with pride and pleasure, and took the bouquet quietly from Ariana. Marshall handed the rings to Brad to make him the ring bearer.

And a moment later, the ceremony began. The assistant mayor managed to make it touching, although he didn't know them, and Marshall looked down at her proudly with damp eyes. They had come such a long way to get here. Melissa was smiling at them, touched by how in love they were. Amelia held the bouquet like a sacred torch during the ceremony, and Brad handed Marshall the rings at the right time. Ariana was amazed he had them. Marshall had gone out to buy them the day before on his own at Cartier, and had accurately guessed her ring size. The ring he'd chosen for her was a narrow gold band. They exchanged the rings then, and hers fit perfectly. Marshall kissed her when the assistant mayor declared them man and wife. And Phillip Armstrong was the first to kiss the bride after that.

They all drank champagne, and at exactly five minutes before noon, the president left for his next appointment. Melissa and the children stayed with them for another half hour, and then they had to leave too. And after thanking the ambassador and assistant mayor, Ariana and Marshall stood on the sidewalk outside the embassy and hailed a cab.

"Wow! We're married," she said as she slipped in beside him.

"Where to, Mrs. Everett?" he asked her with a broad grin.

They decided to have lunch in the garden of the Ritz, and afterward Ariana wanted to go for a walk in Bagatelle, the park near where they had both lived before and were about to again. It was the park where he had first seen her, and everything had started, the day she buried the box.

They had a long, leisurely lunch, drank champagne, and talked about where to go for their honeymoon. Marshall suggested Venice, and she loved the idea. And after lunch, still in her wedding dress, they took a cab to Bagatelle.

They got out of the cab, paid at the gate, and strolled through the gardens. She was still carrying her lily of the valley, and she kept looking at her narrow gold wedding ring and up at Marshall in wonder. She looked totally happy, and so did he. They stopped at the place where she had buried the box, and he had found it and unearthed it. Everything had happened from that moment. She had buried her past, and he had found their future. A lifetime had happened in between, and now they were back in Paris. It was a perfect end to the story. Or in fact, only the beginning.

About the Author

DANIELLE STEEL has been hailed as one of the world's most popular authors, with over 650 million copies of her novels sold. Her many international best sellers include **Country, Prodigal Son, Pegasus, A Perfect Life, Power Play, Winners, First Sight, Until the End of Time, The Sins of the Mother,** and other highly acclaimed novels. She is also the author of **His Bright Light,** the story of her son Nick Traina's life and death; **A Gift of Hope,** a memoir of her work with the homeless; **Pure Joy,** about the dogs she and her family have loved; and the children's book **Pretty Minnie in Paris.**

daniellesteel.com
Facebook.com/DanielleSteelOfficial
@daniellesteel

LIKE WHAT YOU'VE READ?

If you enjoyed this large print edition of
UNDERCOVER,
here are a few of Danielle Steel's latest
bestsellers also available in large print.

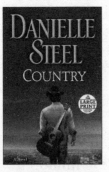
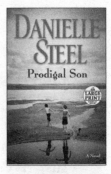

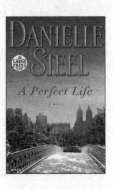